✳· ·•· ✳·•✳·• ✳·

"This is the end of our date," he said. "And you just told me that you won't go out with me, at least not any time in the next ten years, so this is pretty much my only opportunity."

"Opportunity?" Dani raised her eyebrows. "For what, exactly?"

"Well," Jeff said, taking a step closer. "How about you start off by telling me what a great time you had with me tonight."

Dani fought a threatening smile. Dutifully, she repeated, "I had a great time with you tonight. Now what?"

"I reply in kind, of course," he said. "I had a wonderful time with you as well."

"Did you, now?"

"I did," he said.

"I actually did too." She meant it this time.

"So you said."

"True. Are we done here?"

"No." Jeff took another step closer. "Now tell me, what would a stubborn and beautiful girl do to say good-bye to a guy who she didn't want to be out with in the first place? A nod, a handshake, a hug . . ." His voice drifted off and he looked at her with a question in his amused eyes.

Dani laughed. "Sorry, but I don't give hugs on dates."

"What about a handshake, then?"

"Even worse."

"Worse?"

Dani spoke without thinking. "Yes. Nana says that handshakes come from the cowardly and hugs from the weak-minded. She's always saying, 'If a man truly has a spine, he will brazenly kiss you and offer no apology for doing so.'"

Jeff smiled outright. "Well, in that case." He dipped his head and brought his lips to hers before she had a chance to respond.

✳· ·•· ✳·•✳·• ✳·

Luck of the Draw

Rachael
Renee
Anderson

Bonneville Books
Springville, Utah

This is a work of fiction. The characters, names, incidents, places, and dialogue are products of the author's imagination, and are not to be construed as real.

ISBN 13: 978-1-59955-443-3

Published by Bonneville, an imprint of Cedar Fort, Inc., 2373 W. 700 S., Springville, UT 84663
Distributed by Cedar Fort, Inc. www.cedarfort.com

LIBRARY OF CONGRESS CATALOGING-IN-PUBLICATION DATA

Anderson, Rachael Renee.
  Luck of the draw / Rachael Renee Anderson.
     p. cm.
  Summary: Brighton Andrews accepts a bet to date three girls at the same
time, who must be roommates and not know they are dating the same man. After
being thwarted on several attempts, Brighton is forced to take desperate
measures.
  ISBN 978-1-59955-443-3
  1. Dating (Social customs)--Fiction. 2. College
students--Idaho--Rexburg--Fiction. 3. Mormon youth--Fiction. 4. Rexburg
(Idaho)--Fiction. I. Title.

  PS3601.N5447L83 2010
  813'.6--dc22

          2010018874

Cover design by Tanya Quinlan
Cover design © 2010 by Lyle Mortimer
Edited and typeset by Heidi Doxey

Printed in the United States of America

10 9 8 7 6 5 4 3 2 1

Printed on acid-free paper

For Brighton.

You are as fun, smart, and good as they come.
I love you.

✻

Be sure to check out Rachael Renee Anderson's first book.
Divinely Designed

Acknowledgments

✳ · ● · ✳ · ● · ✳ · ● · ✳ ·

This book would still be a document on my computer if it weren't for the wonderful people at Cedar Fort. Thank you, Jennifer, for your suggestions and help along the way; Heidi, for your talent, kindness, and keen eye; Tanya, for your phenomenal design talents; Sheralyn, for your input, friendship, and PR skills. And to everyone else who has aided in the production and marketing of this book, thank you, thank you, thank you!

I also owe a rather large thank you to all my friends, family, and readers who have expressed their interest and enthusiasm. You have no idea how much I appreciate you all. Specifically, there are several people who have helped me a great deal: Valorie, for your fun, inspirational stories and helpful input; Letha, Sarah, and Linda, for listening to my ramblings and helping me propel the story along; Shelly, Lucy, Cora, Leslee, Corrine, Debra, and Jessica, for reading, encouraging, and suggesting; and to Jeff, for humoring this hobby of mine. I love and appreciate you all.

One

Brighton Andrews slammed the apartment door against the turbulent wind and swirling snow. Dang, it was cold.

"Late, as usual." Alex James's eyes flickered in annoyance. "You're lucky we saved you some wings."

Brighton surveyed the pathetic contents of a take-out box resting on the coffee table. "Gee, thanks. Your thoughtfulness astounds me." He tossed his backpack to the floor and wolfed down the two remaining barbeque wings as he made his way over to the refrigerator. Finding leftovers from the week before, he sniffed. They still smelled okay, so he pulled up a bar stool and helped himself to the soon-to-be-moldy chicken and broccoli. "You all knew I had a humanities test tonight. What a joke—I will never understand why it's a required course."

"You only think that because it's the one class you can't ace." Mark Christensen tossed a tattered black rubber rat at Brighton. Although disgusting, ridiculous, and no doubt ready for a proper burial, the four roommates refused to part with the toy rodent. During the past three semesters, it had become something of a treasured mascot, securing a place of honor on a shelf above the TV. Every other Monday, it was taken down and used to sentence one of the roommates to two dates with a random stranger.

"In case you were wondering," said Mark, nodding toward the rat, "you're the lucky one tonight."

Brighton bit back a groan. It couldn't be his turn yet. He had taken out the argumentative know-it-all Karen just before Thanksgiving break, and not enough time had elapsed for it to be back to him again. Brighton picked up the creature and flung it toward another roommate. "I don't think so. It's Grant's turn."

"For someone with an oversized allotment of brains, you sure have a lousy memory," said Kevin Grant. "Remember when you made me ditch classes to drive you to Salt Lake for your med school interview? In case you've forgotten, allow me to remind you. And I quote, 'If you do this one small favor for me, I'll take your place in the laundry bet next time.'" Kevin lifted the rat by its tail, swung it around his head calf-roping style, and released it to land neatly back in the casserole container from which Brighton was eating.

Grant was right—it was his turn. Brighton's audible groan sounded loud and clear. The last thing he wanted to do was go out of his way to meet a stranger and ask her out. He had more important things to worry about. He eyed the grimy rat sitting on what was left of his dinner. Picking it up by the tail, he threw it in the sink and continued to eat. His immune system could take it. Besides, he was starving, and his cupboards were looking about as pathetic as the empty box of wings. He glared at Kevin. "For someone with no brains, you sure have an amazing memory."

Kevin ignored him. "I'd like to suggest a slight deviation from our typical proceedings. You know, to make it a bit more challenging for Andrews."

"What do you mean?" Brighton scraped the bottom of the container. "You can't change the rules."

"I can with a majority vote."

"Says who?"

"Is this America or isn't it? If you have a problem with democracy, you're welcome to move to another country," said Kevin. "Besides, I was the one who invented the bets to begin with. I retain all rule-changing power."

"Fine," said Brighton. "I'll play along. What is this 'slight change' that you want to make?"

Kevin glanced toward Alex and Mark. "Rather than choose one girl, I say we pick three."

"Three!" Brighton choked on his water. "Are you kidding me?

It's hard enough finding the time to take out one girl, let alone three! I was only joking about the 'no brains' thing, but now I'm beginning to wonder."

"If you will let me finish, it'll make more sense," said Kevin. "First of all, because you're taking my turn, you will have four weeks, rather than two. Second, and here's the clincher—the three girls will all be roommates, and they can't know they're dating the same person. Just three girls. Two dates each. That's it. Not to mention you'll get your laundry done for an entire month."

Alex laughed. "Christensen and I will throw in our weeks too, if you decide to keep dating all three."

"Unless, of course, you don't think it can be done, Andrews," Mark challenged.

Brighton mulled the idea over in his mind. Four weeks and no laundry. The thought did offer a certain appeal, and he loved a good challenge. He hadn't lost a laundry bet yet, and there was no doubt he could pull it off. Plus, there was that girl from the library. It could work.

He shrugged. "If anyone can do it, I can, you morons. But I do have one condition. I get to pick the girl and then decide which of her two roommates will be so lucky as to score a date with *moi*."

"Do you have someone special in mind?" Kevin raised an eyebrow. "Because Christensen already has the names and class schedules of three unfortunate women."

"Her name is Katherine Buzzner." Brighton nodded toward Mark, who worked in the admissions office. "Figure out who her roommates are, and we have a deal."

They all agreed, and Kevin showed his appreciation for Brighton's sporting behavior by picking up the phone and ordering more wings.

Two

✻ · ● · ✻ · ● ✻ · · ● · ✻ ·

Rarely in the two years she'd spent in Rexburg, Idaho, had Dani Carlson seen the gentle, relaxed snowfall that might remind her of Colorado. The incessant winds made sure of that, launching the snow on a tumultuous adventure before it careened to the ground.

She shivered in her bulky, fur-lined down coat and smiled tiredly at Katherine Buzzner, her best friend and roommate, as they met together for the lengthy walk back to their apartment. Dani would forever be grateful for the fifth-grade pen pal assignment that had introduced her to Katherine all those years before.

Dani held out a steaming cup of hot chocolate. "I figured we could use something warm on this indecently cold night."

"Bless you." Katherine smiled and accepted the cup.

"I think we must be in some new season that hasn't been invented. Something colder than winter," Dani said, quickening her pace.

"Spend a few months in Alaska during the winter, and this will feel like summer." Katherine hailed from Anchorage, where she had grown up as the daughter of a chiropractor and had the posture to prove it.

"Can you not let me complain for a second? Not everyone is part-Eskimo, you know." Dani took a sip of her hot chocolate and immediately spit it out. "Ouch! Someone really needs to learn how to turn down the temperature on those machines. How is anyone supposed to warm up when it's too hot to drink?"

Katherine held the cup to her lips and blew softly.

"So how was the library? Get any books catalogued today?" asked Dani.

"Don't mock my job. At least I get most of my homework done while I'm at work," Katherine reasoned. "Besides, I now have a date for Thursday night."

"Wow, you've taken multi-tasking to a whole new level," Dani teased. "Who's the lucky guy?"

"Brighton Andrews."

"I take it he's a skier?" Dani said, referring to the popular ski resort in Utah, also named Brighton.

"Very funny," Katherine said. "Actually, he's a pre-med major and spends a lot of time at the library. I've helped him find a couple of books before, but tonight he just came up and asked me out."

"Is he handsome?"

"Handsome, smart, charming—you name it." Katherine tentatively sipped her drink. "Based on the few brief sentences we've exchanged, of course."

Dani laughed. "Sounds like his only flaw would be his choice of major."

"You're the only girl in the world who would think such crazy thoughts."

"Maybe," said Dani. "What time is he coming to get you? I want to be there to meet him."

"You'll have to come to the library then. He's picking me up at four, right after my shift ends."

"So early? He must want to spend as much time with you as possible," said Dani. "Well, since I can't meet him, be sure to take your cell phone and covertly snap some pictures."

Katherine laughed. "Oh, sure. Like that's gonna happen."

"Come on. How do you expect me to follow him around if I don't know what he looks like? I need to make sure he's good enough for you."

"Or you can trust me to determine that on my own." Katherine took a sip of her drink.

"You're no fun. I could have been the next Sherlock Holmes, you know."

"I think you mean Nancy Drew."

Dani glared. "That's it. I want my hot chocolate back."

✢

Dani rushed toward the Romney Building. It would have been a full-on sprint, but six inches of fresh snow covered the sidewalks, and her backpack was weighted with four rather large textbooks. In her hand, she carried a completed calculus assignment and a ten-page English paper. She was already late, and her ogre of a math instructor despised tardiness.

Suddenly her shoe slipped on an icy patch beneath the snow. Her quick reflexes reacted, keeping her from tripping. She'd nearly regained her footing when someone plowed into her from the side. Her papers went flying and she fell to the ground in a disgruntled heap. Closing her eyes and taking a quick breath, Dani fought her mounting frustration. At least her perpetrator had the grace to topple beside her, rather than on top of her.

He jumped up quickly and held out his hand. "I'm so sorry. I was running to class and wasn't watching where I was going."

"Do you always run with your eyes closed?" Dani stared into his startling blue eyes. He had naturally curly, dirty blond hair and was incredibly attractive, even covered in snow.

He smiled. "The wind was blowing snow in my face, and most people are in class right now."

"Class! Oh, shoot!" Dani scrambled up, ignoring his proffered hand. "Now I'm really late." She reached for her backpack and noticed her papers strewn through the snow, some already blowing across the courtyard. Picking up a few of them, she stared dejectedly at the now indecipherable equations. She had thought a few points docked for tardiness would be bad. This was ten times worse.

Turning frigid green eyes toward his blue ones, she said, "It was really nice bumping into you." Without another word, she grabbed the few papers that hadn't blown away and rushed toward the building, brushing snow off herself along the way.

✻

Brighton watched her go, feeling a little exasperated himself. It wasn't like he had run into her on purpose. He noticed a soggy paper she'd left on the ground and weighed his need to get to his own class against his sometimes-irritating conscience. Rolling his eyes, he followed her, entering the building's foyer just in time to see her disappear into a familiar room down the hall. So that's why she was in such a hurry.

✻

Brighton knocked softly on the open wood door, effectively gaining the attention of the man seated behind the battered desk. Two mismatched bookcases packed with books lined one wall, and a large window, overlooking a campus courtyard, framed an aging math professor.

Dr. Richard Green glanced up briefly before returning his attention to some paperwork. "I didn't think I'd see you today."

"I'm not here as a TA." Brighton casually walked in and sat down in the nearest chair, directly across from his former professor and current employer.

Raising his eyebrows, Dr. Green leaned back and placed his hands behind his head. The chair squealed and screamed in protest under the weight of the tall, portly professor. "You intrigue me, boy. What can I do for you?" His sharp, intelligent eyes seemed to probe a person's soul, and Brighton could understand how most people found him intimidating and gruff. Little did they know that under the rough exterior was a wise, kind, and clever man.

"Er, I'm not sure how to say this, but during your one o'clock class, did you have a girl come in late with some soggy remnants of a calculus assignment?" Brighton asked.

"Ah, yes. She did mention that some 'uncouth individual' plowed into her just before class. Although, to her credit, she also confessed that she would have been a few minutes late, regardless." The professor allowed himself a brief smile. "And what do you know of this young lady?"

"Uncouth?" Brighton repeated. "What is she, a drama major?"

"Secondary education, actually. I take it *you* are the uncouth individual?"

"It was just an accident, and yes, I'm the reason behind her ruined homework—not that I'm sorry any longer."

Dr. Green chuckled. "Well, not to worry. She did lose a few points for being late, but I told her she could redo the assignment and turn it in tomorrow morning."

"Tomorrow morning? For one of your assignments?" Brighton grinned. Dr. Green's homework assignments were notorious for taking hours to complete. "That's perfect." His smile lasted only until he heard the professor's next words.

"Considering it probably only took her an hour or so to complete it the first time around, I didn't think it was too unfair. She reminds me of you, in that respect; although *she* is actually humble."

"Well, that's nice. First I'm uncouth and now I'm arrogant. Any other insults you'd like to throw my way?" Brighton asked.

Dr. Green reached for a pen. "Now that I've eased your mind with regard to my student, do you mind if I get back to work?"

"Actually, I do have one more question for you."

"Yes?"

"You happen to have a girl by the name of Danielle Carlson in that same class. Could you, perhaps, describe what she looks like to me?"

"Why?"

"It's a long story, and I can see that you're busy," said Brighton.

"All right, then. Today Danielle Carlson was late, disgruntled, and rather wet. Do you need any more description than that?"

Brighton rolled his eyes and swallowed a groan. Talk about an unlucky coincidence. Forcing himself to his feet, he nodded to his professor. "Thanks. That should do it."

"See you tomorrow." The sound of deep laughter followed Brighton down the hall and out the door, taunting him all the way to the library.

Three

✳ · • · ✳ · • ✳ · • · ✳ ·

Brighton watched as Katherine took a careful bite of her salad and peeked across the table. "This is a nice place."

"Yeah," he said, slicing through his steak. There was no better food than a tender and juicy, medium-rare ribeye. "I've never been here before, but my roommate swears it's the best place around. I try to humor his recommendations when I get the chance—especially when I get to take out a beautiful girl." He winked across the table.

Katherine blushed before changing the subject. "So you're from Colorado?"

"Yeah. A smallish city about thirty minutes south of Colorado Springs called Pueblo."

"Really? My roommate is from Colorado Springs."

Roommates. Perfect. Brighton had been waiting for just such a conversation opening. "Which one?"

"Her name's Dani Carlson."

Of course. *Danielle.* He couldn't seem to get away from that name and it grated on his nerves, like two pieces of Styrofoam being rubbed against each other. He shivered at the thought.

"She's actually been my best friend for years," Katherine said, explaining how they'd met as pen pals in elementary school.

"That's great you've stayed in touch all these years." He searched for a polite way to change the subject. There were still two other roommates. That meant that as far as he was concerned, Danielle, or Dani, was history. "So are you the only one who works in your apartment?"

"No, we all do—sort of."

"Sort of?" *Please don't say Dani.*

"Dani is a snowboarding instructor at Kelly Canyon. She's the only other one with a real job. One of my other roommates, Sandy, stays busy with shows and performances, and Becky just got engaged, so she's 'working' on her wedding plans."

His brain regurgitated the evil word. *Engaged.* How unlucky could he be? Briefly, he contemplated the likelihood of charming an engaged girl into dating him, but grudgingly he dismissed the idea as morally unethical. Perfect. If he wanted to win the bet, he'd have to date Dani after all. He could handle two dates, right?

Glancing up from his food, he caught Katherine watching him. He tried to remember what else she'd said. "Is Sandy an actress?"

"Vocal performer, actually. She loves opera."

"Oh." Brighton nearly choked on his steak, praying he wouldn't have to actually attend an opera in order to meet the girl. There was a reason he struggled with humanities, and it wasn't because he lacked intelligence. "Have you been to any of her shows?"

"We went to one performance, you know, to be supportive."

It was nice to meet someone else who "lacked culture." At least that's what his roommates had told him. But Brighton disagreed. After all he liked *What About Bob?*, and Bill Murray was very classy. "Once was enough for you?"

"For Dani, yes." Katherine smiled. "She said she'd rather jump headfirst into a prickly pear cactus before she'd listen to Sandy scream again."

Brighton held back a laugh. Somehow, he could picture Dani saying those exact words. "What about you?"

"I didn't mind it. Parts of it were well done, and I found it entertaining to watch."

"That's nice." So much for that commonality.

It was only his first of six dates, and already he was mentally exhausted. Instead of enjoying a leisurely dinner with a gorgeous girl, he was subtly probing her for information. How had he gotten himself into this situation? He wanted to strangle Grant.

Glancing across the table, he found Katherine looking at him expectantly. She was obviously waiting for a response of some sort. Terrific. "I'm sorry. Did you say something?"

Katherine smiled and gestured toward their waiter. "He just wanted to know if you'd like some dessert. I've already passed."

"Oh." Brighton noticed the waiter for the first time. "Um, no, thank you. If you could just bring us the check?"

✳

"So how was Prince Charming?" Dani asked as Katherine practically floated into their room. Shoving her calculus book aside, she sat up and crossed her legs. "I hope you took some great pictures."

"Sorry." Katherine tossed her purse on the desk and flopped down on her bed, smiling dreamily at the ceiling. "We went to some archery place and then out to eat. He opened all the doors, said all the right things, and seemed genuinely interested. I haven't been this excited about the prospect of a second date since Jeremy." Her smile faded when she mentioned her former boyfriend's name.

"It's about time," Dani said. "So when's this second date?"

"He said he'd drop by the library sometime next week and let me know."

"The library? Does he not know how to use a phone? Just promise me that if he stops by to ask you out for that same day, you'll say no." Dani didn't want to see another unreliable and flaky Jeremy enter her friend's life. Katherine was unerringly kind and good and deserved nothing but the best.

"Nobody's perfect," said Katherine. "I wish you would realize that and find a good guy yourself."

"I don't expect perfection—just someone who's perfect for me." Dani frowned. "If only that prototype existed."

"You do realize that you have to give them a chance to find that out, don't you?"

"Hey, I've gone out with every guy that has ever asked me out, at least when I've been available."

"Yeah, one date each. You need to try at least a couple of dates."

"I've gone out with someone more than once."

"Really? Who?"

"I don't remember."

"Because you never have," Katherine said.

"Wait! Kyle Skyler! My junior year in high school. I went on a group date with him and then to some dance a few months later."

"High school?" Katherine laughed. "That was four years ago. You're a junior in college now, my friend."

"I know." Dani felt somewhat troubled as she stood up and glanced back at her best friend. "I just haven't met anyone I've wanted to date more than once. Do you think I'm irrevocably messed up?"

Katherine smiled. "No. I think you're just too picky."

"Will it make you feel better if I promise to say yes to the next guy who asks me for a second date?"

"Absolutely."

"Then consider it a promise."

❋

Dani stormed out of her English class, completely irate at the grade she'd received on the paper she had spent hours writing. She despised English, primarily because one teacher would praise her ingenuity, and the next would berate her work. It was all so subjective. Why couldn't every subject be like math? You were either right or wrong, regardless of who was instructing you. *English is for people who don't mind censure*, she'd decided. She, on the other hand, didn't appreciate criticism, constructive or otherwise, and couldn't wait for her English requirements to be met.

"Hey there," a vaguely familiar voice broke through her thoughts. "Aren't you the girl I accidently bumped into the other day?"

Dani turned and green eyes met blue. He was wearing a brown beanie with a white stripe and was even better looking when he wasn't covered in snow. "Bumped?" She raised her eyebrows. "I think you need to try a different verb. Something like *rammed*, *plowed*, or *slammed* is more like it."

"I take it you just got out of a creative writing class," he said.

"Yes, as a matter of fact. Although from the grade I just got on a certain paper, you'd wonder how I ever passed English 101."

"Ah, hence the bright and cheerful mood." He nodded. "Well, I'm glad you seem to have come through our little accident unscathed."

"Yes, I'm dandy," she said, looking over his shoulder. Where was Katherine? She was usually waiting in the foyer by now. She turned her attention back to the guy standing in front of her. "Although, I have to say that redoing the calculus assignment didn't exactly make my night."

He shoved his hands in his pockets and rocked back and forth on his feet. "Actually, when I saw you over here, I figured I'd ask if you'd let me make it up to you."

"You're going to do my next math assignment for me? Or are you better at English, because honestly I could use more help in that area."

"Actually, I was thinking of something a little more ethical."

"Such as?"

"Dinner."

"You want to make me dinner to say sorry for running me down?" Dani asked.

"I can't cook."

"Well, that's an odd way of saying sorry then."

"I meant I'd like to take you *out* to dinner," he said.

"Oh." Dani glanced at her watch. "Actually, that's quite all right . . . uh . . . I'm sorry—I have no idea what your name is."

"Jeff. And you are?"

"Dani. Listen, Jeff, I really appreciate the thought, but I'm afraid I make it a rule never to date anyone who has run me down. Besides, who wants to go on a charity date? Thanks, but I'm afraid I'll have to pass. Maybe you could try knocking into me a few more times to see if I change my mind."

"Would it work?"

"No." Dani shook her head and smiled. "But here comes my roommate so I have to go."

If Dani had to describe a deer-in-the-headlights look, it would be Jeff's expression at that moment. "See you later," he said quickly before rushing down the hall in the opposite direction.

"Who was that?" Katherine asked as she walked over to Dani. "I didn't think you had any friends in your English class."

Dani stared after him, confused. "I don't, and he's not."

"Then who was he?"

"Remember that awful guy I told you about? The one who forced me to redo my calculus assignment?"

"Yes. And from the way you described him, I'm surprised he's not locked up somewhere," Katherine said. "So why was he talking to you?"

"He offered to take me to dinner."

"And you said yes?" Katherine prodded, looking hopeful.

"Of course not! I don't even know the guy. For all I know, he could be an escaped mental patient," Dani said. "Actually, by the way he just acted, that scenario might not be so far-fetched."

Katherine looked disapproving. "You promised!"

"I said the second date, not the first." Dani grabbed Katherine's arm as she pulled her toward the door. "Anyway, I'm starving. Let's go get some lunch."

❊

Brighton found himself deep in thought after his narrow escape. Was this how it would be for the rest of his last semester? Always worrying about who he might run into? Every day seemed to bring yet another negative to the once "exciting" bet, and he mentally kicked himself, yet again, for being so rash.

But at least now he didn't have to dread going out with Dani. Somehow, his early opinion of her had improved slightly. She seemed interesting and lively, and if she'd ever agree to a date, they might actually have some fun. Yet she had refused him. Why? No girl had ever turned him down. At least not without a good reason, which she obviously didn't have. He couldn't figure her out.

Regardless, he wasn't about to lose the bet because of her.

In fact, he rarely lost at anything. From his high school state basketball championship to his acceptance at the University of Utah's medical school, everything had always fallen into place for him. Oh sure, he'd had inconsequential setbacks every now and then—like the time he sprained his wrist waterskiing—but for the most part, his entire twenty-five years had been free from major difficulty. His parents had always said that he had the Midas touch, but for Brighton, it was simply a good life.

"Someday, you're going to encounter a serious trial in your life," his mother had once told him. "I only hope you know where to turn when that happens."

Was Dani going to be his serious trial? He smiled at the absurd thought.

Dani. The name no longer conjured a grimace. Instead, it made him wonder. She was an enigma. Not quite beautiful, like Katherine, but cute in her own way, with those large green-almost-blue eyes that made it difficult for him to look anywhere else. She was also funny and frank. He'd never met anyone like her, and he found himself wanting to know more.

But how? How could he get her to go out with him? There had to be a way.

There was always a way.

❉

"Exactly when are you going to tell me where we're going?"

"When we get there." Brighton propelled Alex toward a muted brown building on the outskirts of campus. "You'll have fun. Trust me."

"The last time you said that, I ended up as a participant in an impromptu comedy audition."

"Well, you're a funny guy," Brighton said.

"Yeah, and I found it especially funny when you stumbled across the girl you were supposed to take out at the same audition."

"I know. It's a small world, isn't it?" Brighton opened a door and ushered Alex inside, hoping his friend hadn't recognized the building or noticed the words "Snow Center for the Performing Arts" written on the outside of the door. Regrettably, it was one of those rare instances when he was out of luck.

"The Snow Building?" Alex came to a standstill.

"I didn't sign you up for an audition if that's what you're worried about. I just need a little moral support."

"I don't think so." Alex shook his head and turned around.

Brighton grabbed his arm. "Please? I'll even buy you dinner after this is all over."

Alex hesitated and Brighton knew it was because he could never turn down a free meal. "Fine. But I refuse to participate in any kind of performance—and I get to pick the restaurant."

"Deal." Brighton ushered him into a suspicious nearly vacant concert hall. "Look, we even get great seats."

"There's only twenty people here." Alex glanced at his watch. "Are you sure you have the time right?"

"Of course," Brighton said. "Come on, sit down. It should be starting any second."

Alex sank into a squeaky faded burgundy seat. "What should be starting?" he asked as the lights dimmed.

Brighton ignored the question.

A girl dressed in a floor-length black dress with her hair pulled back in a tight bun walked up to the microphone on the stage.

Taking the mic from its holster, her silky, languid voice resonated throughout the room. "Welcome to our small, but gloriously entertaining opera workshop. You won't be sorry you came."

Alex looked murderous. "Have your parents never told you the story about the boy who cried wolf?"

"Shhhh, you're being rude," Brighton said, listening as the girl described the operas the performers would be showcasing. The introduction itself lasted a full ten minutes and left him wondering just how long the workshop would take. He hoped it wouldn't be all afternoon.

If only the audience weren't so sparse and the theater so dark, he could have played a game on his cell phone or used the time to study. Instead, he was forced to maintain some etiquette and spent the two incredibly long hours watching the seconds tick by.

When the performers finally bowed, Brighton jumped from his seat to offer a standing ovation, although his applause had nothing to do with the workshop and everything to do with the fact that it was finally over.

Ignoring Alex's fuming expression, he made his way down to the stage, where he congratulated a certain blue-eyed blonde on her performance. Makeup was caked on her face, and like all the other girls, her hair was pulled back in a tight bun. It was hard to tell what she'd look like out of costume. She was also rather petite for the amount of sound she could produce.

Pointing out his friend still seated in the theater, Brighton led Sandy over for an introduction.

"Great performance," Alex said.

"Thanks." Sandy nudged Brighton and gave him a sly smile. "Andy, here, said he was mesmerized as well."

Alex looked heavenward as if asking for patience. "Yeah, well, Andy is quite the opera aficionado. You two probably have a lot in common. He also loves to put on a good show," Alex said, making no attempt to mask his annoyance.

Brighton ignored him and turned back to Sandy. "Hey, we were just about to go grab some dinner. Would you like to come along? You can be my date." The invitation earned him a flirtatious smile from Sandy and another malevolent look from Alex.

"That sounds like fun. Do you mind if I go change first?" She glanced playfully from one to the other.

"Of course not," Brighton said, pulling Alex toward the seats. "We'll be waiting right here."

"I'll be right back." She sashayed off toward the stage.

As soon as Sandy was out of earshot, Alex turned accusatory eyes on his friend. "You're a dead man. And just so you know, you now owe me two dinners—maybe even three."

Brighton shrugged. "Look on the bright side. Maybe she'll give us our own private performance during dinner."

"You can treat me to dinner another night—I mean *nights*. I'm out of here." Alex took the stairs two at a time and left Brighton alone, wondering where all the good friends had gone. Plopping into the nearest seat, he pulled out his zoology book.

Thirty minutes later, Sandy returned, looking stunning. She had changed from her garish costume and had removed half of her makeup, but her expression radiated disappointment. "Where did your friend go?"

Brighton stood. "He had to be somewhere. But between you and me, I'm glad. I'd rather have you all to myself." He winked.

The bright, flirtatious smile returned, and she possessively wrapped her arm through his. "Looks like your wish is my command."

Dinner lasted nearly as long as the workshop. As beautiful as Sandy was, Brighton had no interest in her tales of theater and music—most likely because he also found her to be the most self-centered flirt he'd ever met.

"How did you hear about me and our workshop?" It was the first question she had asked him all night.

He fought the urge to roll his eyes. "I heard someone talking about it. Since I had nothing else going on this afternoon, I figured I'd check it out."

"Did they mention my name in particular?"

"No," he said, his patience waning. But when he saw an annoying pout form on her now not-so-beautiful face, he amended, "You were just a perk."

"Oh." She giggled, leaning across the table and placing her hand over his. "You are such a tease."

Brighton mustered half a grin and wondered, for the hundredth time, where the waiter was with their check. His tip was dwindling by the minute. Would it be rude to go look for him?

The man finally appeared, and Brighton quickly reached for his wallet. "Here's my card," he said before the waiter had a chance to leave.

"You know," Sandy said as if she were sharing some significant secret. "There's another workshop on Tuesday night. Maybe we could do this again." She offered him a radiant smile.

Realizing that one more uncomfortable evening would free him from this girl, he gathered his courage, swallowed the lump of dread in his throat, and nodded in agreement. "Sounds like fun."

"Great," she said. "Now let's get some dessert!"

Brighton stifled a groan. When the waiter returned with the credit card receipt, he forced the words from his mouth, "Do you mind bringing us a dessert menu?"

Four

·•··•*·•·*·

Dani lugged her snowboard up the side of the hill. It was Saturday, and she was on her way to meet her class of four semi-beginner snowboarders. One girl and three boys, ages eight and nine. Typically, she only taught three students at a time, but there had been a last-minute addition—someone who had requested her personally.

Arriving at the designated lift, she leaned her board against a rope and pulled the class list from her coat pocket. "Logan Benson?" she called.

"Right here!" A short, stocky boy left his father's side. He dragged his snowboard with him, grinning. Dani liked him instantly.

"Mackenzie Crotts?"

A young girl trudged over and said shyly, "I'm Mackenzie."

Dani looked down. "Hello, sweetie. I'm so glad I won't be the only girl. Are you ready to snowboard?"

The girl nodded.

"Cody Rhoten?"

"He's right here," said a breathless mother, pulling her son by the arm. "We're not late, are we?"

"Just in time," Dani said.

"Jeffrey Andrews!" According to her friend in charge of scheduling, this was the boy who had requested her personally, although she didn't recognize the name. She hoped he'd been snowboarding at least once or twice like the other children. She didn't have the patience to coddle a true first-timer today.

"Present," a deep male voice called from behind her.

Thinking the voice belonged to Jeffrey's father, she swung her head around. When she saw Jeff leaning on a snowboard, her mouth dropped open in surprise. "You," was all she could think to say.

"Me."

"But you're not eight or nine."

"You only teach kids. You don't even offer private lessons. It took some persuading to convince Kelli to add me to your list, but she finally agreed."

"Kelli is apparently weak-willed," Dani said. "I'm sorry, but you'll have to go get your money back. I don't teach adults."

"I'm really a kid at heart."

"That's obvious."

"Come on. Kelli said it's non-refundable, and you wouldn't seriously do that to me, would you?" Jeff asked. "Besides, I have always wanted to learn to snowboard."

Feeling flustered, Dani looked away and met the curious eyes of the kids in her class. Realizing she was wasting lesson time, she dismissed Jeff from her mind and turned to the other three. "Okay, kids, it looks like this big kid over here will be joining us today. So how about this: I'll give a candy bar to the first person who can beat him down the last run of the day. In fact, if you all beat him, you'll each earn a candy bar. How does that sound?"

"Hurray!"

"Bring it on, scamps. But I'm giving you fair warning—I'm a quick learner," Jeff said.

"You're going down!" said Logan.

Dani smiled. "All right, everyone, first things first. Before we get on that lift and show Jeff how to board, I need to make sure you all know what you're doing. Once you can show me you know how to turn and stop, we'll take the lift to the top."

From the moment Jeff sat down to strap on his board, Dani could tell he was a seasoned snowboarder. He shoved his boots into his bindings and cinched them down with the ease of someone who had done it before. Besides, his board was too expensive to be a rental. When he "tried" to ride down the short slope, his falls were exaggerated and orchestrated, and although he put on a good show for her other students, Dani wasn't fooled.

She watched the other children, mentally noting their strengths and weaknesses. When she felt they were ready, she ushered them up the lift. At the top of the run, Dani plopped down beside Jeff. "Would you mind lending a hand today? Mackenzie could use a little extra help, and I can already tell that Cody and Logan will want to go faster."

"But I'm a beginner," he said.

"Yeah, and so am I."

"My acting skills are that bad?"

"Terrible," she said. "But if it's any consolation, I think you still have the kids fooled."

She finished securing her boot to her board, leaned forward, and stood up. Sliding around to face the kids, she said, "Okay, everyone, just follow me. We need to work on turns the entire way down, so I don't want anyone blowing past me. Got it?" She looked pointedly at Cody and Logan.

"Got it," they both said.

Dani took her time zigzagging down the mountain, stopping often to observe, make suggestions, or wait while a child righted himself. The trail wound down gradually, weaving them through narrow channels, lined with tall pines and bare aspens. It was breathtaking.

She had to admit that teaching the intermediate classes were her favorite. It was usually the time when the kids finally left their fears behind and embraced the joy and thrill of sailing over the snow. The looks on their faces were what had kept Dani teaching every year since she'd turned sixteen.

As they neared the end of the run, she picked up speed, allowing Logan and Cody the chance to show off a little. Jeff proved to be an adept teacher, so she wasn't worried about leaving him behind with Mackenzie. In fact, he had been remarkably patient and fun, winning the kids' adoration with his silly antics and goofy remarks.

Halfway through the lesson, she and Mackenzie coasted off the lift and saw Jeff sitting at the top of a run, holding his board in his gloved hand while he inspected his bindings.

Dani skated over to him. "What's wrong?"

He looked confused. "For some reason my binding came loose when I got on the lift and my board almost fell on the way up. I'm just trying to figure out how and why."

She looked around for Cody and Logan, wondering where they were. Jeff had taken them up the lift ahead of her, and she didn't want them to take off on their own. When she heard snickering, she turned around to see the two boys giggling and pointing at Jeff. Dani bit back a smile and looked back at Jeff. "Well, I'm not certain about the how, but I'm pretty sure there's the why." She gestured to the two boys, who were now laughing.

Their laughter, of course, escalated when an out-of-control skier came off the lift and plowed into Dani, who, in turn, rammed into Jeff. His unattached board flew out of his hands and down the slope, gaining speed as it went. By the time the board had travelled the distance of a football field or two, it had quite the audience; especially when it refused to follow a turn and bounded up and over a snowbank and into a startled pine tree. Or at least Dani figured it was startled. She knew she would be if she'd just been speared with a snowboard.

Dani bit her lip, trying not to laugh. Logan, Cody, and now Mackenzie were about to hyperventilate, and Dani could hear the laughter of several other skiers and snowboarders as well.

Using her hands, she carefully backed away from Jeff, bumping into the skier behind her.

"I am *so* sorry!" said the girl, looking at Jeff's snowboard in horror.

Jeff didn't seem to hear the apology, so Dani stood and offered a hand to help the girl up. "Don't worry about it. He could use the exercise anyway."

The girl looked mortified but nodded and snowplowed away.

Dani turned back to Jeff. He seemed to be in a trance as he stared at his board, which looked to be the size of one of those wooden craft sticks—and not the jumbo kind.

"You just had that waxed, didn't you?" she asked.

"Yep."

"Looks like they did a good job."

"Yep."

"Dude, that was awesome!" Logan shouted while Cody and Mackenzie continued to giggle.

"Oh, you think that was funny?" Jeff finally looked away from his snowboard and at the three kids.

They nodded.

"Well, I think this is funny." He leaped up and picked up Logan, turning him upside down before he dunked his head in some unpacked powder. Cody was next. He went easier on Mackenzie and only swung her around until she squealed.

When Logan and Cody protested the preferential treatment, Jeff said, "If my bindings hadn't come loose to begin with, I wouldn't have taken off my board and it wouldn't be stuck in a pine tree right now." He looked pointedly at the boys, and they immediately stopped complaining.

"At least you'll be hiking down and not up," said Dani.

"Way to find the silver lining."

Dani smiled. Turning to the kids, she asked, "Do you think we can beat Jeff to his snowboard?"

"Not on my watch." Jeff leaped over the edge and headed straight down the mountain, as fast as his heavy booted feet would allow.

"Should we give him a head start to make it fair?" Dani asked as she watched his pathetic progress.

"No!"

She didn't think so either.

The class passed him in no time and Jeff lost, albeit gracefully. After he recovered his board, they were able to snowboard without further incident until their time together was nearly over.

"Well, now that I've got a bunch of professionals on my hands, how about you all head back up the lift for one last run, and I'll stay here to see who gets those candy bars," said Dani.

"Yeah!" the three kids shouted, sliding off toward the lift line.

Jeff smiled and winked at Dani before following after the kids. "There is no way you guys will ever beat me down. In fact, if you know what's good for you, you'll stay far behind me so you don't have to eat my powder."

Dani ambled down to the lodge and purchased four candy bars from a vending machine. Shoving them into her coat pocket, she traipsed back to the end of the run and waited for her class to appear. She didn't have to wait long.

Logan zoomed around the corner first, followed closely by Cody and then Mackenzie. All three of them were giggling when they arrived.

"What's so funny?" Dani asked.

"Jeff tried a jump and biffed it big time!" Logan choked out. "He landed in a huge pile of snow!"

Sure enough, Jeff rounded the corner, covered in snow. As he came closer, he orchestrated yet another fall and landed in a heap at their feet, sending the children into even greater hysterics.

He looked at Dani. "They better not be laughing at me."

"And yet they are."

"We won!" said Cody. "Where's our candy bars?"

Pulling them from her pocket, Dani passed them around to the kids.

"What about me?" Jeff asked, brushing snow from his coat and beanie.

"What do you say, guys? Should we give him one for the best crash of the day?"

The kids were still laughing when their parents arrived to pick them up. Dani even heard Logan say, "Hey, Mom, can Dani and Jeff teach us next time?"

Dani blushed but pretended not to hear as she waved good-bye to her new young friends. She couldn't remember ever having so much fun teaching. She loved her job and the kids she met every week, but today had been particularly fun—almost special even.

Looking around, she found Jeff leaning up against a fence, arms folded, watching her with a half a grin. She walked over to him. "Now are you going to tell me what you're doing here?"

He shrugged. "I just wanted to get to know you better. Since you wouldn't go out with me, I figured this way you'd have to spend some time with me whether you liked it or not."

Dani felt both flattered and irritated. Irritated because his assurance annoyed her and flattered because, well, who wouldn't be? He was one of those guys who could make any girl fall for him—not that she would be another number on his list of conquests.

"Well, congratulations. It looks like you got your wish. I'll see you around." She turned to go.

"Wait!"

She stopped and glanced back at him. "Yes?"

"There's still an hour and a half left before the lifts close. Will you ride with me until then?"

"Sorry. I'm off duty." She started to turn away again.

"Come on, Dani. Give me a chance, will you? Besides, it's not as much fun snowboarding alone."

She nodded. "I get it. You're one of those people that consider it a social sport."

"Definitely. Don't you prefer to go with other people?"

"I guess I fall into the loner category. For me, there's nothing more therapeutic than turning up my iPod and boarding down a snow-covered mountain. Even without the music, nothing can compare to the beauty and serenity up here."

"Would you mind making an exception this once? Please? I did help you with your class, you know. You owe me."

Dani stared into his blue eyes and was chagrinned to discover that she was going to give in. He was handsome, interesting, great with kids, funny, and intelligent. What girl could resist? Besides, it wasn't like she was agreeing to a date. "Okay, fine. I'll ride with you until the lifts close. Satisfied?"

He grabbed his board.

Once they were seated and the noise and bustle of the lift drifted behind them, Jeff broke the silence. "Dani Carlson," he said in a slow, faintly drawn out way, as if he were trying to figure her out by her name alone.

Dani drew her eyebrows together. "That reminds me, how do you know my last name and how did you know I worked here?"

"That day we met, you left a paper in the snow. I followed you to give it back and saw you go into Dr. Green's classroom. I'm his TA," said Jeff.

"For that grizzly? You must have the courage of a knight."

"He's really not that bad once you get to know him. If you want to know the truth, he mentioned that he might offer you my job once I'm gone."

"You're going somewhere?"

"Why, you going to miss me?"

Dani threw an annoyed glance his way. "Are you really as cocky as you seem, or is it just some sort of act?"

"I'm not cocky." He sounded slightly offended and made a pretense of studying the scenery beneath them.

Dani watched him, trying to figure out who he really was. She knew he had an ego—that was obvious. But was he really as carefree as he seemed? She wasn't sure. Not knowing what else to say, she backtracked. "He doesn't know I work here, does he?"

"Who?"

"Dr. Green."

"Oh. Well, after I found out your name, I asked around."

She drew her brows together. "Who did you ask? I'm really not much of a social butterfly."

"I have my sources."

"You sound like a stalker."

Jeff chuckled. "Maybe I am one. Too bad you're stuck alone on a ski lift with me."

"True," she said. "But just to be fair, I should warn you that I'm thoroughly versed in self-defense. But you probably already knew that—from your 'sources.' "

"My sources aren't that thorough," he said. "But congratulations—you've successfully thwarted my evil plans."

"Maybe you could try someone else next time," she said. "In fact, I have a roommate who would be perfect for the role. She's gorgeous and overly susceptible to flattery—and she has absolutely no training in self-defense. On the other hand, she's an opera singer and can carry some amazingly high-pitched notes, which might attract the notice of certain canines, so maybe that wouldn't be the best idea after all."

Jeff shifted uncomfortably in his seat. "Do you always ramble when you're nervous?"

"What? I'm not nervous."

"I take it you don't date very much."

"I date plenty—and this isn't a date."

"I asked if you'd like to go snowboarding with me. You said yes. Sounds like a date to me."

"Sorry, buddy, but this can't be a date. Otherwise, I'd have to—" Dani stopped, horrified at what she'd almost said. Was she losing her mind?

"You were saying?"

"I was saying this isn't a date. Period."

"How about a compromise?" Jeff asked. "For me, it's a date. For you, it's two friends hanging out. Will that work?"

"Whatever." She had no idea why it mattered to him.

"Where are you from anyway?"

"Colorado Springs."

"Really? I'm from Pueblo. We're practically neighbors."

Pueblo. Where had she heard that name before? "Someone else I know is from there. I just can't remember who. Oh, this is going to bug me."

Jeff shifted again and cleared his throat. "So what are you studying?"

"Math, with a certification in secondary education."

"You want to teach?"

"Or just relive my high school years over and over again," she said.

Jeff laughed. "Let me know if they're any better the second time around."

Dani relaxed against the back of the chair, swinging her free foot back and forth. "Somehow, I get the feeling you had a pretty good run the first time around."

"What do you mean?"

"Let me guess—valedictorian, all-around athlete of the year, and student body president. Am I close?"

Jeff's expression turned sober. "That's quite the picture of perfection."

Apparently he hadn't found her description complimentary. "Sorry. I didn't mean it as an insult. I'm just trying to figure you out." When she noticed they were nearing the top of the lift, she said, "In the meantime, I dare you to beat me down the mountain."

"And if I do?"

"You'll be sorry. I am highly competitive and have a dreadful temper."

"Ah, a wolf in sheep's clothing."

"Exactly."

When Dani slid into her car that evening, she couldn't keep the smile from her face. Jeff was easy to be around, and she'd actually had a fun afternoon. He made her feel like she was interesting, fun, and even a little attractive. It was an alien experience, and she wasn't sure what to think or expect. Nor did she have anything to compare it with. Her dating history had consisted of dysfunctional conversation and awkward good-byes.

Katherine had always told her that she had never given anyone a chance, but Dani disagreed. A date was a chance—a chance to see if two personalities could co-exist. When two people spent several uncomfortable hours wracking their brains for a decent topic of conversation, it was not a good sign. And she could never understand the guys who asked her out again. Did they really want to relive a miserable experience or were they simply being kind? Either way, she wasn't interested.

Was it too much to ask that a relationship be easy from the start? She had begun to think it was, but meeting Jeff had proven otherwise. And that gave her hope. Maybe, just maybe, there were other Jeffs out there and someday she'd meet the right one.

Maybe.

❋

Watching Dani drive away, Brighton berated himself. He had lowered his guard more than once. If he wasn't careful, she'd soon have him figured out, and he might as well stamp a well-deserved "L" on his forehead.

That being said, the afternoon had been entertaining and well worth the lost homework time. Dani was amusing, and he found himself disappointed when the lifts closed and they were shooed from the resort. He'd wanted to invite her to dinner, simply to pro-long their time together, but he had a paper waiting to be finished. Besides, he would see her again. The bet made sure of that.

At least he could finally congratulate himself on scoring a date with Danielle Carlson. *Three down, three to go.*

Five

✳ ˙ ● ˙ ✳ ˙ ● ✳ ˙ ● ˙ ✳ ˙

Week three of the bet found Brighton completely swamped. Not only did he waste several precious hours at an opera workshop, followed by dinner with the world's most narcissistic personality, but he also had two tests and a paper to complete before the end of the week. Not to mention an activity to plan for Saturday night.

He had hoped to take Katherine out to lunch one afternoon and show up at Dani's snowboarding class again, but that wasn't going to happen. They'd have to wait one more week, which caused him more than a little stress because the following week was filling up fast too. Somehow, though, he'd find a way. He hadn't endured Sandy for nothing.

Shaking his head to clear his mind, he opened the door to the Romney Building and headed for Dr. Green's office. He needed to grade the math assignments quickly and find some time to get started on his English paper.

Raising his arm to tap lightly on the door, Brighton paused when he heard voices. Evidently Dr. Green wasn't alone. Hoping the discussion would wrap up soon, he casually leaned against the wall adjacent to the door and shamelessly listened to the conversation taking place inside.

"I was hoping you would let me take the test early. Either that, or after I return."

Brighton moved a step closer when he recognized the voice.

"Let me get this straight. You are telling me that you have to leave for two weeks in the middle of a semester?" Dr. Green's voice sounded gruff. "Was there a death in your family?"

"No."

"A wedding?"

"No."

"A sibling being called off to war?"

"No."

"Then why, exactly, do you need to leave for two weeks?"

"My mother is calling it a family emergency."

"Is it?"

"Can I be frank with you, Dr. Green?"

"Please." He sounded exasperated.

"My mother wanted me to attend Harvard, Yale, Princeton, or any other Ivy League school. BYU—Idaho didn't even make her top 500. And because of her low opinion of my choice of schools, she doesn't consider it an inconvenience for me to leave right now.

"My grandmother has taken a bad fall and, unfortunately for her, she's required to stay with my parents until her broken foot has healed completely. Since my parents have been planning a trip to the Cayman Islands and refuse to change their plans, it's up to me, their only child, to take a short leave from school, fly home to Colorado, and stay with my grandmother."

"Can't they hire someone to stay with her?"

"My grandmother is from Texas. She knows no one in Colorado Springs, and I know neither of us would be comfortable with a stranger looking after her."

There was a pause before Dr. Green said, "You do have a scholarship to keep, you know."

"I realize that, and as long as you and my other professors are willing to work with me, I promise my grades won't suffer. I'll do everything I can to stay caught up."

"It's going to be more difficult than you think. Is it really worth it?"

"My grandmother was more of a mother to me than anyone," Dani said quietly. "She needs me."

"Very well," the professor said. "I'll have my TA prepare the test for Friday and get together a list of problems for you to work on while you're away. Will that work?"

"Yes. Thank you." Dani sounded relieved.

"Math isn't the easiest subject to learn from a book."

"I'm aware of that, but I'll find a way."

Brighton tried to make sense of Dani's words. She was leaving? When? He rolled his eyes in frustration. Of course she was leaving. She seemed the one person adept at wreaking havoc with his life. He groaned. Now what?

His thoughts came to an abrupt end when Dani ran into him. "Oh, I'm so sor—" She stopped when she realized who she'd collided with.

"Sorry," Brighton finished as he stepped back. "You were going to say sorry, I believe."

"That's not possible." Dani closed Dr. Green's door behind her. "Isn't that your line?"

"Evidently I can share."

Dani laughed and stepped around him.

"You're leaving?" he asked.

"I have somewhere I need to go."

"I mean, you're going out of town?"

She searched his face, frowning. "I can see I need to add eavesdropping to your list of talents." She started to walk past him once more.

"Mind if I walk with you?"

"Aren't you here to see Dr. Green?"

"Yeah. Hold on." Brighton poked his head through the office door. "Hey, Doc, I'll be right back."

"Just remember I have to be in class in forty-five minutes."

"Sure."

Dani eyed him in confusion before she started walking again. "Was there something you wanted?"

"Just you." He winked.

Rather than smile or blush, Dani halted and turned to face him. "Okay, you need to stop—right now. I put up with it at the ski resort, but I need you to know that I'm not the type of person who likes to hear insincere flattery."

"Okay. Duly noted," he said, taken aback. "But for your information, it wasn't insincere. I really like being with you, and I'd like to know more about your grandmother."

"Why couldn't you have just said that the first time? It sounded much more genuine." Dani turned and resumed walking.

Shaking his head, he quickened his steps to catch up with her. "Is she okay?"

"She's fine. She just needs someone to look after her for a few more weeks before she can be back on her feet again."

"So you're flying home?"

"Yes. I leave Saturday morning."

"I'm sorry."

"It's no big deal."

"Trying to make up two weeks of classes is a big deal," Brighton said.

"Yeah, but so far all of my professors have said they'll work with me, so I'm grateful for that."

Brighton paused in front of the door leading outside. He studied her for a moment before saying, "Like Dr. Green said, math is probably the most difficult subject to learn from a book, so let me give you my cell number. If you get stuck, just give me a call and I can try to help you out over the phone."

"Really?" Dani looked hopeful. "I would really appreciate that. I learn math so much better from teachers."

"I'm the same way."

Dani handed him her cell phone. He was entering the name "Brighton" when she said, "Thanks again, Jeff. I hope I won't need it, but I'm grateful to have it just the same."

Quickly, he erased his first name and replaced it with his middle name, silently thanking Dani for the reminder. Handing the phone back to her, he said, "There, all set. Now where are we headed?"

"The Benson Building." She grinned, naming a building on the opposite side of campus.

"Did I just offer to walk you there?" he asked.

"You did, but if you'd like to bow out . . ." Dani's voice trailed off.

"No, I'm a man of my word." He took a breath and opened the door for her. What was he thinking? He didn't have time for a leisurely stroll across the entire campus. He'd be lucky to make it back before Dr. Green left for class. The absurdity of it all was that he didn't mind the detour. When he had told Dani he liked being with her, he'd spoken the truth.

As they trudged through the cold, Brighton asked, "Why the Benson Building? Isn't that for agricultural sciences?"

"Landscaping has always been a hobby of mine, so I'm taking a design class there."

"You have time for that?"

"I make time for that," Dani said. "It's a general rule of mine to take one class a semester that has nothing to do with my major and everything to do with my hobbies and interests."

"Oh." Brighton wondered if he had ever thought to take a class simply because he'd wanted to. Drawing a blank, he realized that it had never occurred to him. He had been too consumed with his pre-med requirements, and now, here he was, in his last semester, with no chance to change that fact. The idea bugged him, making him feel as though he'd let himself down somehow.

"You've never told me your major," Dani said.

"Pre-med." The words came out without a second thought and Brighton nearly grimaced—not that he could have said anything else. Using his middle name was one thing. Outright lying was another. Thankfully, she didn't seem to make any kind of connection.

"Impressive." Dani gave the expected response, although she didn't sound remotely impressed. In fact, she sounded exactly the opposite. Annoyed? Bothered? Irritated? He couldn't tell.

"Have you decided on a med school yet?"

"I've already been accepted to the University of Utah, which is a good thing, since I'm graduating in April."

"Oh," she said. "Well, congratulations."

"Thanks."

"Do you know what kind of doctor you want to be?"

"An orthopedist."

Dani's expression was blank. "You're interested in surgery?"

"I'm interested in helping people to fix their body so they can get around or return to an active lifestyle."

"Did you break your arm or leg at some point?"

"I sprained my wrist once. Does that count?" He smiled. "Honestly, the decision has nothing to do with some personal life-changing experience and everything to do with seeing a professional athlete hampered by some lousy injury, only to return fully recovered after a knee or shoulder replacement. It's amazing what they can do these days, and I want to be there, learning, contributing, and being involved."

Dani was silent for a moment. "So it has nothing to do with the money?"

"The money is a definite perk, but the incredible technology is what captivates me the most. It's fascinating to think that people can manufacture something like a knee or a hip, insert it into the human body, and teach them to walk, run, or jump again. I am in awe of some of the advances they've made in the past few years."

"Well, I'm glad you're so passionate about what you'd like to do. I hope you love it as much as you think you will," she said. "It's too bad you're not an orthopedist now. I'm sure my grandmother would love to have you for her doctor. She hasn't been impressed with the one my parents found for her."

"What happened to her anyway?"

"She tripped over something and broke her foot."

"While she was visiting your parents?"

"My grandmother doesn't visit my parents, at least not since I left for college."

"So why is she in Colorado?"

"Because my genuinely kind and thoughtful parents flew her out there," she muttered. "After the accident."

"With a broken foot? Was there no one to help her out where she lives?"

"Yes," Dani said. "My grandmother has wonderful friends and neighbors who would have been more than happy to help, but my parents felt she would be better off in Colorado Springs."

"Obviously you disagree."

"Heartily," Dani said. "All Nana wants to do is return home to Texas. She'd be much more comfortable there."

"So why doesn't she just fly home?"

Dani sighed. "It's complicated, but when my grandfather died, my father finagled Nana into creating an irrevocable trust with all her assets, making my father the sole trustee. He now has complete control over all her money, possessions, and property. Turns out it's a great form of manipulation.

"So when my mom decided that all Texan doctors are countrified and antiquated, they threatened to sell Nana's home out from under her and move her to Colorado permanently unless she agreed to see a specialist of their choosing. That specialist happens to be a friend of my father's."

"Seems kind of extreme for a broken foot," Brighton said.

"I thought the same thing, and I'm sure there's more to it than what my parents have told me, but I have no idea what it could be. Unless Nana has offended them in some way, and they're using this as a reminder of who's in charge."

"Your parents couldn't be that heartless."

"You don't know them," Dani said. "I only wish I were free to take Nana back to Texas and stay with her for a good long while."

"Well, I'm sure your grandma will appreciate you for coming."

Dani chuckled. "I've actually joined my parents on her naughty list. She's angry with me for leaving school."

"Didn't you tell Dr. Green that she doesn't want a stranger to take care of her?"

"No. I told him that *I* don't want a stranger to take care of her," Dani said.

"Oh, so you're the Mother Theresa type."

"Not even close. Just stubborn, pig-headed, and overly protective of Nana."

They had reached the Benson Building, and Brighton reached out to pull the door open for Dani. He followed her inside and stopped in the foyer. "I'd better get back before Dr. Green decides to fire me."

"Thanks for walking with me," Dani said. "It was nice talking to you. I feel better somehow."

Brighton's eyes captured hers for a moment. "Is it just me, or do you feel like we've known each other for more than a couple of weeks?"

Dani appeared troubled, and Brighton worried that he'd said too much. "You think we knew each other in a previous life, is that it?"

"No." He shoved his hands into his pockets. "That's not what I meant. You're just . . . easy to be around."

She nodded. "Well, when you aren't knocking me down, you're not so bad yourself." With a wave, she disappeared down a hall.

Brighton mentally scolded himself during the walk back to the Romney Building. He didn't want to scare her away. He needed her to go out with him one more time. *Oh, great. The bet!* How could he have forgotten and why hadn't he thought to ask her out while he was with her? That was why he'd offered to walk with her in the first place, wasn't it?

A timid voice inside his head told him that it wasn't the *only* reason.

�֍

Brighton left the testing center feeling drained and exhausted. His cell phone vibrated once in his pocket, alerting him to a new text message. Now what? Pulling it out, he scanned the message and groaned. It was from Patty, his co-chair on the activities committee, wondering if he'd had time to figure out the food for the social the following night. Great.

Snapping the phone closed, he opted to wait until the next morning to return the message. Right now, he needed an hour or two in front of the television watching sports highlights, followed by a decent night of sleep. He needed to free his mind from thoughts, worries, and stress. Or he would go mad.

Patty would just have to wait.

"Brighton! I haven't seen you around lately."

He glanced up and saw Katherine bundled up in a puffy blue

coat with a matching beanie. She looked beautiful as she crossed the courtyard in the lamplight.

"Dang!" he muttered. How could he have forgotten?

Katherine's eyes widened in surprise. "Pardon?"

"I'm sorry, that wasn't directed at you. I just remembered something I forgot to do," he said.

"Oh. Then I won't keep you."

"Unfortunately, there's not much I can do about it now," Brighton said, disgusted with himself for losing the bet. He hoped the opera workshops had somehow served to culture and educate him because he couldn't handle the thought of enduring Sandy for no reason.

"Bad day?"

"Bad week," he said.

"Do you want to get some hot chocolate and tell me about it?"

He sighed. So much for the sports highlights. "Sure. What are you doing out here so late anyway?"

"I just got out of class."

He nodded. "Ah, the dreaded night classes. I took one of those once and quickly learned my lesson."

"Sadly it was my only option."

"What class?"

"Clogging."

"Aren't you studying sociology?"

"Yes, but I made a promise to my roommate that I would always take one fun class a semester."

He wasn't surprised by her answer and found himself wondering if Dani had ever taken clogging. Somehow, he couldn't picture her tapping across a dance floor. He smiled as he opened the door to the Manwaring Center and followed Katherine inside.

She protested when he insisted on buying her some hot chocolate and a doughnut. If he paid, it could officially count as a date, bringing his final tally to five dates out of six. Eighty-three percent. Not too shabby, but would it be enough to reduce his laundry sentence?

Not likely.

✳

Dani probably should have taken a few days off from the ski resort, but snowboarding was the last thing she wanted to sacrifice right now. The mountains continually called out to her, tempting her with their powdery slopes. It was an escape, really. A time she could forget nagging thoughts or assignments and simply enjoy life and nature.

Friday was not one of those times, however. Not only did she have a particularly trying boy in her ski class, but she was leaving the next morning and had yet to start packing. Her bedroom was a mess, her laundry was piling up, and she hadn't eaten a decent meal in days. It was driving her crazy. She liked things clean, organized, and tidy. When they weren't, she felt out-of-control and anxious.

"Hey, you," Katherine said when she entered her bedroom.

Dani stopped sifting through her laundry pile. "Where have you been? I was about to go out and start digging through snow drifts looking for you."

"I ran into Brighton, and he bought me some hot chocolate."

Dani tossed a few shirts onto her bed. "I can see from your expression that you had a good time."

"I really like him," Katherine said. "I only wish he felt the same way."

"How could he not?"

Katherine sighed. "I know when a guy is into me, and believe me—he's not. I mean, I think he was at first, but something changed. Instead of flirting with me, he treated me like a casual friend tonight."

"Maybe he just had a lot on his mind."

Katherine shook her head. "I don't think so, but don't worry. My heart isn't going to break if he never asks me out again. I just think he's the type of guy I could really fall for."

"Well, if he's not into you, then he's obviously brainless. And you don't want to be married to an idiot, do you?"

Katherine smiled. "I'm going to miss you."

"I wish you could come with me. Nana would love to see you again."

Katherine sat down on the bed next to Dani's suitcase. "I'll never forget that summer I visited while you were staying with her in Texas. Remember when we convinced Nana to buy that hideous blouse with purple ruffles?"

Dani laughed. "At least we had good intentions. At the time, we did think it was beautiful."

"Your poor grandma. I bet she dreaded taking us shopping with her, feeling like she had to agree with our suggestions."

"I know. I used to think she valued our opinions, but I'm sure she just wanted to make us think she did. That's Nana for you. Always trying to undo the damage my own mother caused."

"Oh, I don't think you turned out so bad."

"Thanks to you and Nana."

Katherine started folding the clothes that Dani was tossing on the bed. "And now you get to go off and visit her for two entire weeks. You'll have so much fun!"

Dani searched through her drawers for anything she might have missed. "I just wish it were under better circumstances. She's already upset with me for leaving school."

"She wouldn't be Nana if she wasn't."

"I know."

"Then go. Have a fun two weeks. And with any luck, by the time your parents return, she'll feel well enough to fly home."

"That's what I'm hoping for."

Six

✳ · ˙ ● ˙ ✳ ˙ ● ✳ ˙ ● · ✳ ·

"Danielle, sweetheart!" her mother called as Dani walked through security at the Colorado Springs airport. With the plastic surgeries, breast augmentation, gym membership, and the small fortune her mother had spent on hair, makeup and clothing, Paula Carlson hardly looked old enough to be Dani's mother. Her shiny dark brown hair, dyed to mask the numerous strands of gray, and her brilliant blue eyes, compliments of colored contact lenses, also contributed to her mother's gorgeous, youthful appearance.

It made Dani ill just to look at her.

Paula threw her arms around her daughter. "How I've missed you!"

Rolling her eyes, Dani asked, "How have you been, Mom?"

Her mother sighed. "As you know, it took me awhile to recover from my last surgery, and with your grandmother's accident, things have been incredibly hectic. It's imperative that your father and I get away for a few weeks." The surgery her mother referred to was, of course, the face lift she'd had six months earlier.

"Grandma can be such a burden," Dani said sarcastically.

"Please don't start with me. It's not as though you can't take two weeks away from your precious school to spend some time with your grandmother."

Taking a deep breath, Dani willed herself to keep quiet. Her parents were leaving soon, and she had promised herself she wouldn't argue with them before then. But there was only one way to keep that promise. She literally bit her tongue during the ride home and only partially listened to Paula prattle on about their vacation plans and their "fabulous" new chef, who had suggested a new diet rich in tofu and raw vegetables. Poor Nana.

Dani lugged her suitcases into the house but dropped them when she noticed her grandmother resting in a recliner. Rose Olsen was one of those people whose natural expression exuded kindness and happiness, despite her mood. It was a face Dani had always coveted. Rushing to her side, she threw her arms around the aging lady. "Nana!" she said. "It's so good to see you!"

Nana returned the hug before pulling back and pointing an accusing finger at her granddaughter. "Don't think that I'm not still upset with you for leaving school because of me. How could you do something so scatter-brained?"

"Easy." Dani smiled as she plopped down on a brown leather couch across from Rose. "I had a good excuse to see you, so I came. How are you?"

"Good enough to return home." Nana looked meaningfully at her daughter.

"Now, Mother, you know what the doctor said."

"You mean your husband's golf partner."

"He's your doctor, and one of the best in his field."

"I have no doubt that he is good at what he does," her grandmother said slowly, as if speaking to a child who refused to understand. "But he is also influenced by your husband."

"Are you implying—"

"I'm not implying anything, Paula. I am telling you, like I have been for the past month, I am well enough to return home."

Dave Carlson trotted downstairs, carrying two large suitcases. "Danielle," he said, nodding to his daughter. "It's good to see you." He didn't wait for a response and walked out the garage door.

Dani's pensive eyes followed him briefly before shifting back to her mother, who was speaking to Nana again.

"We'll see how you feel when we return from our trip. We can talk about it then." Paula picked up her purse from the counter. "In the meantime, I'm sure Dani will provide you with adequate care." She smiled a brief, careless smile before strolling out the door after her husband.

"Adequate!" Dani said as soon as the door had closed. "I'm sure I can do better than that!"

"Oh, thank heavens they're finally gone," Nana said. "I'm not sure I could have handled one more day. How I lasted this long without wringing both their necks is a testament to my fortitude."

"It's a good thing I came with a plan, then."

"What plan?" Rose eyed her granddaughter in concern.

"Not so fast," Dani said. "Tell me truthfully. How are you feeling?"

"The brace comes off in three weeks," she said, lifting her injured ankle, "and I get around just fine."

"You have a good, qualified doctor back home to remove the brace and make sure everything is healed?"

"Dr. Simms is a gifted physician and a wonderful friend."

"Then it's settled. We are going to spend two fantastic, fun-filled weeks together, where I pamper you beyond all description. And then I have you booked on a flight out of Colorado Springs two hours before my parents are scheduled to land."

"But your father—"

"Forget about my father," Dani said. "I sincerely doubt he's going to go out of his way to bring you back here again. Not when you're so close to a complete recovery."

"He did it once; he can do it again."

"I don't understand that. Why did they go to the trouble of bringing you here? I would think that flying on an airplane would be worse for your foot. Is there something you're not telling me?"

"Your parents just think they know best." Her grandma stared out the window, appearing abnormally melancholy. Dani almost missed her next words, they were said so quietly. "What happened to her?"

"To Mom?" Dani knew the answer without thinking. It had been etched in her mind from the time she was a little girl, right after her mother underwent her first plastic surgery. "She married a doctor."

"Nonsense," her grandmother said.

"Please. You said yourself that you couldn't have asked for a better child. She married Dad at nineteen. As soon as he finished med school and got his first big paycheck, she hightailed it to the nearest high-end department store and purchased a new wardrobe—even though they were still deeply in debt. I was only six, but I remember her telling me that she needed to fit in with all the other doctor's wives. And she's been fitting in ever since."

"I suppose that growing up with very little money didn't help," Nana said.

Dani shook her head. "I don't think so. She'd be a different person if she'd married your average middle-class man."

"There are a lot of women who marry wealthy doctors and still live selfless lives," Rose countered. "Don't blame the profession."

Dani studied her grandmother. "I'm sure you're right, but I can't seem to help myself. Too much money seems to cause too many problems."

"It can also do a lot of good. There are many wonderful people who use their money to aid others or support good causes."

"I know. But I'd rather lead a normal, simple life—free from the temptations of greed." Dani sighed and stood. "How about we agree to disagree while I go and fix us some dinner?"

"Fine. But before you go, I want you to know that you aren't your mother. And you are far stronger and more discerning than you realize."

Nodding at her grandmother, Dani headed toward the kitchen, pausing to offer one last thought. "You know, it's not just about the money. It's also about time. Dad was rarely around, and when he was, he was always getting pages or calls. I can honestly say that I don't know my own father because he was too busy with the demands of his career. I don't want that for my kids, and I don't want that for me."

Rose smiled at her granddaughter. "You are wise beyond your years, and I have no doubt you'll find a remarkable young man someday." She paused before adding, "Just promise me you won't write off a good, honest man just because he has aspirations to become a doctor."

Dani's eyes widened in surprise before she pivoted and headed toward the kitchen. Her grandmother had always been far too perceptive.

❊

"So I was thinking we could go to Logan," Kevin said to his roommates. "My sister and brother-in-law can hook us up with four snowmobiles, and we can stay in their basement."

"Sure." Brighton stared at his biology book, not comprehending a thing. He needed to study, but his brain refused to interpret the words he'd read several times.

He blamed the wrecking ball of a girl he was unaccountably drawn to. She was like the pocketknife his parents had given him when he turned twelve. Unable to resist running his finger over the shiny metal blade, Brighton had been shocked when blood oozed from his finger. The blade had been sharp, shiny, and irresistible—like Dani. She too was difficult to resist and she too brought problems—albeit unwittingly. It was irrational, he knew, but he held her responsible for his temporary loss of control.

If only she hadn't left.

Because of the wretched bet, his grades had dropped, his social life—aside from his three roommates—was nonexistent, and he was persistently running late. It was like jogging on a high-speed treadmill. Despite all the energy he expended, he was going nowhere fast.

He also felt trapped by his inability to accept defeat. He had pride, after all, and losing the bet was about as offensive to him as getting a B. Intolerable. If only there were some way he could still win. Then he could finally put Dani from his mind and maybe, just maybe, his psychotic world would realign. But that was impossible, not to mention unreasonable. It wasn't like he was going to jump in his truck and meander on over to Colorado Springs for the sole purpose of winning some idiotic wager.

"Andrews! Hello! Are you there?" Mark asked.

Brighton looked up to see his roommates watching him expectantly. "What? Can't you see I'm trying to study?"

"You just keep telling yourself that and maybe it'll come true,"

Kevin said. "From our perspective, you're in la-la land. You've been reading that same page for the past thirty minutes."

"Fine." Brighton closed his book. "What's up?"

"We were just discussing where we should go this upcoming weekend. It's President's Day on Monday."

A long weekend. Brighton suddenly remembered the holiday.

"Yeah, maybe it'll get your mind off losing the bet." Alex was already enjoying the fact that Brighton's loss was inevitable.

The thought came again. *A long weekend.* Brighton chewed on his lower lip. The bet wasn't over until Monday, and his roommates wanted to plan a road trip. It could still work. "How about Colorado?" He tried to sound casual while he watched his roommates consider the new destination.

"We could go skiing," Mark said.

"Not exactly an escape from the cold, but neither is Logan," added Kevin. "And isn't there a ski resort near your house, Andrews?"

"Wait a minute." Alex was watching Brighton with a look of distrust. "Remind me again where Dani is from." Evidently "wolf" had been called one too many times.

"Colorado Springs," said Brighton.

Mark groaned. "You've got to be kidding! You're not seriously considering using our getaway to fulfill your own personal agenda, are you?"

"I'll just sneak away Saturday night for a couple of hours. You won't even miss me."

"You are one pathetic excuse for a friend, do you know that?" Alex said. "Just accept the fact that you lost and be done, man." He turned to Kevin and Mark. "Logan actually sounds pretty good. Let's plan on that."

They nodded their heads in agreement and looked at Brighton. "Well?" Kevin asked. "What's it gonna be—a fun-filled weekend snowmobiling with your best friends or a long, lonely drive to hang out with an aging grandmother and girl who refuses to date you?"

"Well, when you put it that way." Brighton stood and headed for his room. "I hope you all have a great trip. I'll see you Monday night—with my piles of laundry."

Seven

※ ⋅ ⋅ ● ⋅ ※ ⋅ ● ※ ⋅ ⋅ ● ⋅ ※ ⋅

"Sorry I missed your call. Leave a message, and I'll be in touch." Dani debated the pros and cons of speaking. Finally she said, "Uh, hi, Jeff, this is Dani. I was calling about calculus. I just, well, I need help. Could you call me back when you get a second? Thanks, uh, bye." Glancing at the calendar, Dani groaned. It was already Friday afternoon, and she had so much to accomplish before Monday.

In an attempt to keep on track with her homework, Dani had stayed up late most nights to read, write papers, and complete assignments. Despite all the time invested, without the benefits of class lectures and study groups, she found herself falling behind—specifically in calculus.

Normally math was her favorite and strongest subject, but without someone explaining the process to her, she was lost. The words and examples in the book made little sense to her fatigued mind. She needed help, so she had lowered her pride and used her one lifeline—Jeff. Unfortunately, she'd have to wait until he found the time or inclination to return her desperate call.

With a sigh, she pushed her book aside and sauntered to the fridge, where she took a quick inventory. "Nana! I'm going to the grocery store. Do you need anything?"

"No, sweetheart. I'll just stay here and listen to my book on tape, if that's okay."

"Sure. I'll be back soon."

It wasn't until much later, after she and Nana had eaten dinner and watched a movie, when Dani returned to her homework. Jeff had yet to return her phone call, but she was determined to figure out some of the problems before she allowed herself to fall asleep.

An hour later, she still hadn't made much progress. It was midnight, and lying on her bed was providing far too great a temptation. She was exhausted and wanted to throw the math book out the window and crawl under the covers. Perhaps her mind would function better in the morning. She pushed her book off the bed, snuggled up to her pillow, and consigned her worries to the devil.

❊

It seemed like she had only been asleep for five minutes when loud knocking interrupted her dreams. Gradually, her senses awakened, and she realized that someone was pounding on the front door. She peered at the clock and saw that it was three in the morning. What in the world?

Slowly she made her way to the foyer. Adrenaline pumped through her veins, and her heart raced. She felt like she was in a haunted house, petrified of who she might find when she rounded the next corner. The knocking started again, and Dani stared down the now creepy hallway at the dark and ominous wooden door. Mustering her courage, she slowly crept closer and peeked through the peephole, terrified of what she'd see.

Her terror was replaced with shock when she found Jeff shivering on her front porch. He was the last person she'd ever expected to see. Could she be dreaming? Quickly she unfastened the dead bolt and opened the door, blinking at him in confusion.

"You called?" He pulled his arms tight around his chest.

"What?"

"Calculus. You need help." His teeth chattered. "Do you mind if I come in? It's a little chilly out here."

"Oh, yes, of course." Dani opened the door wider to allow him entrance and quickly closed it behind him. Leading him to the family room, she pushed him into the recliner, threw a blanket over the top of him, and flipped on the gas fire. His teeth were still chattering, so she padded into the kitchen and made him a steaming, but not scalding, cup of hot chocolate. Then she returned to the family room and placed it in his frozen hands.

Dropping down on the sofa, Dani willed her brain to function. "You could have just returned my call, you know."

"It's easier to explain in person."

She closed her eyes. "Please don't tell me you drove all this way just to help me with a few math problems. My conscience couldn't handle that."

"Let's just say that you owe me one now."

Dani watched him shiver. "Does your car not have a heater?"

"It's a truck. And yes, it does."

"Then why are you so cold?"

"Just let me finish this hot chocolate and warm up a bit, and I'll answer all of your questions."

"Sorry." Dani stared at him, her mind calculating his real reason for being there. It was absurd to think he'd come merely to teach her a few math problems. Maybe he was headed home to Pueblo and figured he'd stop by on his way to help her out. But why not just drive the last thirty minutes to his own house, sleep in his own bed, and come back at a reasonable hour? It made no sense.

"Please don't tell me I'm keeping you from your home and family because of that message I left on your phone," she said.

He smiled before gulping down the last of his hot chocolate. "I'm thinking you could use a warm drink as well," he said. "You look tired."

"It's three o'clock in the morning."

"Right. That would explain why your hair is sticking out in odd directions."

Dani self-consciously raked her fingers through her hair, coaxing it to a less disheveled state. "Now will you tell me why I found you practically frozen on my doorstep?"

"I drove into town a little after midnight. Your lights were off, and I didn't want to wake anyone, so I figured I'd sleep in my truck until morning. Unfortunately, I was running low on gas, so

I heated up the cab and turned off the car. I woke up freezing a few hours later and figured I'd see how hospitable you'd be in the middle of the night."

"That doesn't explain what you're doing here. Are you on your way to your family's house in Pueblo?"

"Actually, no. But I figured I could always shack up there if you decided to toss me out," he said.

Dani wasn't sure what to say, so she looked at him in confusion, hoping he would elucidate.

He took a breath and let it out slowly. "It's a long weekend and I wanted to get out of Rexburg. Not having anywhere else to go, I decided I'd drop by to see how you and your grandma are doing. My cell phone lost reception for most of the trip, so when I finally heard your message I figured I was inspired to come."

"You drove ten hours just to see how I'm doing?"

"It sounds lame when you put it that way."

"Jeff, I—" Dani closed her eyes, attempting to make some sense of his actions. "You don't even know me."

"I'd like to."

"Why?"

"I have no idea."

She bit back a smile. "You could have waited until I got back, you know."

"You would have just continued to dodge me. This way, you're stuck with me."

"Not if I kick you out."

"True. But if that's what you're planning to do, would you mind waiting until that gas station down the street opens?"

Dani began to snicker, trying to contain the amusement threatening to burst from her mouth. When her giggles turned into full-on laughter, she knew she'd lost the battle. The situation was so unbelievably absurd it became hilarious. Perhaps it was the early hour or her sleep-deprived state. Whatever the reason, she laughed long and hard, giving her stomach muscles quite the workout and even bringing tears to her eyes.

When she finally looked at Jeff, he was staring at her with an unreadable expression. "Most people are grumpy when they get woken up in the middle of the night," he said.

She collapsed back against the sofa. "I'm not exactly normal."

"So I'm noticing," he said. "That's one of the reasons you have me so intrigued."

"Well, I'm sure after this weekend you'll be running back to Rexburg, praying you never lay eyes on me again."

"I take it that means you aren't planning to kick me out."

"That all depends."

"On what?"

"How useful you can make yourself."

"But I'm a guest," he said.

"An uninvited guest."

He raised an eyebrow. "Fine. What would you like me to do?"

"Well, for starters, let's find you a proper bed and let you get some sleep."

"That doesn't sound so bad."

"I'm going to need you well-rested for later today."

He chuckled as he followed her down the hall. "I take it you don't have many visitors."

❉

Dani entered the kitchen and found her grandma sipping orange juice while peering at the morning newspaper's crossword puzzle. "And how are we this morning?"

Rose looked up and smiled. "I feel like a new woman. You've fortified my spirits and brought joy back to my life."

"Then I'm doing the same thing you've done for me so often over the years." Dani pulled out some eggs from the refrigerator. "So what would you like to do today?"

"Actually, I was wondering . . ." Rose paused, looking hesitant.

Dani raised her eyebrows. "You were wondering . . . ?"

A door opened and closed down the hall, making Rose jump. "What was that?"

"You mean, who was that?"

Rose stared at Jeff as he shuffled into the room. "Okay, then. Who is that?"

"Just an uninvited guest," Dani said. "He showed up freezing on our front porch in the middle of the night."

"And you let him in?" Rose's eyes widened in surprise when Jeff sat down next to her and poured himself some juice.

Dani watched her grandmother in amusement. "I didn't exactly want his death on my conscience."

"Gee, thanks." Jeff held his hand out to Rose. "Hi, I'm Jeff. You must be Nana."

Rose eyed him warily before taking his proffered hand. "What brought you to our door, young man?"

"Your granddaughter."

"Oh." Rose's nervousness all but disappeared.

He brought the glass to his lips and swallowed. "You see, back in Rexburg, Dani wouldn't give me the time of day, so I figured I'd corner her in Colorado Springs. You don't, by chance, know how I can get her to go out with me do you? One date is all I ask."

Rose studied him from across the table. "You're pre-med, aren't you?"

Jeff grinned. "She's told you about me, huh?"

"Not in so many words."

He shrugged. "I'll take what I can get."

Rose eyed him with open curiosity. She even put down her pen and pushed the paper aside. "Perhaps if you switched your major," she said. "How set are you on becoming a doctor anyway?"

"Nana!" said Dani.

Jeff drew his eyebrows together. "Pardon?"

Rose continued as if she'd heard no interruptions. "You could become a teacher or an average businessman. Or maybe you could drop out of school altogether. I'm certain you could make a decent wage as some sort of worker or day-laborer."

While Dani glared at her grandmother, Jeff said, "You lost me at changing my major. What does that have to do with going out with your granddaughter? Do you have something against doctors?"

"*I* don't," Rose said. "I'm rather fond of my physician back home. If only he were twenty years older and single."

Jeff redirected his gaze to Dani. "Do *you* have a problem with doctors?"

Dani blatantly ignored his question. She turned around, beat two eggs, and poured them into a sizzling skillet. "I hope you like omelets."

Jeff's breath tickled her neck. "They're my favorite."

She jumped and practically spilled the egg mixture as goose bumps travelled across her back and down her arms. Letting go of the pan's handle, she sidestepped away and busied herself by cracking two more eggs for another omelet.

Jeff casually leaned against the counter next to Dani. "Sorry, Nana," he said. "But your granddaughter has been avoiding me for several weeks now, and she's only just learned I'm pre-med. She may have some personal vendetta against doctors, but that can't be the only reason she won't go out with me. Any other ideas?"

Dani roughly removed the omelet from the pan, dumped it on a plate, and shoved it in front of Jeff's face. "Do you mind psycho-analyzing me another time? I'm starving."

He looked down at the massacred omelet.

"Bon appétit," Dani said sweetly before turning back to the stove.

"Nana, I think you should hurry and apologize," said Jeff. "You are an accomplice, after all."

Rose wasn't paying attention. Instead, she appeared pensive, like she was trying to figure out an answer to a riddle. Finally, she looked at Jeff. "Did you upset her in any way before you asked her out?"

Jeff laughed. "Yes, and most likely every encounter since then. Is that the reason?"

Rose nodded slowly, as though she were preparing him for bad news. "You need to know that Dani is slow to forgive. I'm afraid it's one of her few faults."

"Do you know how I might remedy that problem?"

"Definitely not by using medical terminology," said Rose, picking up her pen and returning to her crossword puzzle.

"Will you two please stop talking about me like I'm not here?"

Dani asked as she placed an immaculate omelet in front of her grandmother.

Glancing from his plate to Nana's, Jeff compared the two omelets before accusing, "Why does hers look so good? She never apologized!"

"Ah, but Nana can do no wrong in my eyes," Dani said.

Jeff took a seat next to Nana. "And just how does one go about obtaining that status?"

Rose patted his hand before taking a bite of her breakfast. "Keep at it, dear boy, and you'll figure it out someday."

Eight

··•··•·*·•·*·

Dani closed her calculus book in satisfaction. With Jeff's clear explanations and examples, she had completed the perplexing math problems in no time. He'd even helped her with the assignment due the following week. She felt an immense sense of relief and reluctantly admitted to herself that she owed it all to the enigma seated beside her.

Glancing over at him, she found him watching her. "Thank you so much. I'm not sure what I would have done without your help."

"Does this mean you owe me one?"

"Room and board doesn't count?"

Jeff chuckled. "I just can't win with you, can I?"

Rose walked into the room wearing her favorite rose-colored dress; the one she typically saved for special occasions. Using her cane, she made her way to Dani's side. "If it's okay with you, I would really like to go to the temple today."

"By yourself?" Dani asked.

Rose nodded.

Dani bit her lip. Why wouldn't Nana talk to her? "Are you okay? Can I help you with anything?"

"You've already helped me more than you know." Rose smiled warmly as she touched her granddaughter's cheek. "It's nothing to worry about. I used to go every week before the accident, and I mainly just miss it. Would you mind terribly?"

"Of course not," Dani said, even though she knew something was wrong. She wished Nana would confide in her. "I hope you know that if there's anything I can do, I'd do it in a second."

"I know," said Nana. "But everything is fine."

"We can take my truck," Jeff said. "But we need to make a quick stop at a gas station first."

Dani looked at him in surprise. "Oh, you don't need to go. You were up half the night. Wouldn't you rather just stay here, relax, and take a nap?"

"No way." He pushed his chair back. "You're not getting rid of me that easily. I'll just grab my keys."

"But—" Dani stopped when a hand gently squeezed her shoulder. Puzzled, she looked up to find Nana shaking her head.

"Let him take us, sweetie. He can keep you company."

❊

Sandwiched between Jeff and Nana on the front bench seat of his small truck, Dani remained thoughtful during their one-hour trip to Denver. She was grateful he had insisted on driving because her thoughts were a million miles away, alternating between the driver of the vehicle and the aging woman beside her. Jeff seemed uncomfortably close, and she was disturbed by how much she enjoyed having him around. On the other hand, her grandmother seemed preoccupied with a problem—one she didn't intend to discuss with her granddaughter.

Dani hated feeling helpless.

But the thoughts refused to take residence elsewhere, and Dani became increasingly anxious and restless. What was Nana not telling her? And what would she do with Jeff for two hours while they waited? She didn't like the idea of spending time alone with him, considering her growing feelings. In ten years, he would be a surgeon—making too much money and working insane hours. Sure, he was wonderful now, but that could all change in an instant.

She had always wanted a simple life in a small town or city. She wanted a little house and a big yard, a tire swing, and a tree house. She wanted a husband to walk through the door every night at a reasonable hour. She wanted him to be close enough to come home for lunch and to make it to their kids' school or sporting events. In essence, she wanted a slow life, a happy life. A wealthy surgeon would never fit into that picture.

Gradually she became aware of a conversation happening around her. Jeff must have asked Nana about her life, or at least that's what Dani surmised as she listened to her grandmother.

"And so we moved to Garysville. Population 900 at the time. At first, I couldn't wait to leave, but after a year or two, I fell in love with the place. It was beautiful, and the people were so close, helping and serving each other as if we were all family. Unfortunately, my daughter, Paula, could never see the charm. The summer after she graduated from high school, she took a job as a nanny for a family in Sacramento. It was there she met Dave, and they were married within six months.

"Danielle, on the other hand, has always been more like me. She loved to come and spend the summers with me while her parents travelled. I always looked forward to her visits, and we had such marvelous times back then."

"You know I'm still planning to come this summer," Dani said.

"I can hardly wait." Nana patted her granddaughter's knee. "And you are always welcome too, Jeff."

"I might just take you up on that." Jeff winked at Dani.

She rolled her eyes. "I'm not sure Garysville is big enough for you. Your overpowering confidence might make everyone feel claustrophobic."

"My ego, you mean," Jeff said. "Don't worry. If I keep spending time with you, it's sure to dwindle by then."

Dani laughed, wondering what he'd think of her beloved small town. Would he love it as she did, or would he make fun of it and call it Mayberry?

Jeff and Dani each offered an arm to Nana as they helped her up the walk to the temple, although Rose didn't appreciate their coddling. "My foot is healed well enough, and with this cane I can walk just fine on my own."

"The sidewalks are icy and wet," Dani said before noticing the walkway was actually dry and clear since it hadn't snowed in days.

Jeff and Nana exchanged looks before he whispered, "I think you should just be grateful she's letting you out of her sight for a couple of hours."

Nana laughed.

After leaving Nana at the front desk, Jeff and Dani meandered back to the truck. "What do you want to do?" he asked.

"I have no idea. If only it weren't so cold outside."

"How do you feel about racquetball?" His eyes challenged hers. "I noticed the words 'Racquetball Courts' on the side of a building back down the road. I'm assuming that must mean they have some racquetball courts inside."

"Racquetball?" Dani asked, looking doubtfully down at her jeans and sneakers. "I'm not exactly dressed to play."

"Neither am I." He turned on the ignition. "If you have any better ideas, I'm all ears. If not, I challenge you to a game of good old-fashioned racquetball."

"Are you any good?"

"No."

"Then you're on."

It didn't take long to find the large gray box of a building. Sure enough, the words "Racquetball Courts" were stenciled across one concrete wall in faded orange paint. They rented rackets and a ball before confining themselves in a small court that smelled of sweat.

"What are the stakes?" Jeff's voice reverberated off the walls, ceiling, and floor.

"Stakes?"

"Stakes. You know—a wager?"

"I don't bet."

"You're just worried you'll lose."

"Maybe I am and maybe I just don't bet."

Jeff ignored her. "How about if I win, you have to go out with me tonight on an official date. And if you win—well, that's not going to happen, so we don't need to worry about it."

Dani felt her competitive spirit engage. "How about when I win, you will stop asking me out."

"I'm not sure if I can handle stakes that high. How about I won't ask you out for an entire week? That seems more fair."

"Sorry, but my terms stand. Take 'em or leave 'em."

"Fine." Jeff threw the ball in her direction. "You can even serve first. We'll do the best two out of three games."

As it turned out, they were fairly evenly matched. After the first hour, they each had one game to their credit and the third was tied at 5-5.

"You're not so bad," Jeff said, holding his hand up for the ball. It was his turn to serve. "For a left-hander."

"You're not so bad either." She tossed him the ball. "I do have a confession to make, though."

"Yes?"

"Well, it just so happens that I know something that you don't." Flipping her racket in the air, she caught it neatly with her right hand. "You see, I . . . am not left-handed." Although she made a valiant effort, she sounded nothing like Inigo Montoya from *The Princess Bride*.

He rolled his eyes. "Are you ambidextrous at sword-fighting too?"

She ignored the question. "Is your confidence shattered?"

"Shaken, maybe, but not shattered. I was going easy on you. That ends now."

She moved to stand behind him. "All right. Let's see what you've got."

Jeff served, held his own for a few additional points, and then lost his serve to Dani. He never gained it back, and she exited the court the official winner.

"You know what this means," she said.

"That you're planning to ask me out for tonight?"

"Dream on, my friend," said Dani, wondering why she felt a pang of disappointment. Would he really leave her alone? Did she really want him to? She tried to convince herself that she did.

"Do I get a consolation prize at least?" Jeff asked.

"No way."

"You're heartless."

A few minutes later, they pulled around to the front of the temple, and Jeff turned to Dani. "Why don't you hang out here while I go inside and wait for Nana? I don't think we'll get in trouble for parking the truck here as long as someone's inside."

Dani nodded but couldn't resist saying, "Yes, I can definitely see one of those sweet elderly temple workers calling a tow truck."

Jeff rolled his eyes and jumped out.

Fifteen minutes later, Dani watched with something akin to sentimentality as he held Nana's arm and led her down the walkway. Again, he had engaged her beautiful grandmother in some sort of conversation, and she felt an unwanted rush of tenderness at the sight. Why did he have to be so nice?

"I think you owe him a consolation prize, dearest," Rose said as she buckled her seatbelt.

Dani glared at Jeff. "You told her about our bet?"

Nana was unfazed. "He did lose to a girl, after all."

"I prefer to think that I lost to a hustler," Jeff said. "No need to make me sound incompetent, though I'm glad you agree with me."

"You mentioned nothing about a consolation prize when I agreed to your ridiculous wager," said Dani.

"I know, but my wounded male ego may never recover without a little TLC."

"And what TLC does this over-inflated ego of yours need?"

"All I want is a simple postponement of our terms. If you'll go out with me tonight, I promise to leave you alone once we're back at school."

"Hey, you aren't allowed to say stuff like that anymore! You lost, remember?"

"Nana. A little help, please?" Jeff asked.

Rose complied without hesitation. "Now, Danielle, this nice young man drove all the way from Idaho to help you with your math and to see you. He's also agreed to not bother you once you return to school. And how do you return his kindness?" She shook her head in disappointment. "I thought I taught you better."

"That's not fair and you know it."

Rose smiled and patted Dani's knee. "Then it's all settled. Besides, I'm in the middle of a wonderful book and would love some quiet time to finish it up tonight."

Feeling trapped, Dani remained silent for the remainder of the ride, noting, out of the corner of her eye, Jeff's smug expression.

Nine

✳ ˙ ● ˙ ✳ ● ✳ ● ˙ ✳ ˙

Jeff pulled his truck into the parking lot, and Dani doubtfully eyed the decrepit, rundown strip mall. Three of the five stores appeared vacant, with broken windows, crumbled bricks, and dismantled signs. And only one place was currently open, with a neon sign blinking the words, "Los Gatos."

"The cats?" Dani wondered whether the health code officials were aware of this restaurant.

"The owners have a soft spot for cats. Every night, they throw all their leftovers into the alley behind the restaurant for all the stray animals in the area—mostly cats."

"Seriously?" Somehow the information did nothing to improve her opinion of the place.

"Scout's honor." He opened the restaurant door and ushered her inside.

"Señor Andrews!" A middle-aged woman with rich olive skin, long black hair, and dark eyes rushed forward and enveloped Jeff in a bear hug. In a thick accent, she said, "You've come home!"

"Just a short visit, Señora Moreno. I was in the area and couldn't resist the taste of your amazing food."

Their hostess released Jeff and turned to Dani. "And who is this? You brought tu novia?"

"Sí." Jeff snaked is arm around Dani and pulled her close.

Señora Moreno's eyes sparkled. "I see. Well then, I have just the table for you." She gestured for them to follow her.

Jeff dropped his arm from her shoulders and casually took her hand as they followed. Dani considered pulling free but was distracted by the feelings coursing through her body. Holding his hand felt so natural—so good. She was confused and torn. She didn't want to like this guy who continued to invade her thoughts and upset her equilibrium.

They were graciously shown to a small, secluded table in the far corner of the dimly lit room. Dani was grateful to see that the inside of the building was remarkably clean and even charming, with sombreros and posters of Mexican beaches decorating the brightly colored walls. The smells from the kitchen made her mouth water and reminded her that she hadn't eaten anything in hours.

Jeff released her hand when they sat down, and Dani made a pretense of studying her menu, trying in vain to focus on the words.

He came to her rescue. "Would you trust me to order for you?"

"Yes, please." She handed the menu back to Señora Moreno. "I'm sure everything is delicious. It smells wonderful in here."

"Gracias." Señora Moreno turned to Jeff. "She's a keeper, this one."

"I know." Jeff winked at Dani before placing their order. After a brief update on the Moreno family, their hostess returned to the kitchen.

Dani felt nervous and uncomfortable, not knowing what to think, say, or do. Instead, she looked everywhere but at Jeff.

"Is it really because I want to become a doctor?" he asked.

Dani's eyes flew to his, and she found him studying her intently. She didn't pretend to misunderstand his question, but how could she explain? Her strong views had been determined by a lifetime of experiences, and this was a difficult topic for her. "My father is a doctor. A very good, successful, and wealthy plastic surgeon."

"Impressive."

"Is it?" She didn't try to hide the hurt and anger. "I don't know my father. He's as much a stranger to me as most of my professors at school. He's always worked insane hours, leaving my mother and me home alone. And to compensate for his absence, my mom became a stranger as well. She turned to material things—becoming consumed with her appearance and status in society. And as she got older, she started getting plastic surgeries to combat the effects of age. She's selfish, vain, and insecure. And I don't remember the last time they went to church.

"As for me, well, I never lacked anything money could buy. My parents enrolled me in the best private schools and made sure I received the best education. I was given a bright red Audi convertible for my sixteenth birthday, which thankfully I was able to trade in for something slightly more sensible. For my eighteenth birthday it was a trip to an all-inclusive resort for me and a friend of my choice. Nana had no desire to go, and the only real friend I've ever had lived in Alaska. Her parents weren't about to let her go off on her own—even at eighteen—so I never used the tickets.

"Nana saved me during those years. My parents allowed me to visit her most summers, probably because they didn't know what else to do with me, and I'm so grateful for that. I was able to see how normal people behaved. She shared with me her time, her love, her wisdom, and most important, her testimony. I'm not sure what I would have been like without her."

"Your grandmother is amazing," Jeff said, reaching across the table to take her hand. "But you know that all doctors aren't like your father, right? And all doctor's wives aren't like your mother?"

"Now you sound like Nana."

"You did say she was wise."

Dani laughed. "Touché." She glanced down at her fingers clasped in his. Wanting him to understand her deep-rooted fears, she said, "I know that there are some rich people that do wonderful things with their money, but even you have to admit that wealth holds a great power to change—and I don't mean for the better. Believe me, I've known my fair share of affluent people, and very few of them live in a normal house, drive a normal car, or lead a normal life."

Dani took a breath before continuing, a little self-consciously, "I remember reading the Book of Mormon one night when I was twelve. I was staying with Nana at the time, and I came across that verse in Jacob, about how it's okay to seek for riches, as long as you seek them with the intent to do good. For some reason, it hit me really hard. When I came back to Colorado Springs, I tried to talk to my parents—to see if we could start some sort of scholarship fund or something. I mean, there are a lot of incredibly poor people in the town where my grandmother lives, and I'd decided I wanted to help some of them out. But my parents looked at me like I was crazy. My mother even mentioned that Nana was perhaps not the best influence. I determined then and there that I would never date anyone who was interested in becoming rich. Least of all a doctor.

"I know it sounds judgmental, but the simple fact is that I prefer the life my grandmother introduced me to. I want that kind of life for my own family. Can you understand now where I'm coming from?"

Jeff considered her with a thoughtful expression as Señora Moreno arrived with their food. After making sure everything was to their liking, she filled their glasses and went to greet some new customers. Dani took a bite of her enchilada. Jeff was right, it was delicious.

He picked up his fork. "I do understand where you're coming from, but I also know that the lack of money can cause a great deal of problems as well. Take the Morenos, for example. They may run this restaurant, but they're far from wealthy. In fact, several years ago, they were ready to file for both bankruptcy and divorce because of all the tension caused by money."

"What happened?"

"Our families have always been close. My father is a financial analyst, and when he found out about their problems, he offered to help them. He taught them how to budget, how to cut costs, and how to invest what little money they had. They still struggle, but at least now they're able to keep their heads above water."

Dani nodded slowly. "The grass is always greener."

"Yes, it is," Jeff said. "Now will you forget our stupid bet and go out with me when we get back?"

"I don't know. Are you going to turn into a selfish, pig-headed, overconfident doctor who drives a sports car and has no time?"

"I don't know. Are you planning to be around to find out?" Jeff asked.

"Of course not." Dani blushed at her unintended implication and turned her attention back to her food. "You've made your point. But I've had this issue on my mind for too many years to be swayed by a five-minute conversation. Anyone who wants to date me will have to prove to me that he has better things to spend money on than multiple sports cars, ridiculously expensive clothes, or a mansion."

Jeff smiled. "So what you're saying is that in ten or so years, when I've finally finished school and am actually making some money, if I show up at your house in a beater truck and take you to my double-wide, then you'll date me?"

"I don't think I could ever date someone with a double-wide," Dani teased.

"Perhaps a nice, moderately-sized, suburban home, then?"

"Only as long as you aren't going bald."

Jeff shook his head. "You have some serious double-standard issues."

After dinner, Señora Moreno refused to bill them for the food, and Dani felt yet another prick of admiration when she saw Jeff hide a hefty tip under his plate.

They were both silent for the drive home, and when they reached Dani's house, Jeff held her hand in his as they meandered up the walkway. When they made it to the door, she gently pulled free and reached for the handle.

"Wait," Jeff said. "Don't tell me you're trying to avoid the doorstep scene."

Dani relinquished the handle and turned around. She hugged her arms to her chest. "Doesn't it seem pointless since it's freezing out here and you're just going to follow me in?"

"This is the end of our date," he said. "And you just told me that you won't go out with me, at least not any time in the next ten years, so this is pretty much my only opportunity."

"Opportunity?" Dani raised her eyebrows. "For what, exactly?"

"Well," Jeff said, taking a step closer. "How about you start off by telling me what a great time you had with me tonight."

Dani fought a threatening smile. Dutifully, she repeated, "I had a great time with you tonight. Now what?"

"I reply in kind, of course," he said. "I had a wonderful time with you as well."

"Did you, now?"

"I did," he said.

"I actually did too." She meant it this time.

"So you said."

"True. Are we done here?"

"No." Jeff took another step closer. "Now tell me, what would a stubborn and beautiful girl do to say good-bye to a guy who she didn't want to be out with in the first place? A nod, a handshake, a hug . . ." His voice drifted off and he looked at her with a question in his amused eyes.

Dani laughed. "Sorry, but I don't give hugs on dates."

"What about a handshake, then?"

"Even worse."

"Worse?"

Dani spoke without thinking. "Yes. Nana says that handshakes come from the cowardly and hugs from the weak-minded. She's always saying, 'If a man truly has a spine, he will brazenly kiss you and offer no apology for doing so.'"

Jeff smiled outright. "Well, in that case." He dipped his head and brought his lips to hers before she had a chance to respond.

It was a soft, brief kiss, and Dani loved every second of it. When he pulled back, she had to keep herself from stumbling forward and wrapping her arms around his waist to keep him close.

"Your grandmother is a very wise woman."

"You kissed me." Her heart was pounding, and she was having difficulty gathering her thoughts. "I didn't mean to imply . . ." She paused, not sure what she was going to say.

"Do you still think I'm spineless?"

"No—I mean, yes—I mean—" Dani turned around and fled inside. "Nana, we're back!"

"So soon?" Rose called from the family room. "I'm not finished with my book yet. Go out for dessert and bring me back something."

"What?" Dani rounded the corner and stared at her grandmother.

"Or a movie. Yes, why don't you go rent a movie?"

"I don't want to watch a movie and I'm not hungry." Dani was now cross as well as flustered. She needed to get away from Jeff. "I'm actually tired, so you know, why don't I turn in and let you finish your high priority book?"

Rose squinted at her silver beaded watch. "But it's only nine o'clock!"

"Good night," Dani said before disappearing into her room and very nearly slamming the door.

❋

Brighton shifted uncomfortably when Rose's steady gaze settled on him. It was as though she could read his innermost thoughts, and it discomfited him.

"What's gotten into her?" she asked.

"Beats me," he lied, shoving his hands into his pockets as he wandered into the kitchen. "If you were serious about dessert and have some ice cream lying around, I can make a mean milkshake."

"I'll be waiting right here."

While he was scooping the ice cream into a blender, he looked up to find Rose watching him. "What's on your mind, Nana?" he asked as he added strawberry jam and milk.

"My granddaughter."

"Join the club." He placed the lid on the blender and pushed the power button. The motor screamed to life, making further conversation difficult. After he had poured two glasses of a thick, strawberry shake, he took one to Rose and plopped down across from her on the sofa.

"Are you in love with her?"

Brighton choked on his shake, having inhaled instead of swallowed. When his coughing fit subsided, he said, "That's impossible to say. We hardly know each other."

"People have fallen in love having spent less time together."

He shrugged. "What does it matter anyway? She won't give me the time of day."

"You should kiss her."

"Tried that. It didn't go over so well."

Rose's eyes twinkled. "Oh, so that explains her behavior tonight."

"Don't go getting any ideas. I only kissed her because she told me that you'd think I was a coward otherwise. I don't think she was too happy with my bravery."

Nana smiled, saying almost to herself, "Well, it's about time Danielle fell for someone."

"I'm afraid you have it wrong."

"I'm never wrong," Rose said, sipping her milkshake.

Feeling Nana's eyes penetrate right through him, Brighton finished his shake, borrowed Dani's excuse, and escaped to the guest room. He closed the door with relief, fell backward onto the black and white paisley bedspread, and stared at the white trey ceiling with black moldings. Everything in the room was either black or white, from the white blinds to the black armchair to the pristine white carpet. It looked nice enough, but it lacked the warmth he was used to in his own parents' home. He found himself wondering how Dani might decorate a house. Were her tastes similar to her mother's? Somehow he doubted it.

Dani. Her name echoed through his mind for what seemed like the hundredth time. He had enjoyed their date that night, just like every other time he had been with her. She was refreshing to be around, challenging his ideas and opening his eyes to things he'd never considered. His career choice, for example. What would life really be like as a surgeon? Would he be working around the clock as she implied, or would he be able to have a normal lifestyle?

He'd never thought about it before. His dreams of becoming a world-famous surgeon, sought after by the elite sports icons, seemed less important somehow. Sure, he'd love to treat athletes with sports-related injuries, but did he really need to be a preeminent surgeon to be happy? Could he be content in a small practice, working with high school kids or the elderly?

There was no doubt in his mind he would choose orthopedics, but he also admitted to himself that he couldn't enter medical school wearing blinders. Perhaps when he got back to Rexburg, he would arrange to meet with a few orthopedic surgeons and find out what life was like for them and what it would be like for him. He prayed he would like their answers.

Brighton rubbed his dry, scratchy eyes in an attempt to bring them some relief. Why was he even worrying about the future? He still had four years of medical school and five years of residency. Nearly a decade. No decisions needed to be made about the type of practice he would join or the hours he would work.

Instead, he should be overjoyed because he had not only won the bet, but come Monday, he could return to Rexburg free and clear from women, dating, and laundry. And he could forget all about Dani Carlson.

If only.

How could a girl be so aggravating and yet so likeable at the same time? She'd gotten to him somehow, like pistachio flavored ice cream. One taste was all it took.

She had barged into his head, made herself at home, and signed a long-term lease. If only Katherine or Sandy had never happened.

Now he was caught in a horrible catch-22 with no idea how to extricate himself. If he wanted to keep seeing Dani, he had to tell her the truth—and then be prepared for her to hate him for all eternity. Either way, he lost. Because of a silly bet, he would lose Dani, and yet he would never have met her otherwise. How he hated the irony.

He snatched a black silky pillow from his bed and threw it hard against the wall.

❊

Dani felt anxious, like a caged raccoon waiting to strike at the next finger that appeared through a hole in the wires. She needed a punching bag, she decided, to batter and pummel with her raw hands. If only Jeff and Nana would go to bed, she could escape and go for a long run, except that it was freezing outside. She needed something, anything, to release her mounting apprehension and worry, to beat down the disgust she felt for betraying her convictions and making a fool of herself.

How could one simple, undemanding kiss upset her emotions and cloud her resolutions? What had probably been nondescript for Jeff had been a 7.0 on the Richter scale for her. The walls she had erected and continuously fortified had cracked, threatening a full-on break. The trouble was, she wasn't sure she'd be able to repair the fractures and resecure the walls.

Why medicine? Why not accounting, computer science, or even philosophy? Those were perfectly acceptable aspirations. Why a doctor? Her heart quelled at the idea of becoming emotionally attached to him. No! She wouldn't—she couldn't. And yet she already had. How in the world would she ever face him again?

Dani turned off the light, opened her window blinds, and sank down in a striped brown and steel blue oversized chair. She gazed at the beautiful winter scene dazzling her on the other side of the window pane. Light from the street lamps illuminated the snow as it cascaded down in soft disarray. Footprints and muck from the streets faded as new, luminous snow covered the old. It was magical, and Dani felt the first stirrings of peace.

Offering a silent prayer of thanks, she allowed her now sane mind to drift once again to Jeff. He was a good person. Was he capable of remaining the same? Once wealth and status entered his world, would he change? She couldn't say.

What she did know was that she responded to him. He was kind, funny, handsome, and adorable. She loved the way he made her feel—beautiful, intelligent, and, yes, even giddy. A girl would have to be mad to not fall for him, at least a little. It was simple, really. She could go back to Rexburg and date him, or she could continue to drive him away.

Dani stood and padded over to her bedroom door. Opening it a crack, she peeked out and tiptoed down the hall, stealing her way into the kitchen. She needed fortification. She needed ice cream. Pulling open the freezer door, she stared at the empty top shelf in confusion. The vanilla was present and accounted for, but the quart of mint chocolate chip ice cream she had recently purchased had disappeared. Her eyes roamed over the other racks with no luck. The ice cream was gone. *Her* ice cream was gone.

Who would do such a thing?

"Jeff!" The whispered accusation and the stomping of her stocking-clad foot sounded loud in the expansive kitchen. Surely he couldn't have eaten her entire stash.

"Present," a deep voice called from across the room.

Dani jumped, and the freezer door slammed shut. Hearing something crash inside the closed door, she glared into the darkened family room. "Darn you!" Carefully, she reopened the door and watched as the last jar of her grandmother's homemade strawberry jam fell onto the cold stone floor and cracked.

Picking up the ruined jar, Dani peered once more into the darkness and hissed, "The jam in the fridge better last the rest of the week and there better be some of that ice cream left!"

"It's kind of difficult to determine volume in a darkened room," Jeff said. "But maybe I should start praying, just in case."

Grumbling, Dani threw the broken jar in the garbage can, grabbed a spoon from the kitchen drawer, and stalked across the tiles to the family room. Opening the blinds to let in some diffused light, she saw Jeff lounging on the couch, cheekily offering her the carton of ice cream. She took the carton, plunked down beside him on the sofa, took a spoonful, and held the carton out for him to do the same.

"So you're not tired after all," he said as he loaded his spoon.

"I took a catnap," she lied. "What's your excuse?"

"Couldn't sleep," he said.

"Why not? You should be exhausted."

"I am."

"So?"

"I've been doing some thinking."

"About?" She took another bite.

"You."

Pausing with the spoon in her mouth, she slowly pulled it out and swallowed. "Well, that clears things up."

"Great. Then I'm off to bed." Jeff started to rise before Dani halted him with her hand on his arm.

"Wait," she said. "I need to talk to you."

He settled back on the couch and waited.

Dani squirmed at the intense gaze peering at her in the dim light. "I—" She paused before trying again. "I mean, you—" Again she faltered, not knowing how to say whatever it was she was trying to say. "Never mind." She had yet to understand her own mind, so she opted for silence, taking a large bite of ice cream to emphasize her decision.

Dani felt Jeff's eyes on hers as she swallowed the ice cream. Unexpectedly, he leaned over and brought his mouth to hers. She gasped in surprise, but immediately responded—almost hungrily. After a few moments, he gently and almost reluctantly pulled away.

Looking into her eyes, he said, "I like you. And I'd like the chance to get to know you better. Will you please let me?"

She wasn't sure if it was the lateness of the hour, her sleep-deprived state, or the pleading, sincere look in his eyes. Whatever the reason, she allowed herself a small nod, too afraid to speak.

"So you will let me ask you out back in Rexburg?" he asked.

She nodded again.

"And you'll say yes when I ask?"

She remembered the promise she had made to Katherine and almost laughed. "I'm sort of obligated to say yes, actually."

He looked confused and maybe even a little hurt—she didn't know for sure. Not wanting him to get the wrong idea, she tried to explain. "I'm sorry, that came out wrong. It's just that I made a promise to my roommate—" She stopped, realizing how absurd she sounded.

He sighed, leaned forward, and rested his elbows on his knees and rubbed his eyes. "I don't want you to go out with me because of some ridiculous promise. If you're not feeling what I'm obviously feeling, then please just tell me now."

When it came to openly sharing her innermost thoughts, Dani's natural instinct was to shy away and divert the conversation to something more light and easy. Unfortunately, her teasing comment had the opposite effect, adding more tension. Why did she have to bring up that ridiculous promise? Glancing at Jeff, she realized she needed to say something.

So she opted for the truth. If she offended him, well, she

offended him. But at least he would know what she was thinking. "The truth is that I don't want to like you. You're exactly the type of person I promised to never involve myself with. But now I am at a crossroads because the fact is that I do like you. I could see myself dating, if only it weren't for—" She searched his eyes, needing him to understand what she couldn't bring herself to say.

"My future choice of profession," he said.

"Yes."

"I'm not asking you to marry me, you know."

She blushed. "I know. But what if—" Then she blushed even deeper, grateful for the darkness. Why couldn't she learn to keep her mouth shut sometimes?

He nodded, even smiled. "What if we just take it one date at a time and see what happens? You never know. Two more dates and we may revert back to despising each other."

"Very true." She laughed, grateful for the return to light banter. "All right. How about this: If you still want to ask me out when we get back, all sense of duty aside, I will say yes because I want to, and we'll see how long it takes for you to come to your senses."

"Sounds good to me." He leaned over and kissed her softly, stood, and lightly grazed her cheek with his fingers.

❊

"You're playing with fire, idiot," Brighton said to himself as he fought for a comfortable position on the mattress. He wasn't sure what had prompted him to kiss her again. Perhaps it was her flustered expression or the way the ice cream lingered on her lips. Whatever the reason, she had responded. And with that response came the unsettling reality that he had fallen—hard.

He had to tell her about the bet, but how? How would he make her understand? Especially when she liked him against her will to begin with. He was a fool who deserved a good flogging, and he was sure it was only a matter of time before Dani would gladly do the job herself.

Ten

Dani breathed a sigh of relief when the private jet her father's medical practice owned touched down at the Idaho Falls airport. A massive storm hovered over southeastern Idaho, hurling snow in all directions and resulting in severe whiteout conditions. It had created some unnerving turbulence during the last twenty minutes of the flight, and she was grateful to be back on solid ground.

Thanking the pilot, she stepped down from the plane into the frigid hangar and located her Toyota Sequoia. Preparing herself for the sluggish, cautious drive ahead of her, Dani turned on the ignition and shivered while she waited for the cold air to turn warm.

A loud knocking on her window made her jump, and Dani glanced over to see the pilot gesturing for her to roll down her window. She obeyed and lowered it several inches. "What's the problem, Jack?" she asked.

"It's crazy weather out there, Miss Danielle," he said. "If you can wait a few minutes, I'd like to put some chains on your tires before you take off."

Dani hesitated. "Is that really necessary? You've got to be freezing, and I have new snow tires."

"I'd feel much better if you'd let me put the chains on. It won't take but a minute or two."

"If you're sure."

"I'm sure."

"Okay. Thank you."

While he was spreading out the chains, Dani let her thoughts drift to the past week—well, mainly to the last day she and Nana had spent with Jeff. He had been his usual engaging and charming self, and the day had been fun, but it had also been disappointing.

She wasn't sure what she had expected from him, but after all that had happened, she had definitely expected something. Anything. Maybe a stolen kiss, an arm wrapped possessively around her during church, or some handholding. At the very least, a meaningful look or two.

Instead, he had just been friendly and considerate. After he left, she'd found a scribbled thank you note in the guest room.

About the same time the heater began to blow warm air through the vents, Jack interrupted her reverie with an abrupt knock on her window and gave her the go-ahead. She waved her thanks, put her worries and thoughts aside, and concentrated on the road. The conditions made her nervous. Thankfully, she merged onto the freeway directly behind a Jeep and followed its red taillights toward Rexburg.

Two or three miles from the exit, the Jeep she was following braked and pulled off to the side of the road. Not wanting to continue blindly, Dani followed suit and watched in confusion as the driver in front of her jumped from his truck and ran toward the snow drifts.

Without thinking, Dani tugged on some gloves, opened her car door, and followed. Her eyes widened in shock when she saw the tail end of a white car practically buried in the snow. The driver she had been following was a young man, probably around her age, who was now frantically attempting to sweep the snow from the car. Dani wasn't sure whether or not anyone was still inside, but ran to help.

The snow was coming down hard, and the car was already deeply buried. Finally, the guy yelled, "I have a tow rope in my jeep. I'm going to hook it up and try to haul this car out of here, just to be sure no one's inside."

"What do you want me to do?"

He glanced back and noticed Dani's SUV. "You got four-wheel drive on that thing?"

Dani nodded. "I've got chains on the tires also." She silently thanked Jack for his overprotective kindness.

"Perfect. Let's use your car then. It will get more traction in this mess. Why don't you pull around, and I'll get the rope?"

Dani did as he asked and was soon backing up toward the buried car. Looking over her shoulder, she saw the man duck down behind her Sequoia. She waited nervously while he attached the rope to both vehicles.

When he gestured for her to move forward, she offered a brief, silent prayer and pushed the gas pedal. Miraculously, the Sequoia gripped the road and pulled the buried car free. She watched the man quickly wipe snow from the driver's window, peek inside, and frantically attempt to open the door. Her heart raced, and she leaped from her car and ran to his side. "Is it locked?"

"Locked or frozen. I can't tell." The man let go of the door handle and stumbled back toward his truck. "I'll be right back."

Dani realized the futility of trying to get the door open on her own and instead beated on the window, hoping to arouse the person inside. She refused to consider the possibility that they hadn't made it in time.

"Watch out!"

She jumped as the man slammed a large hammer into the rear window, breaking the glass into shards that coated the back seat. Carefully, he crawled in through the opening and immediately felt for a pulse. When he unlocked the door and it still wouldn't budge, she called, "Can you kick it open from the inside?"

He moved awkwardly to the front passenger seat, shifted positions, and after three swift, hard kicks, the door flew open, thumping Dani in the stomach and knocking her to the ground. She jumped back up and saw the driver—a teenage girl with long blonde hair, who couldn't have been more than sixteen or seventeen. "Does she have a pulse?"

He nodded. "Barely. She's freezing, her breathing is shallow, and she has a nasty bump on her head. For some reason, the airbags didn't inflate. Will you help me get her out of here?"

"Should we move her?"

"She might be hypothermic. We need to get her warm and to a hospital."

Dani nodded and helped to remove the girl from the car. Somehow, they managed to get her into the back seat of Dani's Sequoia. "The hospital in Rexburg isn't far from here. Why don't you follow my Jeep?"

Nodding, Dani climbed into the driver's seat and cranked up the heat to blow as high and hot as possible. The few miles to the hospital seemed to take hours, but they finally arrived and watched as the hospital staff wheeled the girl out of sight, leaving Dani alone in the waiting room with her fellow rescuer.

Now what? She turned and watched the man sink into a nearby armchair. He was obviously not going anywhere. Shrugging, she followed his lead and took the seat next to him.

Glancing in her direction, he said, "Thanks for your help, uh . . ."

"Dani," she said.

"I'm Kevin."

Dani nodded. "I have no idea how you saw a white car buried in a snow drift, but I have to say that you're the most observant person I've ever met. Do you have X-ray vision by chance?"

He chuckled and glanced at the doors where they took the girl. "Do you think they'll let us know how she's doing?"

"Well, I've never actually been in this kind of situation before, so I can't be sure, but in the movies they only give out information to family members. Maybe if you tell them you're her fiancé?"

He shook his head. "Uh, I don't think so. I've seen *While You Were Sleeping*, and I'm not about to get myself engaged to some random girl and her crazy family."

Dani smiled. "Maybe I'll refuse to give them her license plate number until they let us know how she's doing."

He leaned back in his chair, yawned, and raked his fingers though his hair. "Smart girl. I didn't even think to get a plate number, or search her car for a purse, for that matter."

"If she had a purse, it was stuffed under one of the seats or in the glove compartment because I didn't notice it when I looked around. I hope she's got some sort of identification in her coat pocket. If not, I'm sure they can track down her family using the license plate number."

"My only thoughts were on getting her out of there."

"Considering I would never have seen her car to begin with, I'd say we made a pretty good team."

A nurse walked into the waiting room. "I'm glad you're still here. We can't find any identification on her. Could you tell me where the car is located so we can send a police officer to search it?"

"Is she going to be okay?" Kevin asked, ignoring her question.

The nurse nodded. "She's got a concussion, and she's in the beginning stages of hypothermia, but she's going to be fine—thanks to you two. We just really need to contact someone from her family."

"I have a license plate number if that would help," Dani said, pulling out a notepad from her purse. "Maybe it will save the police officer from having to go out in this weather. Do you need anything else?"

"If you wouldn't mind writing down your phone numbers, in case the hospital or police have any questions, I'd appreciate it."

Dani scribbled her name and number down next to the license plate number and handed the notepad to Kevin. When he was done, the nurse thanked them for their help. "You guys are free to go. No use waiting around here any longer."

"Thanks." Dani watched the nurse walk away. She stood and picked up her purse, but Kevin didn't move. "Coming?" she asked.

"I think I'll hang around here for a bit longer, at least until a family member arrives."

Dani nodded. "It was good to meet you."

"Thanks for stopping. I don't think I would have been able to get her out otherwise." All of his lightheartedness had disappeared, and she barely heard him whisper, "That could've been my sister."

Softly, she touched his shoulder. "It wasn't your sister, and she's going to be fine." Glancing at her watch, Dani noted the time. It was only seven-thirty, but it felt later for some reason. Should she stay? He didn't look so good. "I think I'll stick around with you, if that's all right. But I'm starving. Do you want to go to the cafeteria and get something to eat with me?"

He looked up, appearing grateful. "Yeah, that would be great."

Once they were seated at a table, Dani asked, "What were you doing out on the highway in the middle of that blizzard anyway?"

"I grew up in Shelley and was driving home from my parents' house. Sunday dinner and all that. Well, it was actually more of a late lunch." He sheepishly eyed his plate full of food.

"You go home every Sunday?"

"Usually. My mom is an incredible cook, and most of the time my roommates come with me."

"Not today?"

"Nope."

"Not even for a free, home-cooked meal?" she asked.

"One didn't feel well, one had to study, and one is just plain cranky, although I have no idea why. He just won a bet and doesn't have to do his laundry for an entire month."

"You bet on laundry?" Dani laughed.

"Stupid, I know. But we hate doing it, so it's a great motivator."

"What kind of bet?"

"Sorry, but it's confidential." He munched on some chips.

"Oh, come on. We're stuck in a hospital for who knows how long, and you'll probably never see me again. Please? I could use a good story right now."

"Only if you solemnly promise to never tell another soul."

"I solemnly promise to never tell another soul," she dutifully repeated.

He chuckled. "Okay, but you're going to think bad thoughts of me after this, considering it was my idea."

"How could I think badly about a hero?" she asked sweetly.

He rolled his eyes. "Okay, fine. My roommate agreed to date three roommates at the same time without them knowing."

Dani looked at him in surprise. Was he serious? He looked slightly ashamed so he must be telling the truth. "That's terrible! For how long?"

"One month. Only two dates each—not long enough for anyone to become too attached."

That's what you think, Dani thought. It had certainly not taken her long to become attached to Jeff. "And he actually pulled it off?"

"He did," Kevin said with a nod of his head. "Too bad, too, because he never loses and I thought we'd finally beat him."

"How did the girls not find out? I mean, seriously. I know how girls talk—especially to their roommates. There's just no way—" She shook her head. "I just find it hard to believe that anyone could be so . . ."—she searched for the right word—"blind."

Kevin shrugged. "I've thought the same thing myself."

She shrugged. "Well, maybe he's cranky because his conscience came out of hiding, and he's realized what a jerky think that was to do."

"Who knows?" Kevin gulped down the last of his milk. He glanced at his watch. "Let's go back to the waiting room and see if they've been able to track down the girl's family."

Sure enough, the girl's parents were in the foyer, waiting for their daughter to be moved into a recovery room. Kevin and Dani introduced themselves and received several suffocating hugs as well as an embarrassing number of thank-yous.

When she finally broke away, she drove slowly back to her apartment. It had been a long day, and she was exhausted. Trudging up the walk, she opened the door, dropped her bags on the floor, and slammed the door against the wretched weather.

"Danielle Carlson!" Katherine looked abnormally angry. "Where have you been? Your plane landed hours ago, and when I called your cell phone, all I heard was a series of strange beeps. I even called all the hospitals in the area. When the one here in Rexburg said they were treating an unidentified girl, I nearly had a heart attack until they told me she was a teenager with long blonde hair."

"And she was taller than me too," Dani said. "I'm so sorry, but I didn't think to call from the hospital." Blinking her dry eyes, she briefly explained her adventure, hugged Katherine good night, and fell asleep as soon as her head hit the pillow.

❊

It was a good thing Brighton had already been accepted to medical school because lately his ability to concentrate had become less than stellar—much less. Without permission, his thoughts constantly wandered to a green-eyed sprite of a girl who had unwittingly given him a figurative pounding, and he had no intention of making it a literal one.

The more he considered his predicament, the more flustered he became. She had been home for over a week, and he had yet to come up with a fool-proof plan for how to explain the situation and keep her around at the same time. He'd gone through various versions of the conversation over and over in his mind, but the end result was always the same. She hated his guts.

He had even considered telling her he'd been forced into the wager by a band of murderers—with a ripe sense of humor. If he didn't do as they asked, they would . . . what? Kill his sister? Mother? Father? Grandmother? Yes, grandma it would be.

Hardly. He could clearly see the poster his mother had hung on his bulletin board when he was younger. It pictured a boy whose mouth was wrapped tightly with string and the words, "Big lies can start with a little yarn." It was suffocating just thinking about it.

Or maybe he was just out of breath. He'd been running for nearly an hour and had no idea how many times he'd circled the indoor track. He had planned to run until he'd found a rational answer to the Dani dilemma, but sweat now soaked his T-shirt, and the only solutions he'd come up with were anything but rational. Slowing to a walk, he figured there was nothing else to do—he'd just have to tell her the truth and deal with the consequences. He could only pray she'd forgive him.

❇

Katherine and Dani sat alone in the front room of their apartment, attempting to catch up on some homework. Willing herself to come up with a creative backyard design for her landscape class, Dani stared at the blank paper in her lap. It was no use. Jeff's face permeated her thoughts and consumed what little creativity she had to begin with. Eight days had passed without a word from him.

She sank back into the couch cushions and granted her thoughts a voice. "You know, for someone who was so determined to date me, he sure lost interest fast, didn't he?"

Katherine's long slender fingers stilled on her laptop keyboard. "I'm sure he didn't lose interest."

"You're right," Dani said. "Maybe he bumped his head and is either in a comma or has some form of amnesia. Or maybe the University of Utah un-accepted him to their medical school and he's in the depths of despair. Or, more likely, he sat on a tube of super glue, which exploded, gluing his backside to a chair in his apartment, with his phone and computer out of reach. That definitely makes more sense than him not being interested in me any longer."

Katherine laughed. "Well, if it's any consolation, Brighton—the guy from the library—has now decided that books have nothing more to offer him and there are far quieter places to study."

"You haven't seen him either?" Dani wrinkled her brow. "Did a skunk die in our apartment and we just haven't noticed?"

"Not a chance."

"I don't get it then. What more could a guy want than one of us?" Dani asked. "Maybe I'm just a terrible kisser."

"He kissed you?" Katherine looked at her friend in surprise. "You never told me that!"

Dani winced. "It was no big deal." She wished fervently that she could take the words back. If only she had dated more. Then the image of her kissing someone wouldn't be the equivalent of a UFO encounter on the front page news. Katherine was probably already planning the wedding.

"No big deal?" Katherine asked. "Are you kidding me? To my knowledge, you've never kissed anyone before."

"Well, now you know why. I'm obviously terrible at it."

"Please." Katherine smiled, drumming her fingers on the top of her laptop. "What's his last name anyway?"

"Andrews," Dani said without thinking.

"Dani Andrews," Katherine teased. "Yes, that does sound perfect, doesn't it?"

"Don't you dare."

Katherine laughed and then appeared confused. "Hey, Brighton's last name is Andrews also. What a funny coincidence."

A warning bell sounded in Dani's head. It wasn't the only coincidence. Swallowing, she said, "Isn't Brighton from Pueblo too?"

Katherine's eyes narrowed. "Yes. And aren't they both premed? Do you think they could be brothers?"

"Jeff's only brother is in high school," Dani said, her mind whirling. "Is Brighton about six foot three with curly dirty blond hair and blue eyes?"

Katherine's eyes widened. "Um . . . maybe it's like *Parent Trap*, and they don't know they have a twin."

"Yeah, and Bugs Bunny is my uncle." Dani felt a hurt enter her body, one unlike any she'd felt from her neglectful parents. She fought her mounting emotions while trying to make sense of the situation.

"Do you think he just dates a lot, and it was an unlucky coincidence that he happened to take us out around the same time?"

"If so, why would he give us two different names, and why would he never pick us up at our apartment?" Dani asked, her mind searching for answers. "No, he definitely knew we were roommates. The question is, why?"

Although Dani had never been hit by lighting, she had been electrocuted before. It had happened when she was sixteen. She'd just painted her bedroom and was replacing the faceplates for all the electrical outlets. Her hand had slipped, and her finger had grazed a live wire, sending a jolt through her body. She now felt something akin to that sensation, only worse. Shock, followed by numbness, entered her chest. Her stomach knotted and became queasy.

All because she remembered a conversation with a stranger named Kevin in a dimly lit hospital cafeteria. *The bet.* A silly wager she had once thought terrible and yet slightly humorous. Not anymore. Definitely, not anymore. Her perspective had changed from bystander to target, and now the bet seemed like a horrifying prank pulled by immature, unfeeling boys whom she now detested—especially one in particular.

Looking up, she noticed Katherine watching her in silence and remembered that her friend knew nothing of the bet. Should she tell her? Of course she should. And she did—in great detail, omitting nothing, not even her promise to never tell another soul. As far as she was concerned, all promises were now null and void.

"I guess now we know why he disappeared." Dani was furious. She looked at Katherine for a similar reaction but found her friend deep in thought, appearing mildly disappointed but mostly unruffled. "We've been duped, Kath. Aren't you the least bit upset by all of this?"

Katherine's gaze flew to Dani's. "There has to be some explanation. You can't be sure . . ."

Dani fought a mounting frustration with her friend. "What other explanation could there be?"

Katherine sighed. "I guess you're right. He just seems like such a good, decent guy. I can't imagine him doing something like this and thinking it was okay. Especially considering how involved the two of you became."

"Please," Dani said, her voice like steel. "A kiss to someone like him is the equivalent of a hamburger to a McDonald's employee—completely unexceptional."

"He never kissed *me*, you know."

"Well, you're the lucky one, I guess."

Dani wondered if Katherine had ever felt an emotion as dark as anger. During the two years they had been roommates, Dani had never once seen Katherine exhibit anything close to fury—and right now it irritated her. Dani couldn't handle being nice at the moment. She wanted to hold on to her rage, grip it tightly with both hands, and never let go. It was too good a defense against the pain.

"Where are you going?" Katherine asked when Dani stood to leave.

"To bed. I'm going to need all the sleep and energy I can get when I pummel Jeff, or Brighton, or whatever the heck his name is, tomorrow."

✳

With the previous night's revelations fresh in her mind and a B grade English paper clutched in her hand, Dani's mood from the day before had actually worsened. She stormed out into a relatively decent winter afternoon. The sun was peeking through the clouds, and the snow had melted from the concrete, revealing actual sidewalks. For most anyone it would have been a beautiful site, but she was unimpressed.

Feeling like a nitwit for not putting it together before, Dani decided to forgo lunch. She turned toward the Romney Building and quickened her pace, determined to track down her prey.

A few minutes later she knocked loudly on Dr. Green's door.

"Enter," Dr. Green's voice called.

Pulling the door open, Dani found him typing on his computer. His fingers stopped, and he turned in his chair. "Danielle, hello. How can I help you today?"

Slightly flustered, she said, "Sorry to bother you, Professor, but I, uh, was actually looking for your TA."

"Brighton?"

"Yes." Dani experienced a momentary pang of jealousy that Katherine had been the one he'd favored with his true name. "Any idea when he might drop by?" Her tone was cool and clipped.

Dr. Green studied her for a moment before standing. "I'm actually expecting him any second. In fact, I'm late for a meeting across campus, and if you promise to not search for the answers to your next exam, I'm happy to let you wait here for him."

"I'm not a cheater, sir." Dani walked in his office and stood, stiff and rigid.

Dr. Green nodded while he stuffed a book and a sheath of papers into his briefcase. "I'm aware of that. I was only kidding." He made his way out of the office, pausing at the door. "Would you mind letting Brighton know that I'll be back in an hour if he needs me for any reason?"

"If he's still alive after I'm though with him, I will pass along your message."

He raised his eyebrow. "Feel free to take a seat while you wait." He gestured toward his chair and actually smiled as he left the office.

When the door closed, Dani moved to Dr. Green's chair, wanting to see Brighton as soon as he walked through the door. Wondering how long she'd have to wait, she pulled out a blank sheet of paper and tried again for some landscape inspiration, but her brain offered nothing. So she started doodling, drawing a stick figure with a noose around his neck. She labeled the figure "Brighton."

"Hey Dr.—uh, Dani," he said when he noticed who was sitting in the professor's chair.

"Please don't ever call me doctor again," she said. "You, of all people, should know that it's the last title I would ever want to have."

He ignored her comment. "What are you doing here?"

She opted for sarcasm and artificial sweetness. "I just missed you and couldn't wait another second to see that handsome face of yours. I was hoping you'd show up sooner or later—Brighton." Her pasted smile disappeared, replaced with an expression that reflected quite the opposite emotion.

After the initial surprise and worry crossed his face, Brighton appeared resigned to his fate. Sighing, he sat down in a chair across from her. "My name is Brighton Jeffrey Andrews, so it wasn't a complete lie."

"Oh, what a relief. It's so nice to hear that I was only partially lied to," Dani said, her anger returning full force.

"How did you—?"

"I realize that your little game is now over, and you've won your stupid bet, but I just wanted to congratulate you on pulling the wool over my eyes—and Katherine's too for that matter. At least for a few weeks. And I also wanted to tell you to your face that I think you're a first-rate weasel who deserves nothing more than to be strung up the nearest tree or pushed off a plank into an ocean full of sharks!" Dani was almost shouting by that point.

She had unleashed her fury but instead of feeling better, she felt an almost physical pain. Realizing that traitorous tears were soon to follow, she stood, scooped up her backpack, and ran from the room.

❋

Brighton watched her go, feeling disgusted with himself. Why had he waited so long to tell her? He should have told her in Colorado, where she would have been forced to listen to his side of the story. Nana would have seen to that. Instead, he had wimped out. He had been too busy trying to combat potential disaster that he had inadvertently laid the foundation for the worst-case scenario.

Somehow, she had figured out the truth and even found out about the bet. How? He had no idea. And it didn't really matter. What mattered was that she hadn't given him a chance to explain. She hadn't listened to his prepared apology or seen the genuine look of misery on his face.

Nor had she heard him say that he was falling for her.

Brighton felt like cursing—especially when he saw the stack of homework assignments waiting to be graded. Could this day get any worse?

Dr. Green returned an hour later. Brighton didn't look up or offer any sort of greeting. He had no desire to talk to anyone and wanted only to finish his work and get the heck out of there.

Unfortunately, Dr. Green didn't read minds. "I see you're still alive."

"Just barely," Brighton said, focusing his attention on the paper he was grading.

"She gave you quite the tongue-lashing, I presume."

Brighton grunted noncommittally.

The professor chuckled and took a seat behind his desk. "Did you deserve it?"

"Afraid so." Brighton clenched his teeth together in an effort to remain calm. He was not in the mood to be teased.

Dr. Green's smile faded. "Listen. I have no idea what's going on between the two of you, but it's been my experience that a girl doesn't become that angry if she doesn't care a great deal about the object of her anger."

Brighton looked at his professor in surprise, feeling a minuscule glimmer of hope. And miniscule was better than nothing.

❊

A few days later, a blurry-eyed Dani exited her landscape design class after turning in her hastily drawn backyard plan. It was more of a scribbled mess, but with Katherine's help the night before, she'd been able to come up with something. Venting her frustrations to Brighton hadn't helped much. She felt even worse now than before.

"Hey." The familiar voice halted her scuffling feet.

Brighton was leaning casually against a wall, holding a coil of rope in his hands. She closed her eyes, wishing him away. He was the last person she ever wanted to see or talk to again. "What do you want?" The words sounded more tired than angry.

"Ten minutes," he said. "Please."

Sighing, she followed him into an empty classroom and practically collapsed into the nearest chair. Hugging her backpack to her chest, she waited for him to speak. Instead, he tossed the rope on the desk in front of her. Had he lost his mind? "What's with the rope?"

"Well, if you know how to make a proper noose, you can use it to string me up the nearest tree. I promise not to put up a fight," he said. "Or did you need me to tie the noose?"

"As much as I would love to do exactly that, it wouldn't help anything. You would still be a jerk and I would still be . . ." Her voice trailed off.

"You would still be what?"

"An idiot," she said, standing and slinging her bag over her shoulder.

Brighton stepped in front of her. "Wait. You promised me ten minutes."

She glared at him. "Let me make this easy for you. You agreed to a bet that you worked your tail off to win—even driving all the way to Colorado in the dead of winter. And you won. Congratulations. What more is there to explain?" she asked. "Even Nana fell for you. That makes three girls in one month. You deserve an extra week of laundry or something."

"Four," he said.

"What?"

"Four girls. I took out your other roommate, Sandy, as well."

Dani stared at him incredulously before swallowing the lump in her throat. He was right. Kevin had mentioned three girls, hadn't he? How could she have forgotten that detail? She was even more of an idiot than she had first realized.

In a way she was grateful for his candid admission because the shock and disgust she now felt seemed to hold the tears at bay. *Sandy? Really?* The look on his face told her he wasn't joking. At least he had the decency to look troubled by his actions. She stepped around him and made a beeline for the door.

Brighton was quicker, though. In one fluid motion, he held her arm and pushed the door shut, blocking her only exit. "I'm not finished."

"Please move." Dani forced her voice to remain calm.

"Not until you hear me out," he said. "Then you're welcome to punch the living daylights out of me, and I won't stop you."

It sounded too good to be true.

"Please," he said quietly.

Seething, she returned to her chair and crossed her arms, waiting for him to explain.

Brighton started pacing. "I was trying to figure out a way to tell you, I swear. That's why you didn't hear from me after you got home. But I shouldn't have waited. I just never considered that my roommate would—that you'd find out before I had the chance to talk to you."

Brighton stopped, sighed, and raked his fingers through his hair. Grabbing a chair, he pulled it over and sat down directly in front of her. He leaned forward, as if willing her to understand. "It sounded like an adventure to me, and I stupidly agreed. Normally when we make laundry bets, we aren't allowed to pick the girl we take out, but I had wanted to get to know Katherine for a while, so it sounded like the perfect opportunity to meet her and win the bet at the same time. But then I met you and everything changed."

Brighton hesitated a moment. "I've dated a lot of girls and even had a few girlfriends, but with you, it's different. I feel a connection—one that I never thought was possible. You're fun, interesting, easy to talk to—well, except for right now." He cringed and looked away before continuing. "When you're not around, I wish you were. When something good or bad happens, I want to call you up and tell you about it. Every day since I've returned from Colorado, I have . . . missed you.

"I know it makes no sense, considering we've only known each other a few weeks, but now that I've met you, I can't imagine letting you go." He took a deep breath and seemed to wrestle with his emotions. "Just please, give me another chance."

Silence permeated the room, coating each surface and filling every crack. Dani listened to the stillness, willing it to tell her what to think, what to do, or what to say. She had so many conflicting emotions rolling around in her mind that it was impossible for her to form them into any sort of coherent response. She felt claustrophobic, needing time and space to process everything.

She knew he was waiting for a reply of some kind. The look on his face was vulnerable and worried. It tugged at her heartstrings, and that bothered her. She didn't want to feel sorry for him, nor was she ready to forgive him. But during his speech, she'd felt her anger and misery melt away—replaced by something nearer to hope. It was a traitorous feeling, one she wanted to launch over the nearest cliff.

She shook her head. "Honestly, as much as I would love to believe you right now, I just don't know. I wasn't kidding before when I said that I wasn't the only one who fell for you. Katherine is my best friend and I . . . I just don't know." He looked surprised, almost like he didn't believe that Katherine had feelings for him.

Standing, she said, "I'm going to need some time, Jeff—I mean, Brighton."

He winced at her slip but nodded in response. "I understand." Picking up her backpack, he held it out to her while she slipped it on. Dani could feel his eyes following her as she walked out the door.

Eleven

· · • · ❈ · • · ❈ · • · ❈ ·

Dani knew forgiveness did not come easy for her. After all, she'd been trying to find a way to forgive her parents for how many years? She was also still harboring some negative feelings for Selina Phillips, a horrible girl in her sixth grade class who used to tease and belittle her mercilessly. She knew that to forgive was divine and all that, but she had always struggled with the application of that principle.

That was why she was so surprised to realize, as she navigated the icy streets on her way home from the ski resort, that forgiving Brighton came as naturally to her as loving Nana. In fact, if she were to allow her feelings free reign, she knew she would drive directly to his apartment right now and kiss him long and hard. She missed him that much and wanted to believe he had been sincere. In fact, she did believe him.

But then she remembered her sweet friend and how Katherine had dreamt of Brighton as well. Not to mention Sandy and whatever happened between them. It seemed so wrong to throw her arms around someone who had potentially pained a roommate and definitely hurt her best friend.

And then there was the timing issue. In just over a month, Brighton would be bound for the University of Utah, and Dani would spend the summer with her grandmother before returning to Rexburg for her senior year. Why start something that would morph into a long-distance relationship and eventually fade anyway?

Add to that his future choice of occupation, and Dani was grateful she wasn't running back to him. Feeling her mood spiral downward, she shuffled inside her apartment. Katherine was reading on the couch and looking as beautiful and serene as ever.

"Hey, how was your day?" Katherine asked.

That was typical Katherine. More worried about her friend than herself. It made Dani feel even worse. "Brighton was waiting outside my design class this afternoon."

"What did he say?"

"That he dated Sandy too."

"Sandy? As in our roommate?"

"It was all part of the bet. He agreed to date three girls from the same apartment."

"There were three of us!" Katherine said. "Who thinks of these things?"

"Who *agrees* to these things is the more appropriate question, I think," Dani said.

Katherine's expression once again turned sympathetic. "Did he seem sorry at all?"

Dani squirmed, wondering how much she should tell her friend. "He felt terrible and admitted that it was stupidity on his part, but . . ." She searched for the right words.

"But he fell for you," Katherine finished perceptively.

"Why do you say that?"

"Oh please," Katherine said. "After spending the weekend with you and Nana, it doesn't take a genius to deduce the outcome."

Dani worriedly searched Katherine's eyes. "You've been so calm and collected about everything, and I want to know how you're feeling."

"I'm okay, actually. It was a letdown, to be sure, but I'm more worried about you."

"I really wish you wouldn't say things like that," Dani said, plopping down on the couch beside Katherine." It makes me feel like a selfish brat."

Katherine leaned over and squeezed Dani's hand. "Although

I liked the idea of being with Brighton, but the truth is that we never really clicked. He hurt my pride—that's all. I promise."

"Promise?"

"Promise," Katherine said. "You have no idea how happy I am for you. Despite the bet, I think he's really a good guy, and it's about time someone got to know the real you."

Dani reached over and hugged her best friend. "Do you have any idea how lucky I feel to have been given your name as a pen pal all those years ago? I couldn't have asked for a better friend."

"I feel the same way."

Dani was about to explain her other doubts about Brighton but stopped herself, knowing that Katherine would only disagree. Instead she changed the subject. "Hey, how about we go grab a pizza, rent a movie, change into our pj's, and have a girls' night?"

"Sounds fabulous."

Two hours later, Katherine and Dani were ensconced on the couch, eating pizza and watching *The Scarlet Pimpernel* when Sandy walked in.

"What's up, ladies?" Sandy asked.

"We've decided to take a break from all things responsible and have a girls' night," Katherine said. "Care to join us? We have another pizza over there." She pointed to the dining table behind the couch.

"Heck yeah!" Sandy squealed in her exuberant way as she rushed to her room. "Just let me change, and I'll be right there."

As soon as Sandy was out of earshot, Dani leaned over and whispered, "You do realize she's going to talk through the rest of the movie, right?"

"I'm used to people talking during movies," Katherine said.

"Oh, you did not just compare me to Sandy!" Dani hissed.

"Shhh. I think I hear her coming." Sure enough, the pounding of footsteps sounded as Sandy practically flew into the kitchen.

"Wow. That was fast," said Dani.

"I'm starving! I haven't eaten anything since toast for breakfast."

Dani and Katherine watched as Sandy devoured a slice of pizza. Katherine bit back a smile and tactfully looked away while

Dani teased, "I sure hope you don't eat like that on dates."

Sandy looked up and had the decency to swallow before replying. "There is no way I'd ever let a guy see me eat like this."

Dani couldn't help herself. "Speaking of dates, have you been out with anyone interesting lately?"

Sandy put down a half-eaten slice of pizza. "Yes! I have to tell you about this dream guy I met last night." She went on to describe someone she'd recently met with excruciating detail, even telling them about a small "kissable" mole on his neck. It was not Brighton.

Katherine stopped the DVD, realizing that the pause feature wouldn't last long enough, and Dani found herself wishing she'd never asked the question. But she really wanted to know what had happened with Brighton, so she crossed her fingers and tried again.

"He sounds great. Has there been anyone else?"

It was almost agonizing having to listen to Sandy describe yet another "luscious" man she'd dated. Apparently, Sandy hadn't wallowed after Brighton like Dani and Katherine. The thought was humiliating, but it didn't keep Dani from asking about any other interesting dates.

Finally, Sandy told them about Brighton, or "Andy," as it turned out. Andy Andrews. How adorable.

"So, what happened with him?" Dani asked when Sandy finished her meticulous rendition of her two dates with Brighton.

Sandy frowned. "That's the funny thing. I haven't heard from him or seen him since our second date a few weeks ago. Maybe he lost my number."

A slightly wicked idea formed in Dani's brain. Deciding it was inspiration, she said, "Or maybe he's waiting for you to call him. In fact, I'm willing to bet,"—Dani shot Katherine a meaningful look—"that you'd make his day if you gave him a call."

Sandy picked up the slice of pizza again. "I'm sure you're right, but I don't have his cell number."

"Didn't you say his name was Andy Andrews?" Katherine asked, catching on like only a best friend could. "Dani, isn't that the name of the TA for your math class?"

"I think so," Dani said, reaching for her cell phone. "Let me check." She scanned through the directory. "Yes, here he is." She read off the number while Sandy scribbled it down.

"Thanks, guys!" Sandy said. "I'll have to call him tomorrow."

Dani allowed the devil inside one last act. "It's been a couple weeks since you've been out with him. I don't think you should make him wait any longer."

Sandy finished off her slice of pizza while she considered Dani's words. "You're right, and he was super-cute. Maybe I'll call right now. Would you mind if I didn't watch the movie with you?"

"A cute guy always takes precedence over girls' night," said Dani.

As they watched Sandy walk back to her room, Katherine threw Dani a guilty look. "I can't believe I participated in that conversation."

"It was very uncharacteristic of you," Dani agreed. "But I thank you for it just the same."

❋

Brighton entered the library and went straight to the reference desk, finding a curly haired brunette reading a book. He tapped the counter. "I was wondering if you might be able to tell me when Katherine Beezner is scheduled to work."

"She's here now, restocking books on the second floor in the west wing," the girl said, returning to her book.

"Thanks." He took the stairs two at a time and scanned the rows until he found her. Katherine didn't look up even when he walked over to her.

"Hey," Brighton said, effectively drawing her attention away from the library books.

Katherine smiled when she saw him. "Oh, hi, Brighton. How are you?"

Was she actually smiling at him? He nearly groaned, wishing she would simply yell at him like Dani had done. He would feel sufficiently rebuked, offer an apology, and move on. Instead, she exuded kindness, as though she didn't mind that he had dated both her and her two roommates. He felt foolish.

"Um, I'm fine, thanks," he said. "Do you have a minute?"

"Sure." She led him to a secluded table in a corner of the library. Once they were seated, she asked, "Is this about Dani?"

"No," he was quick to reply. "It's about you."

"Me?"

"Yes, you."

"What about me?"

He shifted in his seat. "Uh, I just wanted to say I'm sorry for everything that happened. You know, the bet and all."

"Oh," Katherine said. "Well, thanks. I appreciate that."

Brighton looked at the floor. Now what? Was that enough and would Dani be satisfied? Probably not. So he tried again. "I just wanted you to know that I would take it all back if I could."

She appeared confused. "Why?"

Was she serious? Maybe he'd heard Dani wrong. "Because it was a stupid thing to do."

She laughed. "Yeah, it was. But something good came from it, right? You got to know Dani."

Brighton was floored. Either his actions hadn't bothered her in the least or she was genuinely the most kind and forgiving person imaginable. Or both. Still feeling the need to say something more, he cleared his throat. "You're right. But I want you to know that I initially took the bet to get to know you. I had seen you working here and wanted to ask you out."

Katherine nodded. "But then you met Dani."

So it was back to that. This conversation was turning into a series of deadends. He sighed. "Look, I just wanted you to know that I'm sorry. You're an amazing person, and I hope I didn't offend you in any way."

She reached across and touched his arm. "Listen, I appreciate the apology, but I'm really fine. I promise. I'm just grateful you had the chance to get to know the real Dani, and I'm happy she's finally found someone like you."

Well, this was going swell. Not only had she laughed off his apology, but now she was comforting him—offering him hope. What kind of girl was she? He found himself searching above her head for a halo. "Are you sure you don't want to yell at me? I'd feel much better if you did."

She laughed again. "I might if we weren't in the library."

"Well, by all means, let's go outside then."

She shook her head. "How about this: I promise to yell at you if you mess things up with Dani. Will that work?"

Katherine couldn't seem to drop the subject of Dani, so he admitted defeat. "And if she won't give me the chance to mess things up with her?"

"Then maybe I'll yell at her."

Now it was his turn to laugh. "Deal."

✳

Dani sat through the last ten minutes of her calculus class, staring at the clock affixed to the orange brick wall. Although the second hand was ticking past each number, she was certain it was doing nothing to advance the minute hand. Forcing her eyes to look away, she glanced to the math problem she was supposed to be solving. It stared back, doing nothing to solve itself, despite the glare she was directing its way.

Dr. Green's voice surged through the classroom. "I'll see you all on Monday."

Finally.

Walking out the door, Dani was surprised when Brighton fell into step beside her. "Touché," was all he said.

She didn't pretend to misunderstand his meaning. "How is Sandy these days?"

"I'm considering changing my number." He opened the door and followed her outside. "Are you free for dinner tonight?"

Dani hesitated.

"Or have I not given you enough time?"

"It's not that." Dani scanned the courtyard for some privacy. Finding a bench, she linked her arm through his and steered him away from the throng of students. "Let's sit for a minute."

He must have noticed where she was taking him. "There are places to sit inside, you know."

"Wimp."

"I was only thinking of you."

"Right," she said as she sat beside him on the cold, stone bench. While she debated where to begin, Brighton watched her with a worried expression. She found it brutally endearing the way he chewed on his lower lip.

"Nana always said that my biggest flaw was my inability to forgive people. Of course, she was talking about my parents at the time, but I've always agreed with her. I don't forgive easily. Nor do I trust easily. It's just not in my nature, and I think I have very few good friends because of that. Sadly, I can count on one hand the number of people who know the real me," she said. "You are one of those people."

"Does that mean you forgive me?"

She nodded. "Yes. In fact, I was surprised how easy it was to forgive you. Maybe after all this time, I'm finally learning something."

"Please don't tell me there's a 'but' coming next."

Reaching over, she gripped his hand and searched his eyes. She had spent the last few nights alternating between praying and crying, but she had finally come to a decision. "I want you to know that I will always consider you a good friend, but I'm sorry that a friend is all I can be. And it's not just because you're going to be a doctor. In another month, we'll be going different directions and we both know the odds of a long-distance relationship working out. It would be so much better to end it now, rather than later.

"I want you to know that I care about you a lot. I think I always will. I just . . . can't date you." She pulled her hand free and offered a silent prayer of gratitude that she'd been able to keep her emotions under control. Barely. Swallowing a lump in her throat, she said, "I don't want to hurt you, but I need you to know that this decision feels right to me."

❋

Brighton had been ready with several arguments. But then out came those last few words, loud and clear, like she'd shouted them though a megaphone. Her decision felt right. How could he argue with that? How did you tell someone that a spiritual revelation they'd received was wrong? He wanted to shake her and tell her to go back and ask again, like Martin Harris had done with Joseph Smith and the Book of Mormon manuscript. But he couldn't. He wouldn't.

Why would the Lord give her such an answer?

It was a new sensation, this gut-wrenching realization that his stupidity had lost him the one girl he had ever really cared about. And, if he were being honest with himself, the one girl he had ever loved.

There had to be some way . . . there was always a way. Wasn't there? But he knew he was only kidding himself. Her words were final, like the last words of the French revolutionaries before they signaled the dropping of the guillotine. Permanent. Concrete. Absolute. Not to mention painful.

And it made him angry.

Angry with Dani for wriggling her way into his heart and slicing it apart. Angry with his roommates for inventing that terrible bet and pressuring him into agreeing to the terms. Angry with God for giving Dani the go-ahead to walk out of his life. And angry with himself for not being able to do a thing about any of it.

He realized Dani was watching him and waiting for some sort of response, but he had nothing to say. If he said anything, he knew he'd burden himself with even more regrets. So instead he nodded, stood, and walked away.

He'd jump in that ocean filled with sharks before he'd ever agree to just be her friend.

Twelve

* * * * * *

The vivid green trees; the fragrant, colorful flowers; and the charming cottagelike homes, surrounded by an occasional waist-high white picket fence, were a welcome sight to Dani's tired eyes. After driving for three days straight, she was finally home.

Stopping off in Colorado Springs to visit her parents had simply not been an option. At least not for Dani. Not only was she sick with a lousy head cold, she was depressed. Her parents, she knew, would do nothing for either symptom. So she bypassed Colorado and went directly to Garysville—a quiet, slow-paced little town, and home to the most meaningful people in her life, with the exception of Katherine. And, if she were being honest with herself, Brighton.

It had been over a year since he'd left her without a word, alone on that cold, stone bench. And yet he was always there, tapping on the door to her thoughts or making himself the hero of her dreams. Would it ever end? Would she ever be able to move on?

And then there was Katherine—her sweet, beautiful, and married best friend. During their final year at BYU—Idaho, Katherine had fallen in love with Damien Sharp, the luckiest guy on the planet, as Dani had reminded him numerous times. They had married in Anchorage, right after graduation. Dani had flown up for the wedding, waited outside the temple, stood in a line at her reception, and hugged her friend good-bye, not knowing when they would see each other again.

While she knew that she and Katherine would always remain close friends, it was difficult to stand by and watch Katherine move on, leaving her behind.

She gazed at the small two-story home, situated quaintly between two large maple trees. A tire swing hung from one of the branches, and Dani was reminded of the wonderful summers she had spent enjoying Nana's large yard.

The wraparound veranda beckoned her with its porch swing. She and Nana had spent hours on that swing, talking, laughing, or simply enjoying a beautiful humid summer evening. That was what Dani wanted—a life like Nana had enjoyed, complete with a loving husband and a small but charming home in a community where people knew and cared about each other.

Would she ever achieve that? Could she have had that? Not with Brighton. He wanted to be a preeminent orthopedic surgeon, working for a thriving, cutting-edge practice in a metropolitan city. Didn't he? She realized then that she had never asked him what he had wanted for his life beyond his choice of profession. Now she would never get the chance.

Knowing there was no use dwelling on the past, Dani pulled her keys from the ignition. Soberly, she made her way up the sidewalk, drinking in the springtime aroma and finally caving to the call of the porch swing. Sitting down, she directed her thoughts to the future.

Four years ago, the principal of Garysville High had assured her there would be a place waiting for her should she decide to make Garysville her permanent home. True to his word, he had called her in January with a job offer and a contract. Without hesitation, Dani had accepted the offer, knowing there was no place she'd rather teach.

Now here she was, about to begin her new career in a place she adored. Why then, did she feel so glum?

"Danielle, how long have you been here?" Rose appeared through the screen door. "I've been worried sick about you driving all this way alone, and here you are, swinging on the front porch."

Dani laughed. "Nana, besides hitting a cow, what could possibly have happened to me in the last hour?" Rose had called her at least every two hours during the last three days, making sure she wasn't too tired, hungry, or bored.

"You know I can't rest easy until I see that you've arrived safely."

Dani sighed. "I know. And I'm sorry. I just couldn't get past this porch swing. It kept calling my name, just like it's now calling yours." Dani smiled as she patted the place beside her.

Rose joined her granddaughter. "I have some dinner in the oven, but I can relax for a minute or two."

Dani slipped her arm through her grandmother's and rested her head on Rose's shoulder. "I prefer burnt food. Fewer calories, right?"

"I have no idea how you came to that conclusion, but I prefer my food to have flavor and taste," Nana said. "Now tell me about your trip."

"You were updated every two hours," Dani reminded her.

"Yes, but there is still an hour unaccounted for."

Dani smiled. "Have I told you how happy I am to be home? And for good this time."

Thirteen

✳ · ● · ✳ · ● ✳ · ● · ✳ ·

"Chad, could I talk to you for a second?" Dani called to a student who was literally trying to run from her classroom. Unfortunately for him, he always chose to sit in the back and now had a throng of students in his way.

"I've got to get to football practice, Miss Carlson," Chad said, trying to elbow his way between two students. "Can we talk later?"

"You really need to think of a better excuse than that. You've used it twice already, so I had a chat with your coach yesterday afternoon and found out that you have a few minutes to spare before practice."

He gave it another try. "But I'm starving." The classroom had finally cleared, and Chad looked longingly at the door.

Dani opened her desk drawer and pulled out a granola bar and an apple. "Here," she said, tossing first the apple and then the granola bar in his direction. He caught them like any good football receiver would. "Now sit."

Chad slumped into the nearest desk. He took a bite of the apple but looked only at the floor, refusing to meet Dani's eyes.

Knowing she didn't have much time, Dani said, "I took the liberty of pulling up all your past report cards, from junior high until now. Until halfway through last year, you were pulling A's, and your teachers raved about your intelligence and promise. During the second two quarters of last year, you averaged Cs. And with the way you're headed so far this year, you'll be lucky to pass at all." Dani studied him for a moment. "Want to tell me why you've decided to give up?"

"I had lousy teachers last year."

Dani raised her eyebrows. "Really? Because you seemed to like them fine for the first two quarters. And I might not be in the running for any teacher-of-the-year awards, but I'm not that lousy, am I?"

Chad only shrugged and continued to eat the apple.

Dani waited in silence for a few uncomfortable minutes before he finally said, "Are we done?"

She sighed and then nodded, watching Chad jump up from the desk and rush out the door. What could she do to help him? He had captured her notice from the first week of school—quiet and aloof, sitting at the back of the room, talking to no one. The fact that he played on the football team had done nothing for him in terms of popularity. It was odd.

Why would a smart kid with excellent grades suddenly decide to throw his future college options to the wolves? He obviously wasn't planning on enlightening her. So what now? She drummed her fingers on her desk. Maybe she could ask around. It was a small town, and one of the other teachers had to know something.

❊

As it turned out, for a small town no one seemed to know anything about the Rutling family. The only information she was able to glean was that they lived about fifteen miles outside of town on a dairy farm and that they kept to themselves. Dani had spoken with two of Chad's former teachers, but beyond cornering him like she had done, they had let it go. Dani wasn't about to do the same.

Armed with so little information, she said a prayer and drove her car west—following the directions Nana had given her. Twenty minutes later, she pulled in front of a small, dilapidated old farmhouse. The roof was in tatters, the faded yellow siding was literally falling off the walls, and the front porch looked as though it were being fed to a community of termites.

Dani's sneakers squeaked their way carefully to the front door. She was worried that the floorboards would give way at any moment. If the exterior was indicative of the interior, she figured it would be perfect for the part of the old abandoned house in a modern day remake of *It's a Wonderful Life*. All it was missing were a couple of strategically placed broken windows.

Bolstering her courage, she rapped loudly on the door, hoping the force of her knock wouldn't bring down the house. The door creaked open slowly, and a little girl with long braided hair, about seven years of age, peeked out with chocolate eyes. *Adorable.*

Dani smiled her friendliest of smiles. "Hello, there. My name is Miss Carlson. I'm a teacher from Chad's school, and I wondered if I could talk to your mom for a minute."

The little girl stared back, blinking occasionally.

Not knowing what else to do, Dani peered down the hallway behind the girl. No one was there. "Mrs. Rutling?" she called loudly.

A woman appeared at the far end of the hall and shuffled toward Dani, wiping her hands on a threadbare apron as she came to the door. Tired eyes scanned the situation before the woman crouched down beside her daughter. She caught the girl's attention by gently touching the child's chin. Mouthing words as she formed the equivalent with her hands in sign language, Mrs. Rutling communicated with the little girl. Her daughter's expression fell, and, bowing her head, she rushed up the staircase.

Mrs. Rutling stood and looked at Dani. "She knows better than to open the door to a stranger," she said. "May I help you?"

Dani refused to be cowed and repeated her earlier introduction. "Can I speak with you for a minute."

"This really isn't a good time."

"I'll come back tomorrow then."

Mrs. Rutling chewed on her lower lip before grudgingly opening the door wider. She must have sensed Dani's stubborn streak. "I'm trying to get dinner on, but if you don't mind talking while I cook, you may come in for a moment."

"Thank you." Dani followed her inside, immediately noticing the decrease in temperature. The week had been unusually chilly, but the house actually seemed to refrigerate the outside air. Subtly looking around, she noticed a broken banister, a parlor door hanging from one hinge, and an antiquated wood floor, desperately in need of sandpaper and polyurethane. The house was clean, though, and a delicious smell was coming from somewhere.

Mrs. Rutling led her into the kitchen and resumed chopping carrots and celery. An aromatic broth boiled and bubbled on the stove, and freshly made bread dough sat rising in the corner. Dani watched how the knife flew expertly in the woman's hand, slicing through the vegetables in neat, even strokes. She wondered if she dared broach the subject of Chad at all. "It smells wonderful."

"Thank you." Mrs. Rutling paused long enough to tuck some frayed strands of hair behind her ear.

Dani pointed to a pile of potatoes waiting to be skinned. "I'd love to help, if you don't mind. I feel silly standing around talking while you work."

Mrs. Rutling looked up in surprise and then embarrassment before gesturing toward the potatoes. "Have at them."

Dani washed her hands, picked up a peeler, and began swiping the brown skins into a garbage can. "I'm here about Chad. I wondered if there's anything I could do to help him in school."

Mrs. Rutling furrowed her brow. "Chad doesn't need any help. He's always been a bright boy and a good student."

Dani stopped peeling and searched the woman's face. "I'm not sure about his other classes, but he's failing algebra."

"What? He loves math and he's great with numbers. It's got to be the teacher. Who do they have teaching my son?"

"That would be me."

"Oh." Mrs. Rutling returned her attention to the vegetables. "Maybe you just aren't explaining things well enough."

"My other students are doing fine."

"There has to be some other reason then. Are you sure you haven't mixed up his assignments or tests?"

Dani ignored the absurd question and offered one of her own. "Have you seen any of Chad's report cards from last year?"

The chopping stopped while Mrs. Rutling considered the

question. "I suppose the last report card I've actually seen was right after Christmas. Chad had a 4.0, just like always."

"Which is why I'm confused at his grades for the third and fourth quarters from last year." Dani put down the peeler and reached for the notebook she'd placed on the counter. She pulled out two pages, handed them to Chad's mother, and watched while she scanned the words and letters. Then she read them again, looking more concerned.

"I don't understand," she said. "Chad told me he was doing fine in school. Why didn't one of his teachers tell me about this last year?"

"They would have, I'm sure, if you'd gone to one of the parent-teacher conferences," Dani said gently.

"I never had any reason to go before." Her voice was barely audible. She sank onto a nearby barstool, biting her lip as she blinked rapidly. Her entire body trembled. "What can I do?"

Dani loathed bringing bad news, especially to an obviously overworked and exhausted mother. "I was hoping that if I could understand the reason behind it all, we might be able to find a solution. The trouble all seemed to start during January of last year. I know it was a long time ago, but can you think of anything that might have upset your son?"

Mrs. Rutling nodded as a tear made a path down her cheek. She swallowed. "That's when his father left."

✻

Driving home, Dani contemplated the distressing information she had learned from Mrs. Rutling. The woman had been timid and prideful yet surprisingly open. Although Dani's own parents seemed permanently messed up, she had to give them a little credit for never walking out on their family.

Trying to imagine what it would feel like to have her father abandon her without even giving a real reason left her drawing a blank. To wake up one morning and find a note saying he needed to get away—for good . . . How did anyone accept that kind of news, overcome it, move on? Especially when the Rutlings had been left with nothing but a decrepit old farmhouse, a staggering amount of debt, and a large herd of cows?

Ruth had sold off their cattle to keep a leaking roof over her family's head and put food on the table. And she'd hoped that the sale of the farm would soon follow. But as it turned out, no one seemed interested in purchasing a dairy farm with no cows in the middle of rural Texas. That meant foreclosure, a dirty and unacceptable word to the proud Mrs. Rutling. It meant beginning anew in a foreign place with no credit, no money, no education, and no job—not to mention four kids.

To her credit, Mrs. Rutling had refused to allow Chad to drop out of school, although he had taken on a part-time night job stocking shelves at the grocery store. She wanted to find a job for herself that could work with her schedule. But home-schooling a seven-year-old hearing-impaired child and being home while Chad was at work or football practice left only small windows of time in which she could work. There seemed to be no solution.

Bleak was the initial word that came to Dani's mind. Followed closely by *unfair, undeserved, horrible,* and *just plain wrong.* Her heart went out to the hardworking, dedicated mother.

An aroma of freshly baked cookies greeted Dani when she wandered into Nana's kitchen and sank down on a barstool. It was amazing how a dose of harsh reality could beat down a person's stamina.

"How did your visit go at the Rutlings'?" Nana moved the delicious looking chocolate chip cookies to a cooling rack.

"Terrible." Dani described the visit in vivid, judgmental detail. "I will never understand how anyone could leave their family. That man deserves to be drop-kicked."

Rose studied her granddaughter thoughtfully before wiping her hands on her apron. "Like wealth, poverty can also influence people to do dreadful things, things they wouldn't have done otherwise."

Even when faced with a pathetic swine of a human being, Nana still found a way to lessen the assault on his character. But Dani wasn't nearly so generous. In her mind, Mr. Rutling warranted no pity. He was a selfish scoundrel and a snake. End of discussion.

Dani also knew that Nana's shrewd answer carried with it a

second meaning. "Like wealth," she had said, meaning that anyone could become such a villain, whether rich, poor, or in-between. Anyone could take a turn for the worse. She might as well have said, "You know all those preconceived notions of yours? Well, they're about as resolute as Jell-O—before it has begun to set."

It wasn't anything Dani hadn't heard before or didn't already know, but she had never seen firsthand the ill effects of poverty. She had preferred to think that living without money meant true, genuine happiness. Livin' on love and all that. It meant creativity and Top Ramen and dancing barefoot in the kitchen to a self-sung, off-key song because the old secondhand CD player just went kaputz. It meant thoughtful, homemade, timeless gifts that adorned a home filled with love. It meant good old-fashioned family time, snuggled around a raging fire on a blustery day.

Her visions had never included leaky roofs and a thermostat set at an unaffordable sixty degrees. She had never pictured a darling seven-year-old who received a lack-luster education because her mother couldn't afford a specialized school for the hearing impaired. And never, even in the deepest recesses of her mind, had she ever considered a father walking out on his beautiful young family because he blamed them for his poverty.

Talk about a fool.

With the way she was feeling, she wasn't sure whether she was accusing herself or Mr. Rutling.

"Do you want to know the irony of it all?" Dani asked her grandmother. "For the first time in my life, I want money. Lots of money. Then I could actually do something to help that poor family."

"Oh, I'm sure you can find a way to help that family without having a lot of money." Nana smiled. "Although having a rich doctor for a husband sure would make things easier, wouldn't it?"

Dani rolled her eyes. "Yes, if only I hadn't blown my chance with a certain future doctor."

"He's married then?"

Dani frowned. "No. I mean—I don't think so." She'd never considered that possibility before. *Thanks, Nana.*

"Well, unless he is, you most certainly have not blown your chance."

"You're so right," Dani said sarcastically. "I should definitely rekindle a relationship with someone who I haven't spoken to in over eighteen months and who lives hundreds of miles away. How do you propose I go about it?"

"The Internet is an astonishing thing." Nana turned back to the cookies. "In just a couple of clicks with a mouse, someone could find information on just about anyone."

Dani's eyes widened. "And just how, exactly, do you know so much about the Internet?"

Nana shrugged.

Dani laughed. "Well, I think you're absolutely right. I'll just write and tell him I've decided that I don't mind being a rich doctor's wife after all and would he please forgive me for breaking up with him and consider dating me again—from Utah. That would go over *really* well."

Nana poured Dani a class of cold milk and handed her a cookie. "You never know until you try."

❋

After Nana had gone to bed, Dani logged onto Facebook and looked up the name "Brighton Andrews." Sifting through face after face, her heart lurched when she saw a curly, dirty blond-haired man with blue eyes staring back at her. Unable to resist the temptation, she clicked on his picture.

Brighton only shares some of his profile information with everyone. If you know Brighton, **send him a message** or **add him as a friend**.

The cursor hovered over "add as a friend" before Dani lost her nerve and shut the laptop.

❋

"You had no business talking to my mother. How dare you!" Dani looked up as an irate Chad entered her empty classroom, practically shouting at her.

"Yes, it was very daring on my part," Dani said, returning her attention to correcting the homework assignments.

"Who do you think you are?"

"Your teacher." Dani set her papers aside and gestured to the desk across from her own. "Sit down, Chad. And for Pete's sake, please stop shouting or you're going to have the principal barging in here."

Glowering, he slumped against the top of the nearest desk and folded his arms. Dani could practically feel his rage.

She chose her words carefully. "I can understand why you are upset. I'd be angry too, but it doesn't mean that what I did was wrong." She held up her hand when he started to argue. "I couldn't just stand by and watch you give up on your future."

"It's my life."

"And you don't think your life also affects others?" Dani asked.

He remained silent.

"Your father—"

"Don't you dare call him that."

"What would you like me to call him?"

"A cowardly jerk."

"Very well," Dani said. "That 'cowardly jerk' knowingly fled a sinking ship, so to speak. According to your mother, the farm hasn't turned a profit in several years. At some point, the bank will be able to seize the property and leave your family with nothing. So tell me, what will you do then? Enter the lottery and keep your fingers crossed?"

Dani didn't wait for an answer. "You're right, though. Your father was a coward and a jerk, but that is not a good reason for you to give up on your future—or the future of your family. Sixteen is not old enough to face the responsibility you now have, but the fact is, your mother needs your help. Having no formal education of her own, she needs you to do well in school, get into a decent college, and earn a degree."

He raised his voice. "And how am I supposed go to college? There's no way we can afford it. And even if we could, you said yourself that I could be in school when my family's forced to leave."

"And you think you'll be able to support them by flipping

burgers or running the cashier at the local grocery store? You think the solution is to flunk out of high school so your mother will let you to take on two or three jobs in order to keep your family in a home that's about to fall down on top of you?"

"It's better than going off to college and leaving them with nothing."

Dani studied him with sympathy, praying for the right words to say. "You won't be leaving them with nothing," she said softly. "You'll be leaving them with hope. A hope that someday you'll be able to fix the mess your cowardly jerk of a father has caused."

Chad looked beaten and miserable. "There is no way I could afford college, especially now that I've destroyed any chance I had for a scholarship."

Dani smiled to herself, taking his dejection as a sign that he was beginning to see reason. "If you can get your grades back up immediately, and do well on the SAT, you still have a chance at an academic scholarship for a smaller college. But even if you aren't able to qualify for one of those, there are thousands of scholarships out there, along with some government grant programs."

Dani leaned across her desk, emphasizing her next statement. "If you promise to get your grades back up by the end of this quarter, I promise to help find a way to get you the money you'll need for college. Deal?"

She saw the spark of hope in his eyes. "And my family?"

"Will never be homeless. If they ever need a place to stay, they will be welcome in our house while you finish your degree."

"My mom has too much pride." He shook his head. "She would never go for that. She even refuses to move us back in with her own parents."

"I think you'd be surprised what a mother like yours would do for her children," Dani said. "But two years is a long time. You never know what will happen to change your family's situation. In the meantime, I want you to worry about school, work, and football, like any normal sixteen-year-old."

Fourteen

❋ ˙˙●˙ ❋˙ ● ❋❋ ˙●˙ ❋˙

Nana was right, Dani thought as she watched car after car arrive in front of her grandmother's house, searching for a place to park. There had to be at least twenty vehicles packed with people—ready to help and serve a family they barely knew. Dani blinked rapidly, telling herself to keep it together.

The season was changing from fall to winter, and the thought of the Rutling family living in that old house without a decent roof had been unacceptable to Dani. The family needed help, and she had been determined to do something about it. That something had turned out to be very little because the response had been overwhelming.

Mrs. Walters had created several donation jars and strategically placed them throughout the town. Mr. Bates from the local hardware store had generously donated many of the materials. Mr. Asay had given them some spare lumber and organized a team of carpenters, skilled and unskilled. And Dani had enlisted several high school students, dubbed them painters, and asked them to bring paintbrushes.

It took only two weeks for them to collect enough money and supplies.

Unbelievable.

Evidently Mother Nature was also willing to help because she seemed to think the cause warranted some warmer weather as well. During their drive to the farm, the sky was blue, the sun bright, and the temperature a mild sixty degrees.

It didn't take too many thumps of the hammers before the front door opened and Chad and his mother appeared.

"What in the world?" Mrs. Rutling followed her son out into the yard, looking askance at the people swarming around her house.

Chad marched toward Dani, his mother close behind. "Miss Carlson, what's going on?"

Dani finished doling out paint before turning to Chad and his mother. "Mrs. Rutling—"

"Please call me Ruth," she said nervously.

Dani smiled. "Ruth, let me put it bluntly. I'm no expert, but from the looks of things, your house is in need of some help. I simply mentioned the fact to Mr. Bates at the hardware store, and before I knew what had happened, word spread, and here we are. Isn't it wonderful?"

"I don't understand," Chad said.

Ruth was horrified. "But this is too much! I couldn't possibly let all these people spend their own money and give up their valuable time. They hardly know us."

Dani reached out and touched Ruth on her arm. "But that's just it. They've always wanted to know you and your family and were thrilled at the opportunity to do something for you. It's okay to let us help."

Ruth raised her hand to her mouth as tears appeared in her eyes. Chad's arm circled his mother tightly, and it was he who finally spoke to Dani. "Thank you, Miss Carlson. We owe you so much."

"Just graduate and get into a good college, and we'll call it even," Dani said.

Chad nodded and gently led his mother back inside the house. Five minutes later he reappeared in some old work clothes, a hammer in hand. "What can I do to help?" he asked Dani.

She led him over to a tall, broad-shouldered, dark-haired man. "Chad, I'd like you to meet Mr. Asay, our go-to person. He seems to know everything there is to know about carpentry, and he was the one who rounded up most of these people."

"Good to meet you," Mr. Asay said, shaking the boy's hand. "My daughter, Becca, goes to your school."

"Yes, sir. She's a cheerleader, isn't she?"

"Yep. She'd be here today if it weren't for some cheer competition in Dallas."

Chad nodded.

"Do you know how to use one of those?" Mr. Asay pointed at the hammer Chad was holding.

"Yes, sir."

"Well, let's find you something to do with it then."

From that point on, the day was a success. The front porch acquired some new lumber, the damaged siding was replaced, new shingles were affixed to the roof, and a fresh coat of paint was applied where needed.

Chad stayed and helped as he could, but Ruth remained inside, no doubt keeping busy with her other three children. Around mid-afternoon, Nana pleaded a headache, and one of Dani's high school students drove her home.

When the sun began to retire, Dani surveyed what they'd accomplished. It was no extreme makeover, but it looked presentable and would keep the family warm and dry through the winter. The yard even looked more maintained, thanks to her grandmother's efforts. The weeds were gone, and the dying shrubs pruned back and readied for winter hibernation. It was fascinating what one day and a slew of wonderful people could accomplish.

Dani was about to send someone for pizza when Ruth appeared around the side of the house, hefting a large steaming pot. Her three other children followed behind, toting some freshly baked rolls, bowls, and spoons. The sight alone made Dani's stomach growl. Ruth must have been cooking all afternoon.

While Dani cleared one of the makeshift work tables, Ruth's sweet little seven-year old, who Dani had learned was named Megan, pulled on her pant leg, holding up a large faded blue tablecloth. Placing her fingertips to her chin, Dani brought them away from her face, hoping she had remembered the word "thank you" correctly.

Megan's twin brother, Morgan, dropped some bowls and

spoons on the table and then darted back inside, while Sarah, Chad's nine-year-old sister, put down some freshly baked rolls and butter before turning around to stare at their house.

"Ruth, thank you! This smells incredible," Dani said, passing around bowls to the hungry crowd.

"No, I'm the one who should be thanking you," Ruth said. "Last winter was bad, but I knew it would be even worse this year. Y'all are an answer to my prayers, and I want to thank you from the bottom of my heart. To come and willingly do this for people you don't even—" her voice broke, and she covered her face with her hands.

Dani put an arm around Ruth and turned to the crowd. "I've had the chance to taste Ruth's cooking, and it's phenomenal. How about we all eat before it gets cold?"

Ruth looked gratefully at Dani through her tears. "I'm sorry. I'm just so overwhelmed, and I don't know how to thank every-one."

Dani smiled through tears of her own. "Come to the Winter-fest in a couple of weeks, and I'm sure they will all feel properly thanked. They've been trying to get you to show up to something since you moved to town."

❉

Dani left the Rutling home feeling happier than she had in a long time. Exhaustion should have enveloped her in a warm hug by then, but it kept its distance, allowing her to relish the euphoric rush of contentment and joy. She knew that as soon as she allowed herself to relax, the fatigue would overpower her energy, but for now, she enjoyed the natural high.

In keeping with her elated spirits, she stopped by the food mart and picked up a package of brownies and some mint choco-late chip ice cream. She hoped her grandmother's headache had subsided and she would be feeling up to a small celebration.

As she drove by the hardware store, Dani was filled with tender feelings for her little town. The outpouring of love and service was unparalleled, and after today she felt a camaraderie with her neighbors and friends like she never had before. Something magical happened when people clustered together for a good purpose. Anger, resentment, and hurt feelings seemed to melt away, like a handful of wet sand slapped with a wave. People integrated, united, and matured.

A tear skated down her cheek, and she touched it in surprise. She was crying. A familiar warmth filled her as the Spirit touched her heart, strengthening her testimony of the goodness of God and his love of all mankind.

Pulling to a stop in the driveway, she wiped away the tears. Today was a happy day, with no place for tears. Grabbing her purse and the grocery sack, Dani ambled up the walk and through the front door, completely unprepared for what she'd find inside.

Fifteen

✳ ⋅ ● ⋅ ✳ ⋅ ● ✳ ⋅ ● ⋅ ✳ ⋅

Brighton opened his apartment door to find his old friend and former roommate standing outside. "Christensen! What in the heck are you doing here?"

"I was in the area," Mark said, wiping his shoes on the doormat. "Mind if I come in? It's freezing out here."

"Of course." Brighton opened the door wider.

Mark tromped past his old roommate and stopped when he saw a girl sitting alone on the couch. He turned back to Brighton. "Oh, uh, sorry. I didn't mean to interrupt. I'll just come back in the morning."

Brighton ignored his friend and turned to the girl. "Hey, Tiffy, I want you to meet an old friend of mine from BYU—Idaho." Brighton smiled and clapped Mark on the back. "I haven't seen this guy in over a year and a half, and he just shows up at my door. Talk about an unexpected surprise. An awesome unexpected surprise."

Mark looked uncomfortable. "I can just drop by tomorrow."

"What? No way! It's not like we're on a date or anything. We're just studying for a test we have on Monday."

Tiffy nodded. "It's nice to meet you, uh . . . Christensen?"

"Mark."

"Ah," she said. "Former roommates, I take it?"

"She's quick, isn't she?" Brighton said. "You can see now why I like to study with her."

"And I thought it was because you had a thing for me." Tiffy smiled, gathering her books together. "Well, it's past my bedtime, boys, and I have early church tomorrow, so I think I'll be going."

It was late, so Brighton walked her out to her car and then returned to his apartment to find out what his friend was doing in Salt Lake. Mark was now studying chemistry on a graduate level at Utah State University.

"Do you mind if I crash on your couch tonight?" Mark asked once Brighton came back inside.

"Only if you tell me what brings you to my neck of the woods."

"I came down with a couple of friends for the weekend. I figured it would be like one of our old getaways, but it turns out my new friends aren't like my old roommates," he said. "They figured it would be a riot to drive down to Provo for some party they'd heard about. I said no thanks and had them drop me by here. They'll pick me up tomorrow on their way home. You don't mind, do you?"

"Of course not. It's great to see you." Brighton walked toward the kitchen. "You hungry? I have some leftover pizza in the fridge."

"Starving," said Mark. "Where are your other roommates?"

"They have lives." Brighton tossed the pizza into the microwave.

"You were alone in your apartment with a girl?" Mark asked.

"This isn't BYU—Idaho, you know. But it wasn't like that anyway. She's just a friend. A very smart friend, as a matter of fact. And those seem to be the best kind to have these days."

"Smart and pretty. Sure you're just friends?"

"Down, boy," Brighton said. "I'm in the middle of med school, and I don't have time to date anyone, let alone someone as high-maintenance as Tiffy. Besides, she's not my type."

"Since when did you start going for the goofy-looking dumb chicks?"

Brighton rolled his eyes. "Right now, no girl is my type. *Capisce?*"

"Even if her name starts with a D and ends with 'ani'?"

"Please. I got over her a long time ago."

"Yeah, and I won the lottery and I'm headed off on a Caribbean cruise next week."

Brighton ignored Mark and handed over some warmed stale pizza. "I'll go get a pillow and blanket for you."

When he returned, Mark said, "Have you heard from her at all?"

"No."

"She's on Facebook, you know."

"Didn't know, don't care," Brighton lied. Of course he had looked her up on Facebook. And of course her picture had brought a stab of pain, so he'd immediately closed the browser's window.

Mark studied his old roommate and good friend. "You've changed. Ever since that day you came home and knocked—"

"It's over, Mark. Just like this conversation." Brighton threw the pillow and blanket on the couch. "I'm going to jump in the shower. Then we can catch up and watch a game before we turn in. Feel free to make yourself at home."

Mark either recognized the tone or caught the atypical use of his first name. "Sorry, man. I didn't mean to hit a nerve."

Brighton simply nodded, turned, and walked down the hall.

Sixteen

✳ ⋅ ● ⋅ ✳ ⋅ ● ✳ ● ⋅ ✳ ⋅

"Nana!" Dani screamed when she saw her grandmother face-down on the floor beside the coffee table in the front room. She dropped her bags, rushed to Nana's side, and pulled out her cell phone at the same time. Quickly she dialed 911 and searched frantically for a pulse. Noting a nasty gash near the temple above her grandmother's left eye, Dani watched in horror as blood drizzled down the side of her head, soaking into the already saturated cream carpet. There was so much blood.

Dani felt ill, wondering how long her grandmother had been like this.

"This is 911 emergency. Do you need police, fire, or ambulance?" a voice registered in her ear.

"Ambulance," Dani said. "And hurry." She answered the operator's questions while working to staunch the flow of blood and reminding herself that head wounds always looked worse than they actually were.

The wait for the ambulance was awful, especially when Dani's efforts to wake her grandmother failed. The faint sound of sirens blared in the distance, and she nearly sobbed in relief when red and blue lights flashed through the bay window.

"Come in!" Dani yelled when a determined rap sounded on the door. She stepped back and allowed the EMTs access to her grandmother. Time seemed to slow and deliberate, as if it couldn't decide whether the seconds were minutes or hours. Lying there on the carpet, Nana looked old, frail, and still. Dani wanted to scream at the medics. *You're the professionals! Get her to wake up!*

But she didn't scream. She watched; she waited. And while she stood there, fatigue seemed to swoop down and envelop her body. She slouched against the wall behind her as her legs threatened to give way. Locking her knees, she turned to the one source of comfort she could access. She closed her eyes and prayed. She prayed for Nana and for the strength to make it through the night.

When her eyes opened, Rose was strapped to a gurney and on her way to the ambulance. Dani forced her legs to move and crawled into her car to follow the ambulance to the hospital in Denton. When they arrived, Nana was still listless and unresponsive. Dani wanted to lean over and give her a good shake.

Rose was rushed through some ominous double doors, leaving Dani alone in the stuffy waiting room. She felt a sense of déjà vu from the last time she'd been in the emergency room of a hospital. Only this time it was a hundred million times worse. This time, it was Nana. Worry and dread sidled up and made themselves at home in her mind.

A receptionist approached with a clipboard. "Are you with the woman they just brought in?"

Dani nodded and accepted the paperwork. Looking around, she found a quiet, vacant corner and sank down on a steel-framed chair covered in orange vinyl. Scanning the questions through weary and dazed eyes, Dani noticed one question that seemed to stand out: "Who is your primary care physician?"

It had been over eighteen months since Nana had casually mentioned his name, but for some reason, Dani recalled it with perfect clarity. Dr. Simms. Pulling out her phone, she dialed the number for directory assistance. There was only one MD named Simms in the area and if she'd wait, they would connect her to his answering service. Dani left a message and waited for the doctor to return her call.

He didn't.

"Dani Carlson?"

She looked up to find an average-looking man with amber eyes and a graying fringe along his temples. The rest of his hair was jet black, including his buzzed moustache and goatee.

"Can you tell me anything about Rose Olsen?" Dani asked, jumping out of her seat. She'd been waiting for over two hours. "Is she awake yet? Is she going to be okay? Will she be able to go home soon?" She wanted rapid-fire answers, like her questions had been, but he didn't comply.

Instead he sighed. "At least you've stuck to questions with yes or no answers." He gestured for her to sit back down and then took a seat opposite her. "Yes and no."

"Yes and no to what?" She was beginning to feel frantic again. Her fingers twisted and turned around each other. "She's not going to be okay? Or yes, she is?"

He searched her eyes grimly, as though he wasn't sure what to say or how to say it. Finally, he looked away. "No. She's not going to be okay."

"What?" It sounded more like a drawn-out squeak than a question, but it was all Dani could muster at the moment.

"My name is Dr. Simms, and thank you for calling my office. It saved hours of tests for your grandmother."

Dani was happy to hear that the doctor hadn't ignored her phone call after all. But then the rest of his words tap-danced through her mind, one letter at a time, like the keys on a keyboard. I-t—s-a-v-e-d—h-o-u-r-s—o-f—t-e-s-t-s.

Dani could only swallow at the implication that her grandmother had a preexisting condition Dani knew nothing about.

"I'm your grandmother's oncologist," he said.

It took several moments before Dani could find her voice. "You're telling me Nana has cancer?"

He nodded slowly. "Glioblastoma multiforme. A nasty form of brain cancer."

Dani's eyes widened in shock, and she bit her lip, shaking her head and trying to cope with the random thoughts ambushing her mind. *When? Why? How long? Not Nana! No!* "You're wrong! Nana is fine—I mean, there are symptoms, aren't there?

Headaches, dizziness, memory loss? Nana's had an occasional migraine, but that was it," she said as the tears started to fall. "How is this possible? It can't be right."

"She was diagnosed over a year and a half ago, a few months before she fell and broke her foot. You remember?"

Dani wiped at her tears with the sleeve of her shirt. "I remember she seemed perfectly fine during the two weeks I spent with her in Colorado."

"She probably didn't mention it to you, but when she fell, she also hit her head. We ran an MRI just to be safe and found a small brain stem glioma, or tumor. Usually people don't know they have a brain tumor until the cancer has worsened to a point where the symptoms manifest themselves, like the ones you mentioned. We caught Rose's case earlier than most, but it was inoperable, and after researching the treatment options, your grandmother declined them all. It's a miracle she's survived as long as she has."

"Why would she refuse treatment?" Dani gave up mopping her tears. Her shirt sleeves were already soaked, and she didn't care any longer. She just wanted to wake up from this nightmare and find out it was just that—a horrible, garish, untrue nightmare.

"The treatments have lousy side effects. They make people feel weak and sicker than they've ever felt before. They can also cause memory loss, headaches, loss of vision and mobility, numbness, and many other things your grandmother didn't want to experience—not when they would have only served to extend her life a little longer. That wasn't the way she wanted to live."

Dani wanted to cover her ears with her hands or duct tape the doctor's mouth shut so he would stop saying such horrible things. She wanted to yell at him and tell him that Nana would have done anything to extend her life—she wouldn't have given up so easily. Not Nana! But instead Dani covered her face and left her ears exposed like any masochist would.

The doctor's voice softened. "She talked about you all the time, you know. She used to say that if it wasn't for you, she'd be ready to go right away, but that God seemed to think you needed her around a little longer."

Dani looked up and choked out, "I need her around a lot longer."

"I'm so sorry."

Dani closed her eyes. "How long?"

"I don't know. Weeks, months, maybe? It's different with everyone. But you should know—"

Dani interrupted. "Is she awake? Can I at least talk to her?"

His expression was grim. "You're welcome to go and see her, but I have to warn you that she's in a coma. From what we've gathered, she must have had a seizure right before her fall, and with the additional head trauma . . ." He shook his head sadly.

"Seizure? Coma?" Dani whispered the words. Just when she'd thought she had heard the worst.

He nodded. "Ever since we discovered the tumor, we've been monitoring its growth. A few months ago, Rose started to complain of migraines. The tumor had grown, and we knew it was only a matter of time before other symptoms appeared, like seizures and dizziness. In a way, she's very lucky—to have the end come so suddenly, I mean. She won't have to experience what so many others do."

"The end? You just said she had months!"

"In circumstances such as these, she may never wake up. She could be in a coma for months, or we could take her off the respirator now, and it might be sooner." He dropped his head. "But that's not your decision to make."

Dani couldn't take any more, not that any news could be worse than what she had just heard. "Whose decision is it?" she asked, forcing the words out.

"Your father's."

"You mean to tell me that my father knows about Nana?" A spark of anger ignited, numbing the despair but only a little.

Dr. Simms studied her, most likely wondering what more he should reveal, what more she could take. Finally, he sighed. "Your father takes care of Rose's finances, so when the hospital bill came for the initial MRI and other tests, she couldn't keep him from finding out the truth. That's why they flew your grandmother to Colorado. They wanted a second opinion from someone they knew and trusted. Unfortunately, he told them the same thing I did—that her tumor was inoperable. They tried to convince her to go through radiation and chemo, but she was adamant." He paused. "She was also adamant that you never find out—at least for as long as she could keep it hidden."

Dani shook her head. The adrenaline boost from her anger faded almost as quickly as it had risen. Now there was only pain. A deep, penetrating ache that seemed to consume every last ray of joy left in the world. "Why?"

He shook his head. "She never told me, but I think she wanted to protect you, to keep you happy for as long as possible."

"She was wrong." Dani felt listless and drained. How could a day that began with such wonder and elation mutate into such an ugly, ghastly beast? It was as though God had given her a miracle and then snatched it away, leaving her with nothing—not even peace. She felt betrayed, deceived, alone.

Dr. Simms studied her with a look of concern. "Would you like me to take you to her room?"

Dani nodded numbly and followed him down a long, stale hallway. Turning this way and that, they wound their way through a maze of corridors, passing room after room, filled with sick people, injured people, or dying people.

Dr. Simms stopped in front of a closed steel door. Room number 117. Dani turned the cold handle slowly, wondering what sort of room her beloved grandmother would breathe her last breath in. She hoped futilely for a vibrant color, reflective of her grandmother's personality. Instead, she found green—a pale, sickly, putrid green, like watered-down toothpaste. At some point, someone had probably concluded that this particular shade was calming, soothing, and peaceful. But it wasn't. Not even close.

And then she saw Nana, beautiful Nana, hooked up to a myriad of machines and tubes and engulfed in a stark white bed. She looked so pale, miniscule, and lifeless. Dani swallowed, praying for strength. Taking the tiny, shriveled hand in her own, she sank into a chair next to the bed and sobbed.

✻

At some point during the night, Dani found the strength to call her parents. They scheduled a flight on the private jet and were at the hospital by the following evening. When her parents rushed into the room, her mother looked fresh and beautiful, reminding Dani of the smelly work clothes she was still wearing from the day before. Was it really only yesterday that life was grand, happy, and wonderful? How fast things had changed.

Paula enveloped her daughter in a tight embrace. "Has there been any change?"

Dani shook her head, grateful for their presence. Her relationship with her parents may not have been the best, but before they walked through the door, she had never felt so alone. Although several concerned neighbors had called, including Ruth, there was nothing anyone could do.

"Well, I guess we don't need to ask how you're holding up." Her father's attempt at humor failed miserably.

"Honey, your father's right. You look terrible and you probably feel worse," Paula said. "Why don't you go home, take a hot shower, and get some sleep tonight? Your dad and I have a room booked nearby, and we'll stay close in case anything changes."

Dani bristled slightly, although she wasn't sure why. Of course her parents didn't plan to linger at the hospital. Logically she knew there was nothing anyone could do. Who knew how long Nana would be lying there in a coma before the disease overpowered her and won? It could be months.

Dani knew she couldn't stay by Nana's side every second either. Her students would be waiting for her at school the next morning and she needed to get some sleep. But part of her rebelled at the thought of leaving, even for a day.

Finally accepting the inevitable, Dani squeezed Nana's hand and left the room.

❋

The following evening after school, Dani walked into the hospital room and immediately noticed a change. Having spent twenty-four hours in a room oppressed by silence had made her aware of every sound. Something was different. There was a noise missing. A whooshing sound followed by a click, like someone snoring lightly.

At first Dani panicked, thinking Nana had stopped breathing. But then she remembered the respirator. The respirator! That was the missing sound. Someone had disconnected the respirator. Why? Dani hurried to Nana's side and leaned in close, listening to the shallow, labored breathing. Why would her father make such a dreadful decision? She didn't understand.

As if on cue, the door opened and in walked Paula.

"Why is the respirator gone?" Dani turned accusing eyes on her mother.

Paula sighed. "She's dying, sweetheart. After speaking with Dr. Simms, your father and I felt it was for the best."

"What about what *I* think?" Dani practically shrieked. "Why doesn't anyone seem to care what I think? I'm so sick of being the one left in the dark, especially considering—" Dani stopped short, clamping her mouth shut and turning away from her mother.

But she'd said enough, and Paula was no fool. "Considering you're the one who loved and cared for her?" Paula asked. "She was my mother, you know. You don't think I care that my own mother is dying and there's nothing I can do?"

Dani remained silent and unfeeling. It was as though her emotions had been sucked dry, leaving her barren and empty, like a discarded candy wrapper. She wanted to understand this person she called "mother" but she couldn't. To Dani, Paula was a complete contradiction of what a daughter or a mother should be.

Paula walked over and stood beside Dani. "She wouldn't have wanted to prolong her life—not like this. That's why she gave your father the power to make these decisions. She knew you never could. Besides, taking the respirator off may not help the end come any sooner for her. It could still be several months, but at least it will allow her to go when she's ready."

"I'm not ready for her to go anywhere." Dani wiped a tear from her eye and turned toward her mother. "Why didn't she want me to know?"

Paula smiled slightly. "How did she put it? Something about

not wanting you to fuss and fret over her and that she'd never have a moment's peace if you knew."

"I could've made things easier on her. I could've helped out more. I could've spent more time with her." Dani shook her head at the injustice of it all. She felt robbed. "I could've said good-bye."

"No," Paula said quietly, in one of her rare moments of understanding. "You of all people should know that you could never have said good-bye—not to your Nana."

❊

Two weeks later Rose Olsen passed away. Dani was in the middle of a calculus lesson when her cell phone hummed "Singing in the Rain." It was the hospital. She had no idea why she had programmed the hospital's ringtone with Nana's favorite song. Maybe she'd thought it would sweeten a sour phone call or maybe she'd finally gone insane. Whatever the reason, it had been a bad idea—like an extra dose of torture.

She didn't have to answer the phone to know that Nana was gone; somehow she just knew. Instead of being at the hospital, holding her hand, Dani was teaching school. *Why, Nana? Why couldn't you have waited a few more hours?* Sentencing her students to a page of problems, she left the room, walked down the hall, and out into the chilly sunshine. Taking deep breaths, she calmed herself enough to return the phone call.

And then she phoned her mother.

Paula and Dave Carlson flew in the following morning. As soon as they arrived, they began the funeral preparations, ordered take-out, and hired a cleaning service. Dani sat back in wonder, for once grateful for their overpowering ways.

Katherine arrived in a rental car on the night of the viewing. Dani met her in the church foyer, feeling a prick of joy at the sight of her friend. She had felt lost and empty for so long that any sliver of happiness was a welcome surprise.

"I've missed you so much!" Dani hugged her friend. "I'm sorry I couldn't meet you at the airport."

"And I'm so sorry about Nana," Katherine said. "How are you holding up?"

"It's been difficult, but I'm doing okay," Dani said. "I'm just so happy you're here."

"I wouldn't be anywhere else. I only wish I could stay longer."

"Me too, but I understand."

Katherine nodded, guiding Dani to a quiet corner. "Are you still angry with Nana for keeping the truth from you?"

"I don't think I'll ever completely understand why she did it, but I'm not angry. In fact, I feel more dead than anything. Like I've come full circle and there are no emotions left to experience." Dani looked down at the ground, watching her feet shift on the carpeted floor. "I miss feeling happy."

Katherine put her arms around her friend. "Well, if you're the Dani Carlson I know, you'll start feeling better pretty soon. You just need someone to knock you down or something. You know—provoke that temper of yours."

Dani chuckled. "I said I missed feeling happy, not mad."

"Was that a laugh I just heard? I think my work here is done now."

"Don't you dare go anywhere before you have to," Dani said, hooking her arm through her friend's. "It would be like taking the sun with you."

"Don't worry. Before I go, I will tape the sun to your head."

The service the following day was short, but sweet, just the way Nana would have wanted. Paula actually offered an affecting narrative of what life was like growing up with Rose as her mother. She even broke down near the end and had to excuse herself from the stand, which both surprised and touched Dani.

The ward provided a small luncheon and not long after, Katherine had to return to the aiport to fly home. She had only been able to get two days off from work. Sadly the two friends hugged good-bye, and Dani watched as Katherine drove off, taking the sun with her.

Dani walked back inside Nana's house, emotionally and physically exhausted. She found her mother in the kitchen, setting plates on the table. "Where's Dad?"

"He went to get take-out somewhere. Neither one of us felt much like cooking."

"Have you ever felt like cooking?" Dani asked. She'd meant it as a joke, but with the way she was feeling, the words sounded more like an accusation.

"I used to cook, you know," Paula said. "I never did enjoy it, though, which was why I was more than willing to hire a chef when we could afford one." She finished setting the table, and Dani followed her into the front room.

Taking Nana's favorite rocking chair, Dani waited until her mother sat down on the sofa before she said, "It was nice, Mom—what you said about Nana today."

"It was the truth. I know she and I grew apart over the years, but I couldn't have asked for a better mother."

Dani smiled and nodded in understanding. This was good. During the last several weeks, she and her mother had found a common ground of sorts. Her mother had been supportive, understanding, and helpful, making Dani wonder if someday they might be able to form a tentative relationship. Perhaps Nana's death would bring about something good.

"When do you plan to move back?" Paula asked.

Then again, maybe not. Dani mentally prepared herself for the argument she knew was coming. "I won't be moving back. My job is here; my life is here; and believe it or not, I'm happy here."

"You can't be serious." Paula stared at her daughter in shock.

"And yet, I am."

Paula leaned forward. "Please put some thought into this decision before you make up your mind so quickly. There's nothing here for you. This small town will suck the life out of you, leaving you alone and living off a paltry teacher's salary."

"This town," Dani said, "has been my lifeline. The people here are phenomenal, and I have never felt such joy and peace as I have felt here. If I die an old maid in Garysville, I certainly won't be lonely. And as for my 'paltry salary,' I'll be fine so long as I can stay in this house."

"This house does not belong to you," Paula said.

Dani grimaced at the rude reminder of her grandmother's

trust. "I know that, but I was hoping you and dad would sell it to me."

"On your salary?" Paula actually laughed. "There's no way you could afford this house."

"I'll rent it from you then."

"You won't be able to afford the rent either."

The implication was clear, and Dani bristled. "What do you want with this house anyway?"

"Absolutely nothing," Paula said. "What we want is for you to move home, get a job in Colorado, and possibly look into graduate schools."

Dani stared at her mother in surprise. Was she serious? "You do realize that I am an adult and perfectly capable of making my own decisions, right?"

"Of course. But despite what you may think, your father and I love you, and we will not lift a finger to help you continue to ruin your life," Paula said. "If you don't believe me, you're welcome to ask your father."

Seventeen

✳ · ˙ ● ˙ ✳ ˙ ● ✳ ● ˙ ˙ ✳ ·

"I'm speaking with Brighton Andrews?"

"Yes. Who is this?"

"My name is Miles Parker. I'm an executor, of sorts, for Rose Olsen's trust."

"For whose trust?" The name sounded familiar, but Brighton couldn't pair it with a face or a location.

"Rose Olsen," Miles repeated slowly, emphasizing the words as though Brighton hadn't heard him correctly the first time.

"Where are you calling from?" Brighton hoped to have his memory jogged.

"Denton, Texas."

"Where?" He'd never head of the city, let alone someone who had lived there. "I'm sorry, sir, but I think you have the wrong person. I don't know of anyone named Rose from Denton."

"She actually lived in Garysville. I live in Denton."

Garysville. Brighton repeated the city in his head, his memory effectively jogged. His thoughts came in rapid succession. *Rose Olsen. Nana. Executor.* "Nana's dead?" he asked. "What happened?"

"Brain cancer, I'm sorry to say."

"I'm sorry too," Brighton said. "She was a remarkable lady."

"That she was."

There was a pause, and Brighton took advantage of the brief

silence to gather his thoughts. *Executor.* The word now held a different meaning for him. "Why, exactly, are you calling me?" More important, why wasn't it Dani calling? "Nana barely knew me. I'm sure she wouldn't have listed me in her will."

"Uh, not exactly. It's actually a little complicated and I would really prefer to talk to you in person. Is there any way you might consider taking a few days to fly out here and settle everything in person?"

"Settle what, exactly?"

"I have you booked on a flight tomorrow. Will that work for you?"

"No, actually, it won't. I have tests all week long that I can't miss."

"When is your last test?"

"Thursday afternoon."

"I'll change your flight to Thursday night and have my secretary call you with the schedule."

"Wait!" Brighton felt like he'd agreed to something without meaning to. "Could you at least tell me what this is all about?"

"As Danielle Carlson will also need to be present, I would prefer to do the explaining in person."

Brighton's mind was reeling. This was crazy. The entire conversation felt like some demented dream. "Dani will be there?"

"Yes."

"I'll be ready on Thursday night."

❋

"Katherine, congratulations!" Dani squealed into her cell phone. "I'm so excited for you!"

"Thanks! I just can't get over the fact that I'm going to be a mom."

"Me neither," said Dani. "But you are going to be the most terrific mother, and she'll be the most beautiful baby in the world!"

"Or he," said Katherine. "It will be several months before we can find out for sure."

"Trust me—it's a she. I don't think you have the lung capacity or the firm hand to raise a boy. Could you imagine? He'd walk all over you. Your baby girl and all her future sisters, on the other hand, will grow up to be sweet, kind, loving, and wonderful, just like their mother."

"There are a lot of good, kind boys in the world, you know."

"And I'll bet you a million bucks that the majority of them are that way because their mothers insisted on it and gave them a good spanking when they acted otherwise."

Katherine laughed before changing the subject. "Speaking of bets, when is Brighton scheduled to fly in?"

"Sometime tonight." Dani felt a knot form in her stomach as she paced the floor. "I'll see him tomorrow morning at Miles's office."

"I take it you haven't talked to him?"

"Nope. I've actually considered calling him, but then I went over the conversation in my mind, and it went nowhere beyond the initial 'Hello,' so I chickened out."

"Are you at least excited to see him again?"

"A nervous wreck would be a more accurate description. For all I know, he could be dating someone, engaged, or even married. I'm not sure how I would handle any of those scenarios. Being the basket case I've been lately, I'd probably burst into tears and humiliate myself completely."

"You're still in love with him, then?"

Dani could hear the smile in Katherine's voice. "I'm not sure about love, but he has been on my mind a lot over the past year and a half."

"And what about the fact that he's almost halfway through med school?"

Dani quit wandering around the room and fell on the couch, her feet dangling off the side. "I don't know. I still don't like that fact, but I'm not sure I'll ever get him out of my mind. It's so frustrating! Especially considering he's probably moved on, and I'm worrying for no reason."

"Only time will tell," Katherine said. "Just like with my baby."

Dani laughed, picturing her friend. "You're rubbing your stomach, aren't you?"

"You know me too well."

Dani smiled. What would she ever do without Katherine? Her friend was a healing balm sent directly from heaven. "Thanks so much for calling me, but I should really get back to packing."

"Let me know how things go with Brighton tomorrow. I'm curious as to what this meeting is all about."

"You and me both." Dani said good-bye. The thought of moving filled her with dread, and thinking of some stranger replacing her in Nana's home made her nauseated.

She wandered into the family room and looked around. Bookcases filled with books and trinkets stared back at her, challenging her to find them a temporary home. Her parents might own the house and everything in it, but Dani wasn't about to watch some stranger dump it all into the nearest landfill. She would take what she wanted and walk out of the beautiful little cottage with her head held high. Her parents would never know what they'd taken from her. And someday, no matter state it was in, she'd buy it back.

Feeling the familiar anger and frustration that seemed to surface every time she thought of her parents, Dani tried to think about something else. She had just grabbed an empty box from the garage when the doorbell echoed through the quiet house. Hoping it was Ruth, who had dropped by nearly every night since the funeral with soup, cookies, or some other yummy treat, Dani dropped the box and went to answer the door. She would love some company, especially Ruth's.

Dani threw open the door with a smile, which faded instantly when she saw Brighton staring back at her. He looked the same as she remembered, yet different—more wizened, mature, and almost sad—but still as handsome as ever.

Her heartbeat quickened, and she found herself struggling to breathe normally. The oxygen levels seemed to drop, and she felt lightheaded, but at least her heart and lungs were attempting to function. Her brain, on the other hand, had shut down completely.

He was the first to speak. "I realize it's not three o'clock in the morning, and I haven't become a human popsicle, but I was hoping you'd let me in anyway. It's been a long week, and I could really use some hot chocolate right about now."

Dani slowly opened the door wider. With a little coercion, she was able to get her mouth moving. "Sorry, but I'm all out of hot chocolate."

He walked inside, shoved his hands into his pockets, and paused in the tiny foyer. "Mint chocolate chip ice cream, then?"

She shook her head and swallowed.

"Water?"

Nodding slowly, she stared at him. Brighton was here. In person. In her home. She'd dreamed about this moment for so long, and yet all she could do was nod and blink at him. Why was she nodding anyway? She couldn't remember.

Brighton cleared his throat. "Yes, you have water?"

"Water," Dani repeated, remembering why she was nodding. Her head bobbed up and down more quickly. "Yes, I have water." But she didn't move, and her hand still gripped the doorknob.

Brighton watched her in amusement before his gaze wandered up the stairs and over to the living room. When he looked back and she was still rooted, he said, "I could always get a drink from the hose out front."

She closed her eyes briefly and took a deep breath. What was wrong with her? Why couldn't she think of a coherent sentence? And more important, why could he? It wasn't fair.

"The hose it is," he said, taking a step toward the front porch.

"Oh, please," Dani said, closing the door and wishing a sixth sense had alerted her to his arrival beforehand. He was probably thinking she was a complete nitwit and feeling nothing but gratitude that she was no longer a part of his life. "I'm sorry. I'm just—I'm just surprised to see you."

"Miles didn't tell you I was coming?"

"Well, yes, but I didn't think I'd have to face you until tomorrow." She winced. "I'm sorry—again. That came out wrong. I just don't know what to say right now—to you. It's been a long time."

He nodded. "I suppose I should have called, but I never asked Miles for your number and figured it would be a good idea for us to talk before the meeting tomorrow. Besides, this way you couldn't hang up on me."

"Why would I hang up on you?"

He shrugged. "Who knows? Maybe for the same reason you sent me packing a year and a half ago."

Dani tensed, not ready for such a personal topic. She tried to keep her voice light. "And what reason was that?"

He watched her for a moment. "I'm still a little unclear. Something about feeling like it was the right thing to do."

"Was it?" The words came out as a whisper. She didn't mean to say them, but out they came regardless.

"You tell me."

She shook her head, trying to clear her mind. The conversation seemed to be caught in a tail-spin, headed for a large volcano filled with molten lava. She felt the need to eject away from it, and fast. "Brighton, I—"

He held up his hand. "Look, you're right. It's been a long time and I didn't come here to rehash the past. Now how about that drink?"

She nodded gratefully and led him down the hall. When she had filled a glass with ice water, she held it out to him, but he wasn't watching. He was looking around at all the scattered boxes.

"You're moving?" he asked.

"Yes."

"Where?"

"Down the street."

"Why?"

She sighed. "Because I can't afford to buy this house." She placed the glass in his hand and led him to the couch in the family room. Since she had no desire to discuss her current feelings, and it was much easier to talk about facts, she launched into an explanation of the recent drama her life had become, thanks to her parents.

When she'd finished her brief narration, he looked confused. "I don't understand. Why are we meeting with a lawyer tomorrow if the trust belongs to your father?"

"I wish I knew."

He shrugged and gestured toward the bookcases. "I'm sorry about the house."

She followed his gaze. "It's okay. Someday I'll buy it back. I hope."

"You plan to stay in Garysville then?"

"It's home."

He nodded.

"How's medical school?" she asked, trying to fill the awkward silence.

"Good. I've got one semester more of classes and next year I'll start my rotations."

"That's great. I'm happy for you."

He looked at her with skepticism. "Are you?"

"Of course."

"Thanks." Another long pause.

Finally Brighton asked, "Why didn't you tell me that Nana had died? I would have come to her funeral. Instead, I had to find out about it through some lawyer." He sounded frustrated.

Surprise flickered across her face. "We haven't spoken in over a year, and you barely knew Nana. I'm sorry, but I didn't think you'd—"

"Care?"

"Something like that."

"I know," he said. "But since your grandmother made sure I'd find out eventually, it would have been nice hearing your voice on the phone instead of Miles's."

"I didn't know he'd called you until after the fact."

Brighton took a deep breath and relaxed against the back of the couch. The tension seemed to subside slightly, and Dani found herself relaxing as well.

"She sent me a card once, the summer after graduation," he said.

Dani was confused. "Nana? She sent you a card?"

"It was more like a letter."

"What did it say?"

"It said, 'Dear Brighton.'"

"Seriously? That's all you're going to tell me?"

"Maybe someday I'll let you read it."

She knew those words meant nothing, but Dani couldn't help the warm sensation that spread through her body at the thought of someday. It felt good and even made her smile. "You still have it?"

"Of course. It's not every day you get a letter from someone like Rose Olsen." He smiled. "So who is this Miles anyway? A friend of your father's?"

"No. He is an executor or trustee or something of another trust. It's all a big mystery and one I'm not supposed to share with my father. I have no idea who appointed him, why you're involved, or what it's all about. Who knows? Maybe my grandfather was a pirate in a previous life and now Miles holds the treasure map."

"I'm glad Nana thought to include me, then. I'm always game for a mysterious adventure."

"I would have thought you'd had your fill of adventures," Dani said pointedly.

He ignored her comment and allowed his gaze to stray back to the bookshelves. His eyes came to rest on a snapshot of Dani and her grandmother. "Had she been sick awhile?"

Dani's expression fell and she shook her head. "I didn't know."

"What do you mean?"

"I mean she knew about the cancer for almost two years and she never told me. I came home one day to find her passed out on the floor with a gash in the side of her head, and a few weeks later she was gone."

"Why wouldn't she tell you?"

Dani shook her head. "I keep going back and forth between feeling guilty for not paying close enough attention to being so angry with her for keeping it a secret. It's like my own personal tennis match inside my head, with the two opposing sides battling it out."

"Well, I hope it ends soon. A tie would be good," he said. "Maybe then you'd feel some peace and closure and be able to focus on the good memories. That's what she would want, you know."

She studied him before daring to speak her thoughts. "I'm glad Nana was somehow able to bring you here. It's good to see you again."

"It's good to be seen."

She laughed. "Want some ice cream?"

"I thought you didn't have any."

She stood and walked into the kitchen. "I said I didn't have mint chocolate chip."

Sitting side by side, they ate what was left of the peanut butter and chocolate ice cream as they talked well into the night. Brighton told her about his experiences at medical school, and she caught him up on her last year of college, Katherine's wedding, and the Rutling family.

Finally she yawned and glanced at the clock. It was almost two o'clock in the morning. "Oh, wow!"

He followed her eyes and stood, stretching his arms over his head. "I better get going if I want to be awake tomorrow."

"Where are you staying?"

"At some hotel in Denton."

"You're planning to drive to Denton tonight?" she asked.

"You mean this morning. And yes, it's better than sleeping in a smelly rental car." He made his way toward the front door. "I guess I'll see you in a few hours?"

"Don't be ridiculous. I'm not about to let you drive all that way right now. You're exhausted, and it's an hour away! I've been sleeping in Nana's room, so you can have my old bed for the night. Then we can drive together in the morning."

"But you live in a small town," he said. "What will the neighbors think when they notice a strange car parked in front of your house all night long?"

She rolled her eyes. "Don't worry. I'll clear up any misconceptions at the next town meeting."

He smiled. "If you're sure."

"Of course. How long will you be here anyway? There's a great little bed and breakfast down the road if you're staying another night."

"I'm booked on a flight tomorrow afternoon."

Dani had a difficult time masking her disappointment. "Oh."

"I'll just go and get my things out of the car."

She nodded. "I'll get your room ready."

Dani and Brighton waited impatiently outside of Miles's office. His secretary had mentioned he was on an important call and asked if they would mind taking a seat for a few minutes. That was twenty minutes ago.

A large stained wooden door stared back at Dani from across the room. Willing it to open, she almost jumped when at last it did and a man waved them inside. He was short, probably in his sixties, with thick, wavy gray hair and a somber expression. Dani wondered if he ever smiled.

Casting a sidelong glance at Brighton, she saw him shrug as he followed her inside. Miles briefly introduced himself, shook each of their hands, and directed them to two chairs across the desk from his own.

He didn't waste any time. "Before I tell you why you're here, I need to give you some history. Danielle, I have actually known your grandparents for a very long time. Your grandfather and I used to be good friends before he passed away.

"I am also a real estate lawyer. Ten years before he died, a commercial development opportunity came my way. Your grandfather had just received a decent inheritance from the passing of his own parents, and I encouraged him to invest. He did, and although it took nearly ten years for the project to come to fruition, the payoff was exceptionally large. Your grandfather suffered a heart attack two months later.

"Rose was naturally devastated and wanted me to take your grandfather's percentage. She was content with her home and her life and had no idea what to do with all the money." Miles actually smiled when he related this memory. "I refused, of course, but gave her a few options. She chose to give it to you, Danielle—or at least partially."

"What?" Dani was stunned as the story unfolded. "But my father—"

"Doesn't know about this money," Miles explained. "After your grandfather died, your father pressured Rose to set up an irrevocable living trust with all her assets and list him as the trustee. According to him, it was so Rose wouldn't have to worry about her finances ever again. Living trusts are a good thing, but

I encouraged her to list herself as the trustee, rather than grant complete control to your father. I would have been happy to help her manage everything.

"In the end, Rose went against my advice and did as your father asked for a few reasons. She was sick of arguing with your parents, she had very little experience dealing with money, and she didn't want to impose on any more of my time. She was also worried that he would eventually find out about your grandfather's money and want control over those funds as well. So before she signed over all her assets, she had me create a separate irrevocable trust with your grandfather's money, with the intent to keep it hidden and out of reach from your father.

"So we set up what was called an irrevocable charitable remainder trust. The trust was created with you as the beneficiary, Danielle, with the clause that you would become a co-trustee once your grandmother passed away. I am the other trustee. Basically, it's our job to manage and invest the money."

"Which means?" Dani asked, confused. All of his words were becoming muddled in her stupefied brain.

"You can see why I wanted you both here in person, now, can't you?" Miles took a breath. "A charitable remainder trust is interesting. It's designed to benefit both the charity and the beneficiary." He directed his next words to Dani. "In essence, you will receive a lifetime income from the trust. Six percent, to be exact. Then, when you die, the principal amount will go to the charity designated in the trust. Right now, it's The Church of Jesus Christ of Latter-day Saints."

"I don't understand. Nana knew my phobias about money. Why didn't she just donate everything to the Church?"

"She felt like you could use the money for yourself and others. You know—your own charities."

"I don't understand," Dani said. "I don't have any charities."

"Your grandmother had me create an addendum to your income payout. Although you will receive six percent, you are required to use five percent of that money on a charity or on someone other than yourself. She felt this would give you the freedom to help others and make it so you weren't as angry with her for listing you as the beneficiary." Miles paused while he eyed Dani. "You know, most people would be thrilled to be left with any amount of money."

"She's not most people," Brighton said. "She wasn't kidding when she said she had money phobias. I'm not sure there's a name for her sickness, but let me assure you, she's a medical marvel."

Dani ignored his comment, still trying to process all the information. "What is Brighton's part in all of this?"

Miles actually chuckled at the question. "Three months ago, Rose came to me and wanted to add yet another addendum to the income portion of the trust. I thought she'd lost her marbles, but I humored her nonetheless."

"What clause could have possibly included me?" Brighton looked rather amused.

"You are now a—how did Rose put it?—a co-trustee for Danielle's five percent. In other words, you are the person who must sign off on all of her personal charities."

"What?" Brighton and Dani said at the same time, although Brighton was laughing and Dani was still confused.

Miles chuckled. "I realize this is a lot to take in, but Ruth did leave a letter for you, Dani, hoping it would help you to understand her reasons."

"She left a letter for me?" All thoughts of trusts dissipated as Dani reached for the letter. Her hands were shaking when she grasped the envelope tightly between her fingers. "When was this written?"

"She gave it to me right after she added Brighton's name. She asked me to give it to you during our meeting." He hesitated. "After she was gone."

Dani stared at the envelope in her hands, not knowing how to feel or what to say or even think.

Miles continued, "Other than needing a signature from each of you, nothing needs to be decided or done today. It is up to both of you to work things out and let me know where you want the five percent donated. Then, with each withdrawal you take, I will need you both present to sign."

"Present?" Brighton asked.

"Meaning that you both need to be in the same room together, whether it's with me or a notary," Miles said.

"Is there any way to take myself out of the trust completely?" asked Brighton.

"Of course. After the first two years, you will automatically be removed, but if you want out now, just say the word, and you're out. But I have to tell you that Rose did add one more contingency. Should you refuse to be involved, the Church will be removed as the primary charity beneficiary and another added in its place."

Dani looked at Miles in confusion. "Let me get this straight. If Brighton decides he doesn't want to be involved, you're saying that the Church will no longer receive the principal amount when I die?"

"Yes."

"Who will?"

"A plastic surgery charity."

"What?" Dani shot out of her chair. "You can't be serious."

"Unfortunately, I am, and believe me—they do exist. Your grandmother Googled it."

"Unbelievable!" Dani practically crushed the envelope in her hands. "Of all the manipulative tricks." Glancing down at Brighton, she said, "I'm sorry, but like it or not, you will be present to sign off on all my—I mean *our*—charities." Dani turned and fled the room, unable to hear another word.

Eighteen

✳·•·✳·•·✳·•·✳

Dearest Danielle,

I know you are unspeakably angry with me at the moment. I'm not sure when you'll find out about my illness, but I hope and pray that I'm able to keep it from you until the very end. If I have my way, it would be after I'm good and gone, but I don't see how that is possible. Unfortunately, cancer doesn't tend to let its recipients off the hook so easily.

I know you, sweet granddaughter of mine, and I am certain I wouldn't have a moment's peace once you discovered that I was sick. You would be constantly fretting and worrying about me, and I don't want that to happen.

You've brought me so much joy with your smiles, your laughter, and your zest for life. I never want to see that joy turn to sorrow, the laughter fade, and the sadness take away your smiles. I want to remain happy to the very end, and you're helping me do that. I know you are beating yourself up, thinking you could have made my life easier, but the truth is that you did. Your stories and our talks helped me to forget and find joy in the moment. I will always treasure the time you've spent with me, and I hope you can forgive an old woman her secrecy.

Speaking of secrecy, I'm sure you now know about the

trust. I never told you before because I know your views on money and I didn't want to fight or argue with you about being the beneficiary. I hope that you will find good ways to use the money. I also want you to keep some of it for yourself and your future husband, children, and posterity.

Danielle, I want to emphasize that you are not like your parents. Far from it, in fact. I believe that even though you are now wealthy, you will still teach high school, still live modestly, and still do good. Only now you have the means to do so much good! Be sure to have a little fun in your life, though. Take some fun vacations, see the world, buy a cabin in the mountains or a houseboat on a lake, for all I care. Share those things with others and build some lasting memories with your family and friends. When you become old like I am, it's those memories you hold onto the most.

As for Brighton's involvement, well, I wish I could be there to see your face. I'm smiling just thinking about your reaction. I'm sorry, my dear, but I couldn't resist. You've been pining for that boy ever since you pushed him out of your life, and knowing how stubborn you are, I knew you would never do a thing about it. So I had Margie, down at the library, show me a thing or two about the Internet. I discovered that a certain Brighton Andrews is living with three other roommates in an apartment in Salt Lake City. Once I knew he was unmarried, I decided to intervene. You see, I can now meddle as I wish with no repercussions. You go right ahead and yell at me all you like.

I don't know if Brighton is the one for you, but at least this opportunity will allow you to find out. So go ahead and set up your charities together. If you and Brighton don't connect, he can sign off on them and move out of your life for good. But at least you'll know for sure.

I love you so much. All I want is for you to be happy. I hope you know that, and I hope you can come to forgive an old lady for her intervening antics.

All my love,

Nana

❋

Dani was sitting under a tree, holding the letter against her chest and crying, when Brighton found her. Frantically, she brushed at the tears and jumped up, folding the letter and shoving it into her pocket as she made her way over to him. "I'm sorry about how I acted in there. You must think Nana and I are both certifiable."

Brighton smiled, pulling her in for a hug. "If you want to know the truth, I've always known you were certifiable. It was just surprising to find out that Nana was too."

Dani stepped out of his warm embrace and slugged him lightly. "You sure know how to make a girl feel better."

He put his arm around her and guided her back toward the car. "So what did the letter say?"

"It said, 'Dearest Danielle.' "

"I should have seen that coming." He pulled open the car door and waited for her to climb inside.

They drove in silence for a time before Brighton broached the subject of the trust. "So, charities . . ."

"I know of one I would like to start," she said.

He waited for her to continue.

"I'd like to start some scholarship funds, beginning with some of my high school students, like Chad Rutling. He's a bright kid and deserves to go to college. I've been searching out various scholarships, but most of them aren't enough for tuition, let alone enough to pay for living expenses. It would take several of them to get Chad through one year of school. If I could set up a fund that would pay for four years of tuition and books as well as some supplementary income, it would be wonderful. Not to mention a huge load off Ruth's shoulders."

"Okay," Brighton said. "What else?"

"I'd also like to buy their farm, anonymously, of course, and deed it directly back to them. They would never let me help other-wise."

"Are you sure she even wants the farm?" he asked.

"Why wouldn't she? Their family needs a home."

"Yeah, but from what you said, even though your neighbors

were good enough to make some repairs, it's only a matter of time before it will need some serious overhauls. Not to mention the fact that they aren't milking cows anymore. Wouldn't they be happier with a small, less run-down house in town?"

"Good point. I'd never considered that." Dani thought about his words. Who knew what Ruth would like? She might enjoy being closer to town on a more manageable property. "I suppose we could just buy the farm from her and let her decide what to do with the money. She might be happier somewhere else."

Brighton steered the conversation back on track. "I take it you'll want to make the scholarship fund anonymous as well?" he asked. "Although, I'm not sure how you'll keep everything a secret for long. It would be too much of a coincidence for them not to be suspicious. Especially when no one moves into the farmhouse."

"They can speculate all they like, but they'll never know for sure it was me." Dani furrowed her brow. "I just realized that I forgot to ask Miles exactly how much money we had to work with. Maybe we can't afford to do both. I have no idea how much five percent of the principal is."

"How much would it take to purchase the farm?"

"My guess would be a couple hundred thousand."

Brighton laughed. "You should be okay then."

"How do you know?"

"Because I asked that question after you ran off," he said. "The principal is just over 25 million, which means that every year you have approximately 1.25 million to shell out to whomever you wish. It also means that your take-home income is somewhere in the ballpark of 250 thousand. You'll have to ask Miles about the tax ramifications on those numbers, but in the meantime—congratulations. You are now richer than most doctors."

"Two hundred and fifty thousand dollars?" Dani gasped. "You're telling me that my grandfather made twenty-five million off of one real estate investment?"

"It wasn't quite that much at the time," he said. "It was still huge, but it has also been tied up for over ten years in some fairly aggressive funds, so it has grown a great deal. The Church is going to love you when you finally keel over."

Dani glared but Brighton just shrugged.

She took a breath. "Okay. So every year, we have to come up with a way to spend 1.25 million on someone else."

"Actually, *you* do. All I have to do is sign." She glared at him again, so he quickly amended, "But I'm more than happy to help you spend the money if that's what you want."

She shook her head in wonder. "I had no idea it'd be that much."

Dani's head started to spin as she grasped the magnitude of the responsibility she'd been given. Not only did she need to come up with the right places to spend the money, but there would probably be mounds of paperwork, planning, and organizing involved. And how long would Miles choose to stay involved? He obviously didn't need the money and he'd certainly want to retire at some point. What then?

And then there was Brighton.

She glanced over at him uncertainly. "Miles said you're only stuck helping me out for two years. Are you sure you don't mind?" Despite what she'd said earlier, she didn't want him to feel trapped.

"Are you serious? I just found out that we have over a million dollars to spend for charity. Talk about a once-in-a-lifetime opportunity. Besides, Nana included me personally, and there is no way I'd consider letting her down—she might come back to haunt me."

"What about medical school?"

"I have three weeks until I start back up. We can brainstorm and get some preliminary work done in that time. Then, once Miles gets the paperwork together, I can fly back on a weekend or weekends to sign. I don't see a problem there."

"And Christmas?" She didn't want to spoil his plans.

"Not to be insensitive, but you don't have anywhere to go, do you? I can't imagine you want to spend it with your parents after all that's happened."

Dani frowned. "That's not entirely true. Ruth invited me over for dinner with their family."

"And you said . . . ?"

"That I'd think about it."

"Think about this, then," Brighton said. "Come home to Colorado with me and spend Christmas with my family."

"No way!" she said. "I'm sure your family is wonderful and all, but I'd rather go to the Rutlings. At least I know them."

"Don't be ridiculous. We've only got three weeks, and I already told my family that I'd be coming home. In fact, I would be there right now if it weren't for this little detour. We'll just get you on my flight and powwow during the break."

"I can't fly anywhere this afternoon. I called a substitute for today, but I still have to teach through Wednesday of next week."

"We'll book a flight for you next Wednesday or Thursday then. It will give my mom a chance to get everything ready anyway."

Dani looked at him, her eyes pleading. "I can't come to your house for Christmas. It's a holiday, and you should share it with family, not some strange outsider. Please don't ask me to do that."

"What about the day after Christmas? That would still give us two weeks to brainstorm."

Dani knew she couldn't ask him to leave his family to fly back to Texas, but she also hated the thought of intruding on what little time his family had to be together. That being said, she and Brighton needed to have some serious discussions, and she didn't want to make all the decisions alone.

"My dad would probably be a great help," he added, interrupting her thoughts and finally swaying her.

"Okay. If your family won't mind having a stranger around, I'll plan on coming the day after Christmas," she said.

"I wish you'd consider coming for Christmas too, but I won't push you."

"Thank you." She looked out the window, nervous and worried. "You have no idea how much I appreciate your help. It's nice to know I'm not in this alone."

He reached over, picked up her hand, and lightly squeezed her fingers. "I just can't get over the fact that you're now wealthy."

She relished the feel of her hand in his, hoping he wouldn't let go anytime soon. "Yeah, feel free to call me a hypocrite." And she wasn't just referring to the money.

Nineteen

✳ ˙ ● ˙ ✳ ˙ ● ✳ ● ˙ ✳ ˙

Ruth stopped by on Saturday evening, bearing homemade cinnamon rolls slathered with just the right amount of icing.

Dani smiled. "You are an angel in disguise. These look heavenly, and I'm starving. One day, you really need to teach me how yeast works." Dani opened the door wider and waved her inside. "I'm so happy you're here because I could really use some company tonight. Or do you need to be somewhere?"

"Chad is holding down everything at home, so I can stay awhile, if you'd like."

"I'd love that," Dani said. "I was just working on some lesson plans, but I can't seem to concentrate. The house is too quiet."

Ruth gave her a sympathetic look and followed her to the front room. "What's keeping you from concentrating?"

"A guy."

Ruth raised her eyebrows. "I didn't know you were interested in anyone. Does he live near here?"

"He lives in Utah."

"How did you meet him?"

Dani smiled at the memory. It was funny how the passage of time could transform a once humiliating incident into something humorous. What had initially angered her now made her want to laugh. Regardless, it made for a good story, and Ruth proved to be an excellent listener.

When she finished the tale, Ruth nodded in understanding. "It's funny how we all have different perspectives. You were turned off by someone who wanted to be successful and I—well, there was a time that I would've given anything for a man like that."

Dani's smile vanished and she looked at her newfound friend with concern. "I'm so sorry. I didn't mean to remind you—"

Ruth held up her hand. "I didn't say that to earn your pity. I simply wanted to point out that regardless of who you marry, there are no guarantees in life—just like there are no guarantees that the weather will stay sunny and warm because you want it to."

"I know." Dani nodded. "Nana tried to tell me that for years."

"I wish I had gotten to know her better. She sounded like a wonderful person."

"You would have loved her."

Ruth searched Dani's face. "So this Brighton—he's come back into your life?"

"In a way."

"Does he have a good heart?"

"I think so."

Ruth smiled. "Then don't let him get away."

❋

What had begun as nervous butterflies had morphed drastically into something that felt like a convergence of vultures feeding off her innards. Wanting nothing more than to flee back down the terminal hallway and jump on the nearest flight to anywhere but Colorado, Dani forced her feet to move forward, down the escalator, past security, and into the baggage claim area, where Brighton had said he'd be waiting.

Reading the electronic screens, she struggled to push through the mass of holiday travelers, emerging at last, unscathed, next to the carousel. Dani wavered between hoping the crowds would thin so she could catch her breath to being grateful for the camouflage they provided. If Brighton couldn't find her, she wouldn't have to face him again or invade his home.

It was strange what could happen to a girl when she admitted that she was falling for someone. If there was ever a time when Dani wanted to be her most clever, intelligent, and wonderful self, it was right then. Instead, she felt like a tongue-tied moron.

"Hey." Brighton stepped up next to her, somehow locating her among the throng of people. "It's a madhouse in here, isn't it?"

Dani only nodded, knowing any words she might speak would come out sounding clumsy and inane.

"Have a good flight?"

She could tell he was trying to fill the awkward silence, but she couldn't seem to help her nervous stupidity at the moment. So she nodded again.

"Okay, then," Brighton said slowly, grinning at her. "Either you're extremely claustrophobic and the fear has you petrified, or you are a robot made to look like Dani Carlson. Which is it?"

Dani simultaneously laughed and blushed. A few seconds later, she was grateful to see her suitcase finally appear. She bent to retrieve it, but Brighton was quicker and picked it up first.

"I got it." He grabbed her hand and pushed his way through the crowds, pulling her along behind him. When he continued to hold her hand even after they escaped the baggage area, Dani tried not to let his touch add to her nervousness. If only she could think of something intelligent to say.

"Feeling less claustrophobic now?" he asked once they were both seated in his father's truck. He shook his head and chuckled. "I have no idea why you're so worried. My family is happy you're coming—they're all looking forward to meeting the one girl who rejected me."

She nearly sighed in relief. Sarcasm. She could do sarcasm. "You know, it's a good thing you met me. Your head would be far too big otherwise."

"And she's back." He winked. "I was getting a little worried."

"That makes two of us. It's just that I'm feeling like a misfit toy about to crash the after-Christmas party in Santa's workshop."

"You'll fit right in." He reached for her hand again. "We're a family of misfits."

"You've never told me much about your family."

"What do you want to know?"

She shrugged. "What I'm getting into. You know, how many siblings you have, their names, possibly some small tidbit of information I might use against them if it comes to that."

He laughed. "I'm the oldest, as you've probably surmised from my level of maturity. Joy came next. She's five years younger than me and was aptly named because my parents experienced so much joy when they found out they were having another baby. For a while, they were worried I'd be an only child. She's a freshman at Colorado State and she has a ridiculous love of chess. Drex is the baby of the family. He's now a senior in high school and plays football, basketball, and runs track. Basically, he's a jock."

"And your parents?" Dani asked. "The only thing I know is that your father is a financial analyst."

"Yes, my dad is all about the numbers. He can relate everything to math, and any advice he offers comes equipped with a numerical metaphor or something. He loves to golf and can't walk past the TV without checking some game score. My mother is the kindest person in the world. She's always doing something for some friend, family member, or neighbor. She's perpetually happy and loves cooking and gardening. She even keeps a greenhouse out back so she can garden all year round."

"Really? That's amazing," Dani said. "I like her already."

"And what about everyone else?"

"The jury is still out on your dad, since I'm not an avid sports fan and I forgot my calculator, but as for your brother and sister, well, that depends. If your sister can beat you in chess and your brother can outplay you at football or basketball, we should get along fine."

"She might, but he can't."

"Please," Dani said. "You've been out of competitive sports for nearly six years, whereas your brother is in the middle of the season, no doubt in great shape."

"What are you saying?"

She shrugged. "I'm saying I'd put my money on Drex."

"That's it. You just got bumped to the end of the shower line tonight. You'd better start praying for some lukewarm water."

"That's okay. I take my showers in the morning."

Twenty

* · • · * · • · * · • · *

"Dani! It's so wonderful to finally meet you!" Brighton's mom was petite and adorable, with cropped dark hair and light eyes. She had a genuine smile and surprised Dani when she pulled her in for a hug. "I'm Lynette, by the way."

"It's nice to meet you. Thanks for having me."

A younger and taller version of Lynette walked in the foyer and looked Dani up and down. She turned to her brother with raised eyebrows. "Punched any holes through the wall lately?"

Brighton glared at his sister and pushed his way through, carrying Dani's bag.

"What was that all about?" Dani whispered to him.

"Ignore her," came his reply.

But Joy had overheard. "Oh, he never told you about that?"

"Joy." Her mother gave her a speaking glance. "Would you mind checking on dinner?"

"Sure. Dani and I can always chat later." She strode off down the hallway toward the kitchen.

Dani followed Brighton and his mother to her room. As they walked through the main section of the house and down the hall, she decided she loved their home. It was a small rambler, but homey and comfortable, with wood floors and tastefully neutral-colored walls. The wood-burning fireplace crackled with freshly added lumber and the Christmas tree was decorated with homemade ornaments and strings of popcorn. It looked like a page directly out of a *Family Fun* magazine.

In the hallway, she noticed two framed cross-stitches, obviously sewn with little fingers. She fingered them wistfully as she passed by, reminded that her own mother's pristine walls had never held anything created by her.

Lynette led them to the first door on the right. The small room boasted walls covered with University of Utah sports paraphernalia. A charming window seat was nestled under a large bay window, and a door in the corner led to a small bathroom. It was perfect.

"This is Brighton's old room. I keep meaning to redecorate it and make it into a proper guest room, but I can't bring myself to alter it. Not yet, anyway," Lynette said.

Brighton placed Dani's suitcase on the floor and put an arm around his mother, pulling her in for a side hug. "Of course she can't change the room of her favorite son."

Lynette smiled. "In junior high, he sprained his ankle running track. We took him to the emergency room to make sure it wasn't more serious, and he met a doctor who had gone to medical school at the U of U. He thought the doctor was so great because he gave Brighton a completely unnecessary brace for his ankle so he'd be able to show off his injury to all his friends. In case you couldn't tell by his room, he suffered the symptoms of hero worship and decided that he wanted to go to U of U and become an emergency room doctor. Later he changed his mind to orthopedics, but it has always been U of U," Lynnette said. "Now why don't you get settled in while I'll finish up with dinner? I'm sure you're both famished."

She walked away, leaving Brighton leaning against the wall nearest to the door.

"If this is your old room, where are you staying?" Dani asked, worried that she was kicking him out of a comfortable bed.

"My mom set up an extra bed in Drex's room."

"Oh," Dani said, sinking onto the bed. "Thanks."

"No problem." He watched her in silence. When Dani started to squirm self-consciously, he said, "Sorry. It's just strange having you here."

For some reason, his words reminded her of the comment Joy had made earlier. She searched the walls of the room. "I don't see any patches on the walls. Did you really punch a hole through one of them?"

"I'm going to kill Joy." He backed out of the room. "Let me know if you need anything. If not, just follow your nose to the kitchen when you're ready. My mom is a terrific cook."

"That's fine," Dani called after him. "I can always ask Joy."

Sighing, he stopped and took a step forward. "If I promise to tell you later, will you please not bring it up with my sister? She has a knack for mutilating facts."

"You promise you'll tell me later?"

"I promise," he said, leaving her alone.

Taking a deep breath, Dani closed the door, retrieved her suit-case, and grabbed a change of clothes and her toiletries bag. After a quick shower, she took her time getting ready.

Lynette was wonderful, but Dani was still nervous about meeting Brighton's dad and brother. Social situations had always unnerved her because it took time for her to feel comfortable around people. Perhaps that was why she had so few genuine friends.

Regardless, she knew she couldn't hide in Brighton's room all night, so after checking her reflection, she took a deep breath, opened the door, and smelled her way to the kitchen.

"Whatever you're making smells wonderful," Dani said. "Is there anything I can do to help?"

"Actually, if you wouldn't mind filling up that pitcher with water, I'd appreciate it," said Lynette.

"Of course." Dani was grateful to have something to do, especially since Brighton wasn't around.

"Where's Drex and your husband?" Dani asked, trying to make conversation.

"We invested in snowblades for our four-wheelers this year. Drex and Jerry are out making the rounds through the neighbor-hood. They try to make me think they do it to be considerate and neighborly, but I know better. I've caught them racing or pushing snow at each other too many times to know their motives aren't completely selfless." Lynette removed a dish from the oven. "Bright went out to find them and bring them home for dinner."

"Joy went too?" Dani placed the pitcher on the table and turned back to Lynette.

"She got a call from her boyfriend and escaped to her room for some privacy."

"Brighton never said she was dating anyone."

"Probably because he's hoping it won't last very long. She brought him home one weekend when Bright was here, and he made it clear he wasn't impressed with him. She's been slightly miffed ever since. I think that's why she went a little overboard on her teasing earlier. She's trying to get back at her brother for the way he treated her boyfriend. I'm sure you understand all about sibling rivalry."

"Actually, I'm an only child. But I have lived with roommates. Does that count?"

"Oh, I'm sorry. I don't remember Brighton ever mentioning that."

"It's hard to believe he mentioned me at all," Dani said, curious as to what he'd told his parents about her.

"Oh, he didn't have to say much for us to know he'd fallen for someone."

"He didn't?" Dani's heart beat faster.

"Brighton's body language and mood are as readable as a picture book for toddlers," Lynette said. "He was quite the sourpuss that summer after graduation."

"Oh." Dani felt uncomfortable again. Surely it wasn't because of her—his mother must have misinterpreted things. Although Dani remembered that summer well, and she too had been somewhat of a scrooge. Nana had gotten after her more than once to give that "poor boy" a call and put an end to her misery.

Suddenly, the garage door flew open and chaos ensued. A tall, lanky, high-school aged boy surged into the room, trying to slam the door behind him as a couple of snowballs ricocheted off the door and onto the kitchen floor. He lost his balance and fell to the floor as he dodged one of them. Jumping back to his feet, he slammed into the door while Brighton tried to wedge himself inside.

"Show no mercy, Bright!" a voice called from inside the garage. "You get him back out here and we'll show that punk of a kid exactly what happens to someone who messes with us."

Lynette and Dani watched in amusement as Drex slipped on the now wet and slick floor, allowing Brighton to leap inside and stumble to the floor next to his brother. A wrestling match followed, and within moments Jerry was there, carrying a large pile of snow. Gingerly stepping around his wrestling sons, he grabbed Drex's hood and shoved the pile of snow down his son's back.

The holler that followed brought Joy running in to see what was going on. "What in the world?" she asked.

Lynette glared at the boys. "Will you three please grow up and stop dirtying what once was a clean floor?"

Her voice caught Brighton's attention. When he noticed Dani standing next to his mother, he immediately let go of his brother and leaped up from the floor. Dusting the snow from his shirt, he said, "We're done now."

Drex sat up and frantically tried to pull off his coat in an effort to remove the snow that now covered his back. "This is not over," he said. "Although I'm not surprised it took two of you to take me down."

"Only because you had a head start and ran away like a coward," said Brighton.

"Drex, when are you going to learn to not mess with your dad?" Jerry asked.

Joy was giggling. "What happened?"

Jerry looked at his daughter. "Drex thought it would be hilarious to plow his four-wheeler into that flimsy willow tree down the road when I stopped to talk to Brighton. I had just taken off my hat and gloves, and my coat was unzipped. Brighton hadn't bothered to wear a coat at all, but Drex, of course, was still wearing his hooded parka, so the cold snow shower didn't bother him. You know the rest."

Drex grinned, picking himself up. "Yeah, and it took both of them to get back at me." A nudge from his brother landed him back in a heap on the floor.

Jerry laughed, and Brighton walked toward Dani as if nothing had happened.

Dani turned to Lynette. "Are they always like this?"

Lynette nodded and added dressing to the salad.

"Maybe I should be glad I grew up without siblings. I'm suddenly feeling very mature."

Jerry laughed and shed his coat and boots, walking over to their houseguest with his hand outstretched. "You must be Dani. I'm glad you were able to make it."

"Me too," Dani said, shaking his hand.

"What are you doing dating my brother, anyhow?" Drex asked. "Don't you know any better?"

"Oh, we're not dating," Dani was quick to say, feeling her face infuse with heat.

"Not yet anyway." Brighton winked.

Lynette smiled at the interchange before announcing that dinner was ready. By the end of the evening, Dani found herself wondering why she had been so nervous to come. Brighton's family was just like him, drawing her out and making her feel at home—the kind of home she'd had with Nana. They stayed up late talking, bantering back and forth, and playing games. Aside from a few uncomfortable comments from Joy, Dani thoroughly enjoyed herself.

Joy and Drex eventually dragged themselves off to bed, leaving Jerry alone with Brighton and Dani in the family room while Lynette mopped the kitchen floor.

"Brighton told us about this trust fund of yours and the family you want to help back in Texas," said Jerry.

"Yes," Dani said. "But we still need to find some good ways to spend the rest of the money. Brighton was hoping you might have some ideas."

"I plan to leave those decisions to the two of you, but I'd love to see where they have that kind of money stashed. I might be able to recommend some investments with a better rate of return. After all, the larger you can grow the principal, the better."

"I know." Dani relaxed against the back of the couch. "Miles mentioned that the money was already invested fairly aggressively, but if you want to have a look, I'll see if he can send me something. I'd love to find investments with better returns—nothing too risky though."

"Better returns?" Brighton turned to his father. "You know, when we first met, she despised wealth. Then she decided it might come in handy to help out people she cared about. Now, she can't get enough." He shook his head. "Nana has created a monster."

"Just think of it as a phobia cured," Dani said, returning her attention to Jerry. "I'll call Miles tomorrow and see if he can email you some kind of summary."

"I could have a lot of fun investing that kind of money," Jerry said almost wistfully as he covered a yawn. When he caught sight of his wife putting away the mop, he rose to his feet. "Well, I'm beat. We can talk again after I've had a chance to look over everything."

"Thank you," said Dani.

"It's my pleasure," he said, taking his wife's hand.

"Good night," Lynette called.

Dani watched them fondly until they disappeared down the hall. She couldn't remember the last time she'd seen her parents hold hands, let alone talk and banter back and forth the way Brighton's parents had.

She caught Brighton studying her. "Your family is great," she said. "I really like your parents."

"Sorry about Joy."

"Why don't you like her boyfriend?"

His lips twitched. "What else did my mom tell you?"

"You don't want to know."

Brighton sighed and reached for her hand. Playing with her fingers, he said, "He just rubbed me the wrong way. My parents would never say, but I don't think they like the guy either. He's pompous, has no motivation in life, and lets Joy cater to him like she's his servant or something. Granted, I don't know him well, but the entire weekend he was here, he prattled on about himself, cut Joy off several times, and didn't offer to do a thing to help out around here. Frankly, I have no idea what she sees in him."

"Have you told Joy any of this?"

"Not in so many words."

"You should, you know. She obviously looks up to you. Maybe you could open her eyes to something she's missing."

"Or maybe I could follow the example of my parents and let her make her own decisions."

"That means you need to treat him the way your parents do."

Brighton grimaced. "That's not going to happen."

"Then talk to her. She deserves to know why you don't like her boyfriend. And who knows, maybe she'll actually listen and stop teasing us so much."

He leaned closer and grinned. "I think your motives might be more self-serving than you let on."

"I'll admit she was starting to drive me crazy tonight," Dani said. "But I also think she deserves to know why you don't like the guy."

"Fair enough. I'll try to talk to her before I head back to school."

"Tomorrow would be better."

He laughed. "I don't think so. I kind of like seeing you blush."

"Very funny." Dani glared at him, pulling her hand free. "Speaking of uncomfortable topics, you do realize that it's later, don't you?"

He looked at her in confusion.

"You said you'd tell me about the hole in the wall later," she said.

He sobered. "Tonight's not later enough."

"Why do I get the feeling that later implies years down the road?"

"You're quick."

"Come on," she said. "I've just endured teasing from your sister because of you. The least you can do is to tell me what provoked you to put your fist through a wall."

Brighton shifted uncomfortably, raked his fingers through his hair, and finally said, "You."

Her eyes widened. She figured Joy had been referring to some embarrassing episode in his youth. "Me? What does that mean?"

"It means that after you told me you wouldn't date me, I went back to my apartment and, uh, renovated a little. End of story."

Dani stared at him, opened-mouthed and speechless, not understanding completely. Had he really cared that much, or was he merely angry that for once something didn't go his way? Had it been as difficult for him to walk away as it had been for her? And more important, did he still care?

His admission had obviously made him self-conscious because he stood and said, "I'll see you in the morning."

"Wait." Dani jumped up and grabbed his arm. She had no idea what she wanted to say, but she didn't want him to walk away. Not like that. Impulsively, she stepped closer and took both of his hands in hers. Lacing her fingers through his, she said, "Tell me, if I were to walk out the door right now and you knew you would never see me again, would you be tempted to, uh, renovate again?"

His gaze captured hers. "I think the entire house might have to come down."

"Really?" All the teasing had left her voice and she searched his face for the truth.

"Really."

Reaching up, she moved her fingers to the back of his neck, tugged him toward her, and kissed him quickly before pulling back and looking down at the carpet. What had she done? She wanted to run to her room, shut the door, and be on the first flight back to Texas in the morning. But then she felt his arms encircle her waist and draw her toward him. Maybe it hadn't been such a bad idea after all. She rested her head against his shoulder, savoring the warmth of his embrace.

"Do you think that . . . maybe you might . . . be able to give me a second chance?" His hesitancy was adorable.

She snuggled closer. "Funny. I was just wondering the same thing about you."

Apparently, her answer was a good one because he leaned down and kissed her thoroughly.

Twenty-one

··•···•·*·•··*·

Dani awoke the following morning feeling happy and ener-
gized. She stretched, savoring the softness of the comforter and
down pillows. Why were beds so much more comfortable in the
morning? Rolling to her side, she glanced at the alarm clock on
the nightstand. Nine-thirty! Yikes! She couldn't remember the
last time she'd slept so late. Jumping out of bed, she rushed to the
bathroom to get ready.

When she wandered into the kitchen twenty minutes later, she
found, to her embarrassment, that she was the last person awake.

"Hey, sleepyhead," Brighton said. He was holding a newspaper,
and Dani noticed a plate scattered with syrupy pancake crumbs on
the table in front of him. "Care for some cold pancakes?"

Lynette smiled from behind the island. "Don't let him tease
you. I have some fresh batter right here and was just waiting until
you woke up."

"I don't know what happened. I never sleep in this late," Dani
said, walking to the chair Brighton had pulled out for her.

"Brighton has that effect on people," Joy said from the other
side of the table. "You know, keeping them up past their bedtime
and all."

Her comment, obviously meant to provoke, left Dani blush-
ing, Brighton grinning, Jerry and Drex laughing, and Lynette
scolding. Wanting nothing more than to flee back to the solace of

her room, Dani sighed and sank down in the chair, staring mean-ingfully at Brighton. If he didn't talk to Joy soon, she was going to run back to Texas on foot.

Dani ate quickly and escaped to the den with the excuse that she needed to call Miles. Taking her time, she checked her email on the family computer. Chad Rutling had sent her a message.

Miss Carlson,

Just spotted a For Sale sign in front of your house. What's up with that?

Dani sighed, wondering when Ruth would tell him. Or was she waiting for Dani to break the news? Knowing Chad was concerned about his family, Dani pondered on an appropriate response. She wanted to ease his worries, but knew she couldn't say much.

Chad,

Talk to your mother. She can tell you why the house is for sale. As for everything else I'm sure you're stressing about, STOP! You're still going to college, and your family will be fine while you're away. Trust me!

Miss Carlson

She clicked the send button and then phoned Miles. Within the hour, she was scrolling through the pages of funds and invest-ments he'd emailed her. She had always loved math, but the num-bers staring back at her made her feel brainless and overwhelmed. How did anyone go about managing all that money? She prayed that when Miles retired, she would be able to find a good, honest, and intelligent person to replace him.

"Hello, sunshine." Brighton poked his head through the door.

She looked over her shoulder at him. "I'm not sure my disposi-tion matches that description at the moment."

Coming up behind her, he rubbed her shoulders while he stud-ied the computer screen. "I still can't believe you're a millionaire."

"I'm feeling very overwhelmed—like I'm not smart enough for the responsibility I've been given."

"You're smart enough," Brighton said. "So are you going to use your salary to buy Nana's house back?"

"I'm not sure."

"You could do it anonymously, you know," he said. "Your father wouldn't know it was you until after the fact."

"I know, and I've actually been thinking about it—but not for me." Dani turned in her chair to look up at him. "Don't get me wrong. I'd love nothing more than to move back into Nana's house, but I've actually been doing a lot of thinking. Remember what you said about the Rutling's old farm? Well, what if I were to buy Nana's house and anonymously gift it to Ruth? Not only is it the perfect size for her little family, it's also in town, and as long as they don't have a mortgage payment, I think they could afford to live there while Chad finishes college—especially if Ruth can find a part-time job somewhere."

Brighton walked over and leaned against the desk. He searched her eyes. "You want to give Nana's house to someone else?"

She swallowed. It sounded dreadful when he put it that way. "Yes."

"Are you sure?"

"I've talked to a realtor, and the only other homes for sale in the area are a small one-bedroom trailer home and the Rutling farm. There's nothing else." She looked down at the floor. "They need it more than I do."

"You must really like this family."

"It's crazy, I know, but they're wonderful people who don't deserve what's happened to them. It feels right for me to help."

"Where will you live?"

"I'll rent a room for now, and maybe someday I can design and build my own house. We both know I can afford it now."

He nodded.

Wanting to change the subject, Dani said, "I was also thinking about your friends, the Moreno family. You mentioned that they're struggling, and I thought we might be able to pay off the loan on their restaurant or even their house. What do you think?"

"I think that you're going to run out of money if you keep this up," Brighton said. "You should spend the money on people you want to help, not on people you think I would like to. It's your trust fund, after all."

"But I want some of it to go to people you care about," she said. "So here's what I've been thinking. What if we establish a few scholarships for deserving high school kids, purchase Nana's house for the Rutlings, and pay off the Morenos' mortgage? I'd also like to donate some money to the elementary school so they can hire an aide for hearing-impaired students. Besides Ruth's daughter, there are two other children in the area with hearing disabilities. I know it won't be as good as a specialized school, but it's better than nothing. That would also provide Ruth the freedom to get a part-time job during the day. What do you think?"

For an answer, he leaned over and kissed her. "I think you are amazing. And thank you for thinking of the Morenos. My dad knows more about their current finances, so we can pick his brain—later." Brighton pulled her up beside him.

"But I promised to give him those summaries." She pointed to the pages resting on the tray of the printer.

Brighton picked up the stack of papers. "I'll give these to my dad while you get your coat, gloves, hat, and snow pants."

"Why?"

He smiled. "You, oh wealthy one, are taking me snowboarding."

❄

That afternoon was one Dani would always remember. The powder on the mountain was knee-deep, the sun was shining, and the sky was a brilliant blue. Add to that the snow-covered pines scattered across the Rocky Mountains, and she couldn't have asked for a more gorgeous backdrop to a perfect day.

They raced, talked, laughed, threw snowballs at each other, and Brighton even pilfered a kiss or two—or more. Dani lost count halfway through the day. She couldn't remember feeling so happy, and she owed it all to Nana. Because of her, Brighton had burst back into her life and filled an empty void she hadn't realized needed filling.

As they drove back down the canyon, she knew, with a surety she'd never felt before, that she was in love with the man seated beside her. It had come so easily, almost stealthily, and she refused to fight it any longer. The future still held a mass of uncertainty, but for now she was content.

�֎

By the end of the week, everything was falling into place. After talking with Jerry about the Morenos, Dani and Brighton made the decision to relieve them of their restaurant mortgage as well as purchase Nana's house and anonymously gift it to the Rutling family. The rest of the money would be used to fund scholarships and allow the school to employ an ASL teacher.

"Paying the restaurant mortgage shouldn't be difficult," Miles said to Dani one afternoon. "I'm hoping I can get it taken care of before you leave Colorado. That way, Brighton won't have to fly out to Texas any time soon."

"Sounds good." Dani stifled a yawn. "Do you need anything else from me?"

"I'll call if I do, but you've given me enough to keep me busy for a while."

"Thank you so much for all your help."

"My pleasure."

Dani ended the call and leaned back, stretching her legs. She felt a profound sense of relief and gratitude for the people in her life with greater knowledge and expertise. What would she have done without them?

Brighton walked into the office, carrying a plate with a sandwich in one hand and a cup of ice water in the other. Noticing her cell phone sitting on the desk, he asked, "Finished already?"

"Already? I've been on the phone with Miles for the past three hours." She picked up her phone and studied the screen. "I'm shocked this thing still has some battery life."

"I expected you to be in here all day." He placed the plate and glass on the desk next to the computer keyboard.

She sighed. "I'm sure there will be many future conversations, but we hashed through everything he could think of, so now all we have to do is sit back and wait to hear from him again. We should be able to sign for the Morenos' mortgage before I leave, but it will take a couple of months before Ruth has her new house. By next fall the schools should have their aide, and he's not sure about the scholarship stuff yet."

Standing, she wrapped her arms around Brighton and snuggled close. "Thank you so much for all your help. And thank your dad too. You've both been wonderful."

"Yes, what would you do without me?" Brighton teased. Dani drew back slightly, and he looked worried. "What is it?"

She thought for a moment. "I want to say something to you, but I'm probably going to mess it up, so please just hear me out." She sidestepped away and leaned against the desk. "This past week has been one of the best weeks of my life. I've come to really . . . care about you and your family. You've all been so welcoming."

"Joy included?" he asked.

"I'm hoping the teasing dies down in time."

"I like that word."

"What word?"

"Time."

"Okay," she said slowly, trying to understand what he was saying.

"It means you aren't planning on pushing me away again, right?" He moved closer.

Dani held up her hand. "Will you please stop interrupting me? Now I completely forgot what I was going to say."

"You were about to tell me how you can't live without me and that you want to keep spending time with me. At least that's my interpretation."

"Oh, for crying out loud." Dani turned to look out the window. "Never mind." She found that any clarity of thought she had was now gone, leaving behind a mixed-up mess of confusion. Why did he have to be so irritating?

Brighton chuckled, walked up behind her, and turned her around to face him. "I love you too." His mouth covered lips that were parted in surprise and his arms drew her to him.

She found herself on sensory overload. Not only was he kissing her thoroughly, but he had told her he loved her. Her! Here, in his father's office, in the middle of the day—only weeks after he'd come barreling back into her life. It was unbelievable. The kind of feeling she'd expect to have after winning the lottery. Only so much better.

"As much as I hate to interrupt this lovely little interlude, Mom needs your help," Joy's icy voice cut into their perfect moment, making Dani pull back abruptly and look anywhere but at the two siblings.

Brighton grabbed Dani's hands, keeping her close. "I'll be there in a sec."

"It sounded urgent," Joy said, not moving.

Turning his head, Brighton glared at his sister until she finally shrugged her shoulders and left the room.

"I really don't think she likes me much," Dani said.

Sighing, he released her hands. "I'm sorry. I tried to talk to her yesterday, but it didn't go well, as I'm sure you can imagine. I don't know what her problem is. Personally, I think she's just mad at the world right now and taking it out on us."

"Well, thanks for trying." Dani turned back to the window, feeling cheated. Joy had successfully spoiled a truly perfect moment, and Dani wanted to both cry and wring the girl's neck. "Your mom needs you. We can talk about this later."

"We can talk about a lot of things later," Brighton said before ducking out the door.

Twenty-two

Dani awoke to a loud rapping at her bedroom door. Groggily, she rolled over and glanced at the clock. Seven-thirty. What in the world? She had become used to sleeping late and knew she'd have some actual rude awakenings when her high school classes began again in a few days. Flopping back onto the pillow, she called out, "The house better be on fire!"

Brighton cracked the door and asked, "Is it safe for me to come in?"

"That all depends on how you feel about getting your ears boxed."

His head appeared. "You do realize we live in the twenty-first century, don't you?"

"Do you or do you not have a good reason for waking me up early on my last day of Christmas break?" Dani asked before pulling the covers over her head.

"I just checked the weather report and Monarch got eight new inches last night," he said.

Dani lowered the covers and looked over, thinking there was no place she would rather spend her last day with him. "You talked me into it. I'll be out in a few minutes."

As it turned out, Drex and—much to Dani's irritation—Joy wanted to go snowboarding as well. The four of them jumped in Jerry's truck and headed up the canyon where Drex, with his care-for-nothing personality, showed off his jumping prowess and entertained them all with some failed landings and his goofy personality. Joy, on the other hand, became progressively more boorish as the day advanced.

At some point, Dani halted to rest her legs and Joy skidded to a stop directly above her, spraying her with fresh powder. Dani forced herself not to cringe when the snow landed on her bare neck. What was with that girl?

"Oh, did I get snow all over you? I'm so sorry!" Joy said. "Maybe you should take a break and go get dried off. There are some restrooms in the lodge." She pointed toward the small ski lodge adjacent to the lift at the bottom of the hill. "There's probably only time for one more run anyway, so we can meet up with you afterward."

"No thanks," Dani said, too stubborn to remove the snow that was now trickling down her back. "I was getting hot anyway, so you actually did me a favor. See you at the bottom." Directing her board downhill, she rode to the lift where Brighton was already waiting.

Thankfully, it was a two-seater lift, so Drex would be the one to "enjoy" Joy's company and Dani could relax with Brighton.

"Looks like you've been having some fun." Brighton swiped some snow from her jacket.

"A blast," she said, pulling off her glove to remove what was left of the snow at the base of her neck.

"You're supposed to land the jumps on your feet, not your head," Drex joked.

"You would know." Dani was thankful they hadn't noticed her encounter with Joy. She removed her boot from its binding and moved in next to Brighton in the lift line.

"Mind if I ride up with Dani for this last run?" Joy asked Brighton as she came up behind them. Dani was stunned. Why couldn't Joy just leave her alone? Dani glanced at Brighton and nearly throttled him when he shrugged and moved aside to let Joy by.

"Thanks for sharing," Joy said to her brother just before the chair swept them up.

Determined to not be provoked, Dani took in the scenery and made what she thought was a safe comment. "It's beautiful, isn't it?"

"Beauty is in the eye of the beholder."

"You disagree?" Dani found it hard to believe that Joy didn't think the views were breathtaking.

"I wasn't talking about the scenery," Joy said, making it impossible for Dani to mistake her meaning. "I noticed that my brother was sure quick to forgive you."

"Does that bother you?"

"Why should it bother me?"

Dani turned in the chair, exasperated. "What is the deal? Do you have something against me, or is this some sort of revenge to get back at your brother for not liking your boyfriend?"

"Please," Joy said. "I couldn't care less about what Bright thinks of Pat."

"Really?" Dani preferred to keep the focus on Joy. "Because if I had an older brother who worried about me the way Brighton worries about you, I think I might care."

"Well, you're not me."

"Thank goodness for that," Dani muttered.

"What did you say?"

Dani looked away, willing herself to remain calm. "Are we close to the top of the lift yet? For some reason, this ride seems really slow."

Joy lapsed into silence, much to Dani's relief. What had she done to irritate Brighton's sister so much? Over the course of the week, Joy's teasing had transformed into something nearing disdain, and she had no idea why.

Unfortunately, the silence didn't last long. Joy seemed to find it necessary to unleash her frustrations once more. "What are you trying to do? Do you want to hurt my brother again? Is that it? Do you like making people miserable?"

"What are you talking about?" Dani asked. "I'd never hurt Brighton. I—" Dani stopped herself before saying too much. Instead, she revised, "He's the best thing that's ever happened to me."

"Ever considered that the reverse is not so true?"

"Meaning?" Dani couldn't help but ask, even though she really didn't want to know.

"Meaning that you are both worlds apart from each other, with different backgrounds and different goals."

Dani blinked, trying to understand. "I think you're wrong. We have a lot in common and we both have similar goals."

"So you're okay with moving away from your favorite Texan town? I guarantee there are no hospitals near you with a decent orthopedic practice. Or are you planning to ask Bright to give all that up and move to Podunk-ville? Ever thought about that?"

Dani said nothing and looked away, feeling both angry and depressed. Angry because Joy was a brat and depressed because, of course, what she'd said was valid. But why did Joy have to be so cruel? Why couldn't she see that Dani would never dream of asking Brighton to give up his goals?

"You know," Dani said quietly, praying for patience as they arrived at the top of the lift. "He just thinks you deserve a lot better than Pat. And you do. You deserve someone more like your brother." She couldn't leave the seat fast enough and immediately shoved her boot in the binding and cinched it down. Not wanting Brighton to think there was anything wrong, she yelled to him as he came off the lift, "Race you to the bottom!"

She heard him call her a cheater as she left them behind and sped down the hill as quickly as possible, trying to get her emotions under control before she'd have to face Brighton again. She needed to find a way to forget Joy's words, at least for the moment, and to focus on something else. If not, she would be an emotional wreck during the last day she spent with Brighton.

So she thought of ways to enact revenge—like putting purple hair dye in Joy's shampoo, switching her contacts with a new, more powerful prescription, or putting a red sock in her next laundry load of whites. Yes, it was catty and ridiculous, but by the time Dani arrived at the bottom of the run, she found she could smile once more.

She was even able to keep up the happy pretense during the drive home and through dinner. Joy had been blessedly quieter than usual, which helped, but Dani still felt the need to keep her distance. When the plates were cleared, Lynette thoughtfully shooed Brighton and Dani out the front door, telling them to go and enjoy their last night together.

For that one consideration, Dani would always adore Brighton's mother.

As they walked to the truck, Brighton reached for her hand. "Was there anywhere in particular you wanted to go?"

"Nope. Anywhere is fine with me."

He opened the door and waited for her to sit down before walking around and sliding in next to her. "What about a movie?"

"Sure." Dani looked out the window and unwittingly allowed Joy's accusations to reenter her mind. She wanted to kick herself. Her good mood was now fading fast, and she found herself thinking thoughts that would surely doom her to misery. What was she doing here anyway? She hadn't needed to come. She and Brighton could have discussed the trust over the phone. They could have made decisions over the phone. Why then, had she flown to Colorado?

Dani shifted uneasily in her seat and admitted to herself that she'd wanted more from Brighton than his help with the trust. She had wanted him in her life again, and she'd gotten her wish. But, as Joy had so rudely pointed out, what kind of future was in store for them? Tomorrow, they would both go their separate ways and then what? Keep in touch through text messages, email, and phone calls? For how long? With his lofty career goals, there was no way he would end up in a small Texan town, or any small town for that matter. Could she really handle living the life of a prestigious doctor's wife? Could she be happy?

Brighton must have noticed she wasn't paying attention because he said, "What about *Dumb and Dumber III*? It just came out and I hear it's a great show."

"Sounds good," she said, still lost to her thoughts.

"Earth to Dani!" Brighton waved a hand in front of her face.

Blinking, she turned to look at him. "Sorry, did you say something?"

"You realize that you just agreed to watch *Dumb and Dumber III*, don't you?"

"I did not!" she said. "And there better not be a number three!"

Brighton chuckled. "Somehow, I knew you would have poor taste in movies. And no, there is not a third, although should one ever come out, just remember you already agreed to see it."

"Funny."

"Okay, so a movie is out. How about hot apple pie instead? Would that help you to refocus your attention on me?"

"Did someone say pie?"

Brighton chuckled as he backed the truck out of the driveway. Within fifteen minutes they were seated at a table, waiting for their order.

"So, you're leaving tomorrow," Brighton said.

Dani fiddled with her napkin. "As are you."

"Are you going to miss me?"

"Just a little." She held her thumb and pointer finger about an inch apart.

"Oh, I think it'll be more than that."

Dani offered a smile that didn't quite reach her eyes. With the jumbled thoughts working their way through her brain, she couldn't quite return his lighthearted banter. It was frustrating. She wanted their last night together to be fun and memorable, not dramatic and sad. Picturing Joy with her head stuck in a snowdrift and her feet flailing in the air didn't seem to do the trick this time.

Brighton's smile disappeared, and he leaned across the table, reaching for her hand. "What's up?"

She shook her head. "Nothing."

"Come on, Dani. I'm not an idiot."

She sighed. "I know. It's just that I've been doing some thinking, but I'm not ready to talk about anything yet."

"Does that 'anything' involve me and our future, by chance?" he asked.

"What future?" she countered, not able to keep the sadness from her voice.

"What do you mean, 'what future'?" He pulled his hand free and drew back, watching her with one of his rare serious expressions. "Please don't tell me you're about to break up with me again."

Dani closed her eyes and wondered how she'd gotten herself into this conversation before she'd had time to sort through her own feelings. "May I ask where you see things going between us?"

He remained silent for a time. "To be honest, I have no idea how everything will pan out, but I know how I want it to end. And that ending includes you in my life—forever."

Dani swallowed against the raw emotion that pelted her insides. "I don't know what to say."

"Say that you want the same thing," he said, the fear showing on his face.

"I do want the same thing," she said. "It's the panning out part that worries me. I see you going your way and me going mine, and I can't see a place where we'll come together again."

"So we *make* us come together again." He was losing his patience, and who could blame him?

"And how do we do that, exactly? Orthopedic surgeons by default tend to gravitate toward larger cities, and I am a Garysville, Texas, kind of girl. I just don't think I have it in me to live in metropolitan USA with a workaholic for a husband."

"I see," he said. "So what you're saying is that you want to just give up? Without even trying to work out a compromise?"

"I'm saying that I don't know!" Dani leaned across the table, trying to make Brighton understand. The waitress arrived with their order and filled their glasses. Looking away, Dani waited impatiently for her to leave.

"Have you even prayed about me at all?" Brighton asked quietly after the waitress had gone.

His question troubled her. "I used to, but not recently."

"Used to?" He sounded surprised.

Dani was grateful for the distraction. "If you must know, I used to pray that you would stumble back into my life somehow, since I couldn't seem to get you off my mind."

"Really?" He almost smiled.

"Don't let it go to your head."

"Too late."

Dani sighed. "That doesn't mean that things are meant to work out between us, you know. I would hate for one of us to give up something we love and end up hurt and angry down the road."

"So you're asking me to give up you instead," he said. "That's worse than anything."

"You tell me, then, what the answer is." Dani was tired of worrying about a problem with no foreseen solutions.

"I will. Just as soon as I figure out what it is," he said. "In the meantime, eat your pie and stop thinking such ominous thoughts."

✳

That night Dani knelt down beside her bed and offered up a heartfelt prayer to her Heavenly Father. She told Him that she had fallen in love with Brighton and pleaded for direction. Was he someone she could marry, and if so, would God mind stepping in to smooth the way or at least show her how? *Please, please, please help*, she begged.

Although there weren't any miraculous visions or answers, Dani did feel a familiar warmth flow through her body, and she was reminded once again that God loved her and was watching out for her. Peace and gratitude filled her heart as she climbed into bed and picked up her scriptures.

A quiet knock tapped on the door, and Dani wondered who it could be. Brighton had already said good night. "Come in!" she said, peering over the top of her book.

The door opened and Lynette let herself in, closing the door softly behind her. "Sorry to bother you, but I wanted a chance to talk to you before you left in the morning."

What could Brighton's mom possibly want to talk about? Dani scooted over to make room on the bed. "Of course. Have a seat."

Lynette walked over and sat down next to Dani. "First of all, I wanted to thank you for coming."

"I should be thanking you," Dani said. "I barged in on your family time, and you've made me feel so welcome."

"Well, most of us have tried, at least," she said. "I'm sorry for Joy's behavior. But the rest of us feel like you're part of the family."

"Thank you. That means a lot to me."

Lynette fell silent and contemplative, staring down at her hands. She linked and unlinked them several times before she began to speak. "That summer, after Brighton graduated and moved home, he was different. He seemed to have lost his natural exuberance for life, and although he wasn't depressed, he wasn't completely happy either. He just wasn't himself.

"At first I worried, praying that he would find a girl to make his heart whole again, but then I realized that the change wasn't necessarily a bad one. The trial he was battling helped him mature in ways nothing else ever had, I think. Don't get me wrong, he had always been a wonderful son, but I worried about the strength of his testimony. Did he have a close enough relationship to God?" Lynette blinked at the tears forming in her eyes.

"After that summer, I knew he did, and I was so grateful for that knowledge. I watched as he turned to God for help. Several times, I would peek into his room to say good night and find him down on his knees. I loved how he grew that summer, but at the same time, I missed the old Brighton—my teasing, happy, problematic son—and I wondered if he'd ever be back.

"These past few weeks, he has been. Only he's better now than ever before. He's not only grounded in the gospel, but he has that spark back, the light in his eyes when he smiles." Lynette looked at Dani through her tears. "I just wanted to thank you, dear sweet girl, for what you have done for my son."

By that point, Dani was crying as well. She didn't trust herself to respond, feeling like words would somehow mar the spirit in the room, so instead she reached over and hugged Brighton's mom until they could both pull themselves together.

Wiping the moisture from her face, Lynette stood up and made her way to the door. When she reached it she turned around and said, "I don't want you to think I'm pressuring you into marrying my son or anything. I just wanted you to know that you have impacted his life for the better and that he truly does love you." Lynette smiled before closing the door softly behind her.

Hugging a pillow to her chest, Dani whispered, "Thank you, Lynette—for everything."

Twenty-three

It took several weeks, but life in Garysville eventually gravitated back into a predictable pattern. Dani finished boxing up her things and moved into the apartment across town, her high school students grudgingly accepted new homework assignments, and she ended each day with the best part—a lengthy phone call from Brighton.

The Moreno family was now free from the debt on their restaurant, the school was looking into hiring an aide, and the scholarship funds were being researched. If only the purchase of Nana's home would go as smoothly. According to Miles, it would be March before the Rutlings found out about their new home, which was frustrating.

Not having anything else to do, Dani decided to take Ruth and her family some homemade chicken noodle soup one afternoon in February. Stopping by the grocery store on her way, she picked up a package of rolls and then made her way to the register. An older woman from town, Cessily Walters, was dressed in a violet suit jacket, black slacks, and purple pumps, and was talking with George Casper, the owner of the small store, while he totaled her purchases. Overhearing Ruth's name, Dani scooted in behind Cessily, pretending to peruse a magazine while waiting for her turn.

"It's just plain unbelievable," Cessily was saying. "To think they have to up and leave with so little notice. Why, if I were that woman, I would divorce that man quicker than a striped lizard on hot asphalt."

"Are you talking about Ruth Rutling?" Dani couldn't help but ask.

"Oh, Danielle darling, I didn't see you come in." Cessily smiled a greeting. "And yes, I am. With you being such good friends with her, I'd have thought you would've known."

"Known what?"

"Well, that scoundrel husband of Ruth's went and emptied her bank account last month."

"What? How?" Dani was appalled at the news.

"It was a joint account, you see. He hadn't touched it since the day he left, and sweet Ruth was hoping he'd come right back; so she didn't open an account of her own right away and plum forgot to do it later. I'm sure she never dreamed he'd do such a sinful thing!"

Dani assumed Cessily knew this because her husband happened to own the only bank in town. "Isn't there any way to get it back?"

"Oh, she could sue, to be sure, but with what money? By the time it was all over, she'd owe more to some lawyer than any money she could recoup."

"That's horrible!" Dani said. "Ruth hasn't said a thing to me."

"I'm sure she didn't want to worry you, my dear." Cessily patted her hand.

"A darn shame is what it is," George said. He was tall, with buzzed gray hair, and Dani couldn't remember ever seeing him without an apron. "That woman is sweeter than honey and doesn't deserve to be dealt a hand like that."

"No, she doesn't." Dani eyed Cessily's large basket of food that had yet to be rung up. "George, I don't mean to be rude, but I need to be somewhere." She handed him a five-dollar bill. "Just keep the change."

Forcing herself to drive carefully so the soup wouldn't spill, it seemed like hours before Dani finally pulled up in front of the old farmhouse. Grabbing the rolls and pot, she made her way to the front door and rapped loudly.

Chad answered. "Hi, Miss Carlson."

"Is your mom here?"

"Yes. She's, uh, packing." He shoved his hands in his pockets and looked at the ground. "So much for things looking up."

"Don't say that," Dani said, pushing past him. "And don't worry. We'll figure something out." She put the soup and rolls on the kitchen counter before Chad led her upstairs to the master bedroom.

Ruth was taping a box closed and looked up in surprise. "What are you doing here?"

"It's true, then? Your husband really took everything?" Dani sat on the bed next to her friend.

"Oh, the perks of living in a small town." Ruth smiled and shook her head. "He left us a little. Enough to get us to Tennessee at least."

"What's in Tennessee?"

Ruth sighed. "My parents. They're letting us stay with them until I can get us back on our feet."

"That's good, right?" Dani asked.

"If I can endure hearing about the mess I've made of my life, and how my mother told me not to marry Justin, I'm sure it will work out fine. I'm just grateful we have somewhere to go."

"If only I had Nana's house. You could've moved in with me."

"You are a dear," Ruth said. "Everyone has been so wonderful to us these past few months, and we've felt so at home here. One day, I hope I can bring us back."

Dani nodded, unsure of what to say. "When do you need to be out?"

"We have two weeks."

"What can I do to help?"

❖

"They're moving!" Dani said into her cell phone later that night when Brighton's name registered on the caller ID.

"Am I supposed to know what you're talking about?" he asked. Dani could hear the smile in his voice.

If only there was something to smile about. "The Rutlings!" she said before briefing him on the situation. "What should I do?"

"There's nothing you can do, not until your father agrees to sell the house. But at least they have somewhere to go, and if all goes well, it's only a matter of time before they move back."

"What kind of reaction is that?" Dani paced back and forth across the wooden floor. He could at least demonstrate some sympathy. "Don't you care at all?"

Brighton sighed. "Of course I care—mostly because you do. But there's nothing you can do about it. All I meant was that their situation could be a lot worse."

She sighed. "I know. I just feel like it's all my fault."

There was a moment of silence before Brighton finally spoke. "I'm not even going to try to understand why you feel that way. Instead, I'm going to tell you one of the reasons I called."

"You mean it wasn't because you wanted to hear me rant?" Dani sank onto a loveseat, the only piece of furniture in her so-called family room.

"Afraid not."

"And it wasn't because you missed me and just had to hear my voice?" She found herself grinning, loving this man who could so easily restore her good mood.

"I said one of the reasons," he said. "That was the other."

"Flatterer."

"It's not flattery if it's the truth. Now do you want to hear the other reason or not?"

"You have my complete attention."

"Paz Moreno called my dad tonight."

"Really?" Dani's interest was piqued. "What did he say?"

"Once Dad got him to stop raving in Spanish, he found out that the Morenos had been refunded their last payment, along with a letter and statement explaining the payoff of their loan."

Dani was confused. "And he was angry?"

"More like worried. He figured the mortgage company made a mistake, and he was apprehensive about what would happen when they corrected the error and thought no payment had been sent. When the customer service rep could only tell him that the mortgage had been paid in full, he immediately hung up and called my dad, wondering what he should do."

"What did your dad say?"

"He told Paz to calm down and he would call the mortgage company himself to find out what had happened. After waiting twenty minutes, he called Paz back and explained that there was no mistake. Someone had anonymously paid off his mortgage, and there was no way of knowing who."

"What did Mr. Moreno say to that?"

"He started crying, asking who would do something like that for them and how could he ever pay them back. He had my own father, who never cries, tearing up by the end of the conversation." Brighton paused. "I just thought you might like to hear the results of your incredible altruism."

"You mean Nana's altruism," Dani said. "She's forcing me to spend that money on others, you know. If I had my way, I would now be the owner of my own small island in the Caribbean."

He chuckled. "I'm sure you would. But thank you just the same. You just brought one family a whole lot of joy—and me as well," he said. "You know I love you, right?"

"Yes," Dani said, blinking away the tears in her eyes. "And I love you too."

Brighton cleared his throat. "So, is there a new projected signing date for the house? I'm ready to fly out and see you."

"Two weeks," Dani said.

"Gee, where have I heard that before? Oh, I know. Two weeks ago."

"Blame my father."

"I do."

❋

Because Dani couldn't rush the sale of Nana's house and refused to tell Ruth anything, she was forced to help load the Rutlings' aged van with what few possessions they could fit and tearfully watch them drive away. Half the town had come out to say their good-byes and bring some sort of parting gift for the sweet family. It was a touching scene, and Ruth went through an entire box of tissues before she left.

Frustrated, Dani watched the van turn the corner, wishing there were some way to make them stay for just two more weeks. Instead, she clutched a paper containing an address, phone number, and email—her only remaining connection to Ruth. She just hoped and prayed that Miles could work his magic and that Ruth would accept the generous gift.

Feeling helpless, she slid into her car and called Miles. He answered after the first ring. "I just watched the Rutlings drive away, and I feel sick. I was calling for an update. Please tell me that in a few weeks I'll be able to watch them drive back."

Miles sighed. "I'm sorry, but your father keeps delaying everything. Now we are looking at April."

"What!" Dani said. "I don't understand. What kind of delays?"

"According to him, he doesn't like the idea of selling to an anonymous buyer, so he keeps coming up with ridiculous excuses. Thankfully, no one else has shown any interest in the house. Otherwise, I'm sure he'd sell to them in an instant."

"Why does he care? He's getting his money either way."

"To tell you the truth, I'm worried he has somehow found out about the trust and might know that it's you who's trying to buy the house."

Dani felt even more ill. She pressed the phone closer to her ear. "How?"

"I have no idea, but I think it might be time for you to have a conversation with your dad. Rest assured, the trust is yours, and there is nothing he can do to take it away from you."

"He can refuse to sell me the house."

"Yes. Unfortunately, he can do that."

❋

Brighton let out an exasperated sigh, and Dani could practically feel his frustration through the cell phone. "Is this ever going to be over? I would like to see you sometime before the end of the year, you know. If I'd have known it would take this long to begin with, I would have flown out to see you by now. This two more weeks thing is for the birds!"

"I miss you too."

He took a breath and lowered his voice. "The Rutlings are gone, I take it?"

"They left this morning," Dani said. "Although the more I think about it, the more I wonder if this might be a good thing after all."

"How so?"

"I'm willing to bet that Ruth will be more eager to accept the house after she's lived with her parents for a few weeks."

"Sounds like another set of parents I know."

"No kidding. And speaking of parents, what in the world am I going to say to my father?"

"Tell him to sell you the house or you'll sue the daylights out of him. I'm no lawyer, but I'm pretty sure what he's doing is illegal," Brighton said. "Or better yet, give me his number, and I'll tell him. I've been meaning to ask him if I can marry his daughter anyway."

"That will go over well." Dani tried to calm her racing heart. *Did he just say marry?* The thought both thrilled and terrified her. "You've found a solution to our future then?"

"It's a work in progress," he said. "By the way, I've been meaning to ask you how you are with compromises."

"What's a compromise?"

"I'm pretty sure you know what it is. What I don't know is if you have ever willingly participated in one."

Dani frowned. "What's that supposed to mean?"

"That you're used to getting your way."

"And you're not?"

"All right, all right. I just need to know that you're willing to negotiate."

"If it means having you in my life—yes, I might consider other options," she said. "What do you have in mind?"

"Not so fast. I'll let you know when I'm good and ready. In the meantime, quit stalling and go call your pathetic excuse for a father."

✸

"Hello, Danielle." Her father answered right away, much to her annoyance. She would have preferred to leave a message and give herself more time to come up with a solid argument. "I don't remember the last time you called me."

"I've been busy."

"So it seems. What can I do for you?"

Dani didn't waste any time. "I want you to sell me Nana's house."

"I thought you couldn't afford it."

"I've found a bank willing to loan me the money," she lied, wanting to know if he'd found out about the trust.

"For Pete's sake," he said. "Just come out and say that you can now afford to buy the house."

"I thought I just did."

"And you need a bank to lend you the money?" His voice was filled with sarcasm.

She sighed. "I want the house and you don't. I don't under-stand what the problem is."

"Your mother and I both want you out of Garysville."

"Why?"

"Because it's a go-nowhere town. We've already allowed you to choose your own college, degree, and career, thinking you'd come to your senses when you realized how poorly teachers were paid and how little you could do with your life on that salary. But you're just as stubborn as ever. And now your grandmother has gone and left you with money, making the situation worse. Is this some sort of idiotic rebellion against your mother and I?"

"I don't understand why the trust would make things worse. I'm now bringing in a much higher salary. Isn't that what you wanted for me?"

"Rose has enabled you to stay in Garysville," he said.

Realizing that her anger was getting her nowhere, Dani took a breath and tried to calm down. "I'm happy here. Why can't you see that?"

"You have so much more potential," he said. "No daughter of

mine is going to wind up as a lowly high school teacher, married to a farmer or some other lowlife. I want you home where you belong."

"This *is* my home." She was losing her temper. "And you can't make me change my career choice. Do you realize how ridiculous you sound?"

His voice sounded hard and final. "I will let the house sit vacant before I'll sell to you. End of discussion."

Thinking of Ruth, Dani was frantic. If only there was another house available. But there wasn't, and there was still the fact that it once belonged to Nana. That reason alone propelled Dani's next words. "The house isn't for me," she blurted.

He was quiet for a moment. "Who is it for, then?"

"A family who needs it more than I do. I was planning to deed it over to them immediately."

"And where are you planning to go?"

"Where I am now. In an apartment across town."

There was silence on the end of the phone while Dani waited for her father to speak. Not realizing she'd just handed him an ace, she listened when his reply finally came. "I will sell you the house on one condition."

"What?"

"You promise to move back home to Colorado after the school year ends," he said. "For good."

❋

Who knew that a twenty-four year old millionaire could still be manipulated by her father? It was ludicrous, but in this situation, true. Dani had reviewed her miniscule options over and over again only to come up blank. Brighton and Miles had no answers for her either. The farm was in foreclosure, which meant months of legalese to purchase it back from the bank; not to mention the fact that it would only serve to restore the Rutlings to a dilapidated old shack far from town. And the nearest decent home for sale was in a neighboring town, thirty miles away.

Ruth's family belonged in Garysville, where the people had grown to love and care about her.

Dani felt trapped, desiring nothing more than a scenario that would allow her and Ruth both to remain in Texas. But that wasn't going to happen. Her father had too much control over the situation. Deep down, she knew she had to succumb to his demands if she really wanted to help the Rutlings.

After deliberating for several days, Dani finally decided to agree to her father's ridiculous terms. She would buy Nana's house, deed it to Ruth, and pray tirelessly for Ruth to accept the gift. The last thing she wanted was for her sacrifice to come to naught. And then, after the school year ended, she would move back to Colorado Springs.

The agreement was that she would stay with her parents for the duration of the summer. She knew they planned to launch a full frontal attack to convince her of the error of her ways, but she would be prepared to deflect their criticisms and arguments. Should her parents refuse to listen to reason, there were always earplugs.

Thankfully, they had realized that they couldn't puppeteer their daughter completely. So after the summer, if she still wanted to teach, she would be free to move wherever she pleased—except Texas, of course. They wanted her nowhere near Garysville. For some preposterous reason that Dani couldn't begin to comprehend, her parents loathed that little town. It bordered on psychosis.

At least her parents couldn't remove Brighton from her life as well. No matter how much her parents would scorn a poor college student from a middle-class family, she would never allow them to come between her and Brighton. Ironically, the thought of moving to a big city with him no longer filled her with dismay. In fact, it seemed downright wonderful compared to the alternative of bunking with her parents.

Thinking of Brighton made her yearn for his presence, now more than ever. She wanted to be held in his arms and listen to his droll comments, and she wanted him to kiss and coerce her sadness away. Unfortunately, she would have to wait yet another two weeks.

How she hated that specific duration of time.

Twenty-four

Brighton wanted to wring Dave Carlson's neck. Of all the pompous, over-bearing, arrogant, manipulative people.

As fate would have it, Brighton had finally worked out his rotations for the following year. It had been a complicated and problematic process, but he had arranged for most of them to take place in the Dallas area—not a location he could now reverse. He was hoping to surprise Dani with the good news that they would be mere hours apart, but thanks to her parents—well, his plans had now been thoroughly quashed. What a mess.

His cell phone rang.

"Miles said he'd have the paperwork ready a week from Saturday." Dani's voice sounded anything but excited. "Are you free that weekend?"

"You could sound happier at the prospect of seeing me again," he said, not knowing how to cheer her up. He'd dealt with an angry, flustered, prideful, and even nutty Dani. But sad? He wasn't quite sure how to deal with that emotion, especially from three states away.

"If it were up to me, I'd make you fly out here tomorrow. We could spend the next week and a half together, sign the blasted paperwork, and fly to Vegas."

"What's in Vegas?"

"An assortment of wedding chapels."

Brighton chuckled. "There's a temple in Vegas too, you know."

"Do you think they'd have an opening on such short notice?" Dani asked. "If so, I'd definitely prefer that option."

"And what about your high school students?"

She sighed. "Fine. We can wait until the end of May and elope to the Salt Lake Temple since you'll still be in school. How does that sound?"

"Why the sudden desire to get married?" And more important, why didn't she sound more excited about the prospect?

"My parents can't make me live with them if I'm married to you."

Ouch. So he ranked only a little higher than her parents. Talk about a menial position. "I've imagined better proposals."

"I'm sorry. I'm just feeling a little . . . cranky."

"Really? I would never have guessed."

He heard her take a deep breath. "What if my parents find out about you and decide you're not right for me either? Evidently there's no stopping them when they think they know better."

"What could they possible do?"

"I have no idea, but I used to think the same thing about Garysville," she said. "Moving is one thing, but you . . . I just couldn't handle it if they came between us as well."

Feeling marginally better that his status had somehow risen above her favorite town, he sighed. "Don't worry. There's no way they could keep me from you. Now get some rest, and I'll call you tomorrow."

Brighton hung up the phone, feeling less assured than he sounded. If her parents disapproved of him, would they really contrive something to keep Dani away from him? He wouldn't put it past them. In fact, they probably already had a husband selected for her. Someone from an affluent, prestigious family—someone with the last name of Kennedy, Vanderbilt, or Rockefeller. Someone who would one day become a successful lawyer or doctor.

At least he fit one of the criteria. But was it enough? Would that be enough to compensate for his middle-class background or nondescript surname? On the other hand, at the rate Dani was defying their wishes, maybe they would actually be thrilled to welcome him to the family.

It was like a nearly finished puzzle, when all that remained were sporadic gaps here and there, gaps that were easily filled with the lingering pieces. Perhaps the situation wasn't as dire as it seemed. Maybe, just maybe, Brighton was in a previously unknown position of influence. And there was only one way to find out.

He needed to find some time to pay a visit to his future in-laws.

❃

"All right, people, time's up!" Dani called, listening to her students groan as they dropped their pencils to their desks. "Oh, please. You studied hard for this test, and I'm sure you all performed brilliantly."

More groans.

Dani laughed. "Okay, okay. Now turn in those tests and have a marvelous weekend."

"We all know *you* plan to have one," one girl said as she passed by and tossed her test into Dani's outstretched hands.

Dani couldn't deny it. Glancing at her wristwatch for the umpteenth time, she smiled at the thought that Brighton's plane would land in less than four hours. Her plan was to rush back to her apartment, change, and drive as fast as she dared to the airport. If she was ridiculously early, so be it. Perhaps her presence would act as a magnet, urging the plane to fly faster.

❃

Unfortunately, the magnet she'd pictured in her mind was turned the wrong way, and the plane was delayed—only thirty minutes—but it seemed like hours as Dani sat near the security checkpoint, drumming her fingers and searching for Brighton's blue eyes.

Then suddenly, there they were.

Leaping from her chair, she nearly upset the pedestal table in her haste to throw herself into Brighton's arms. He dropped his bag and chuckled as his arms tightened around her.

"Oh, this feels so good," she murmured, burrowing close and breathing in his scent. How could someone smell so good after spending several hours on a plane? "I've decided that you are not allowed to leave on Sunday."

"Sounds good to me. Who needs medical school anyway?"

"Not you."

"Not me." He tilted her chin toward him and kissed her right there in the middle of the airport. Dani loved that he didn't care about all of the people drifting about.

"Now how about we get out of here? I'm starving." He hefted his bag to his shoulder and searched the signs. "Where'd you park?"

Good question. Dani looked around, trying to remember. Where did she park? In her haste to see Brighton, she hadn't paid attention and had simply parked in the first place she found. Where was it? "Um . . . I remember driving up a level—or two. Let's just find the parking garage, and I'm sure it will come back to me."

"Okay," he said. "North or south?"

"North or south?" There were two garages? She'd never been to this airport before, so how was she to know? "I know I parked in terminal C parking," she finally offered.

"Considering we are in terminal C now, that's good," he said, watching her face. When he realized she really was clueless, he said, "Seriously? You don't remember where you parked?"

Dani bit her lip and shook her head. Turning around, she glanced up and down the corridor in both directions, hoping to see something familiar. Both hallways looked identical.

Brighton rolled his eyes and pulled a quarter from his pocket. "Heads we start with the north—tails the south." He flipped the coin and caught it neatly in his right hand, turning it out onto the top of his left. "North it is." He grabbed her hand and pulled her alongside him.

Ninety minutes later, they located a white Toyota Sequoia on the second story of the south parking lot. Brighton brought her around to the passenger side, where he opened the door for her.

"It's my car," she said. "Shouldn't I be the one to drive?"

"I'm sorry, but your driving privileges have been revoked. Seems you've been spending too much time in a town with one traffic light."

"Two traffic lights," she muttered as she crawled into the seat. "And to think I was just about to commend you on your patience."

"Oh, believe me, I have patience," Brighton said. "I've waited nearly two years for you, haven't I?

They ate at the nearest restaurant they could find before driving two hours back to Garysville, where Dani dropped him off at the town's only bed-and-breakfast-type establishment. In actuality, it was a beast of a house owned by a widow named Mrs. Batty. She rented out her best rooms to visitors and fed them a hearty breakfast every morning; it was her way to stave off the loneliness of living on her own. Most guests felt like they'd spent the night in something better than a five-star hotel.

Knowing Mrs. Batty insisted on an early bedtime for herself, Dani had procured a key in advance, and now she quietly snuck Brighton up the stairs to the second room on the left.

He doubtfully eyed his surroundings.

"Trust me. It's Mrs. Batty herself who will make your stay seem wonderful," she promised. "She's . . . unforgettable."

Kissing him softly good night, she left him in a rose-papered room, smelling of vanilla, with a gold-leafed four-poster bed, white lacey drapes and an overstuffed cherry wood armchair.

*

They spent Saturday morning shut away in Miles's office before grabbing some lunch and driving back to Garysville, where Dani spent the remainder of the afternoon acquainting him with her dear little town. She showed him around the high school and inside her classroom, gave him a tour of Ruth's abandoned farmhouse (the back door lock was broken), and walked hand-in-hand with him down Main Street. They ordered take-out from the diner and watched the sun descend below the horizon from Nana's front porch swing.

Dani wanted to call back the sun and never let it set.

"What time is your flight tomorrow?" she asked.

Brighton took her empty plate, stacked it on top of his, and set them aside. She snuggled close when he wrapped his arm around her shoulders. "I've answered that question about half a dozen times. Do you really not remember?"

"I was hoping your answer would change. Two o'clock seems indecently early."

"It's two o'clock in the afternoon, not morning."

"Like I said—way too early."

He chuckled and kissed the top of her head. "So, how do you plan to survive the summer with your parents?"

She looked up at him. "By spending every spare second with you, of course."

Brighton's forehead wrinkled as he studied the horizon.

"Unless you'd rather I didn't," Dani said, suddenly worried.

Removing his arm from her shoulder, he turned in the swing to face her. "I need to talk to you about something."

Now she was petrified. The weekend had been going so well. Why was he so serious all of the sudden? "Just promise me you're not planning to break up with me."

He rolled his eyes. "You're such a girl."

"Well, considering I *am* a girl . . ." Her voice drifted off. "Is that a compliment or an insult? Because it sounded a tad offensive, if you want to know the truth."

He chuckled. "What do you expect? You immediately jumped to some dramatic conclusion before you actually listened to what I have to say."

"I just wanted to rule out the worst possible scenario," she said. "What's wrong with that?"

"What's the point in ruling out a scenario that's not even possible?" He had a way of making her insides turn to mush.

With relief, she took his hand in hers and played with his fingers. "Well, you looked so serious—it kind of scared me."

"Good."

"Good?"

"Good," he repeated. "I'm glad that the idea of me breaking up with you would scare you."

"And why wouldn't it?"

"I just . . ." He pulled his hand free from hers, raked his fingers through his hair, and leaned forward, resting his elbows on his knees. "After the whole thing with your father, you changed. I wasn't just a guy you cared about, a guy you hoped would somehow fit into your future. Suddenly, I became a person you wanted to marry immediately. I kind of feel like the only reason you decided you wanted to marry me was because you were forced to, that I was the lesser of the two evils." He sighed. "I just want to know that you would have chosen me regardless."

Dani looked at him in surprise and then directed her focus inward. Was that true? If all the events over the past few weeks had never transpired, would she still want to drop everything for Brighton?

Her brow furrowed in concern while the "what ifs" drifted through her mind. How did she really feel about the man seated beside her? There was no doubt in her mind that she loved him, but it really bothered her that she couldn't honestly answer his question. Would she really have chosen him over her dream small-town life?

"Earth to Dani," Brighton said.

"Sorry," she said. "You just asked some questions that made me think."

"And what are you thinking?" he asked when she paused again.

"I'm thinking that there is no doubt in my mind that I love you and want to be with you, but to be completely honest, I have no idea how things would have played without my father's interference." She stared down Nana's street. "I suppose that once I got over the shock of his ultimatum, I kind of figured that it was an answer to my prayers. Like Heavenly Father was giving me a nudge in the right direction—a direction I might never have taken on my own."

"Okay," Brighton said. "Not exactly what I wanted to hear, but at least I have God on my side."

Dani's heart warmed. He was amazing. How could Garysville or any small town even compete with a man like him? Linking her arm through his, she slid over and laid her head on his shoulder. "I know I didn't give you much of an answer to your question, but if you could give me some time to work through my feelings, I'm sure I can give you a better response."

"Only if you promise that the response will include nothing about breaking up," he said as he wrapped his arm around her once more. "I'm pretty sure I'd beat you with a wooden spoon if you tried to break up with me a third time."

"Now who's being the girl?"

❋

Dani sat on the front porch steps next to a stack of uncooked pizzas as the Rutlings' tired old van puttered to a stop in front of their new home. Jumping up, she ran to hug Ruth and welcome her back.

"I don't know how, but I know you're behind this somehow," said a teary-eyed Ruth.

"If that were the case, I would have done something before you left two months ago," Dani said. "I'm just so happy you're home."

"Hi, Miss Carlson," Chad said, looking happier than she'd ever seen him. "It's great to see you. I take it you have the keys?"

"They're supposedly in the mailbox on the front porch," Dani said.

Ruth eyed her speculatively but didn't say another word, much to Dani's relief. She didn't want unanswerable questions to spoil this happy day.

The only drawback was that in five short weeks, Dani would be leaving. With the exception of the high school principal, she hadn't told anyone yet, not wanting to tarnish her final weeks in Garysville. Her experience had given new meaning to the saying "you can't really understand another person until you've walked a mile in their shoes." Although Dani wasn't battling a terminal disease, at least she could now better understand why her grandmother had chosen to keep her illness a secret.

Two small arms wrapped around Dani's waist. Looking down, she saw Megan's sweet face staring up at her. Crouching down to the little girl's level, Dani hugged her and signed, "Welcome home." She'd made it a point to learn a few signs while Megan was away.

The little girl clapped her hands in delight and turned to throw her arms around her mother.

"In case you couldn't tell, she's rather excited," Ruth said.

Dani gestured toward the house. "It only has three bedrooms, so I'm afraid your kids will all have to share."

"Does the roof leak?" Chad asked.

"No," said Dani.

"Does the air conditioning work?"

"Yes."

"Is that tire swing safe?" Morgan pointed toward one of the maple trees.

"Definitely."

"It sounds like heaven to us." Ruth effectively ended the barrage of questions.

Walking around to the back of the van, Dani hefted a bag and followed the family inside. The furniture from Ruth's old house had been brought over earlier and placed in the garage, waiting for Ruth to sort through at her discretion. Between her old furniture, and what remained in Nana's house, Ruth would have no problems turning Nana's house into their new home.

A few neighbors showed up, carrying pies or plates of cookies, expressing their delight in seeing the Rutling family back where they belonged. Grabbing the pizzas from the front porch, Dani invited everyone to stay for dinner. While they ate, she felt a certain amount of melancholy, knowing her time with these wonderful people would soon come to an end. How she would miss this place!

Once the kitchen had been tidied up, Dani was quick to excuse herself. The Rutlings were probably exhausted from their long trip, and she knew they still needed to unpack. Promising to come back the following night for dinner, she hugged Ruth good-bye.

"Dani." Ruth followed her outside, her eyes bright with unshed tears. "Thank you."

"I did nothing." It was the truth; Miles had handled everything.

"I'm sure that's not true." Ruth turned slowly to study the house. "Normally, I wouldn't even consider accepting such unbelievable generosity, but I'm not sure how much longer we could have stayed with my parents."

Ruth paused and lowered voice. "I thought that after an initial scolding, they would leave well enough alone, but that didn't happen. Day in and day out, they ripped me to shreds and reprimanded my children for the most ridiculous things. They treated Megan the worst of all, like she was responsible for her loss of hearing," she said, her voice breaking. "I searched desperately for a job, needing to get my children away from their grandparents, but there was nothing."

Ruth turned around to face Dani, wiping tears from her eyes. "I know there are people in far worse situations, and I should have been thankful to have a roof over our heads, but you have no idea the gratitude I felt when I heard from that lawyer." She paused. "Everything has fallen into place for us—this house, a hearing impaired aide at the elementary school, and a job waiting for me as a teller at the bank."

"You have a job?" Dani asked. What wonderful news! She would have to remember to give Cessily Walters a hug the next time they crossed paths.

Ruth nodded through her tears. "I'm not sure how you did it, but whatever part you've played in all of this, I want to thank you. From the moment we met, you've been an answer to my prayers."

As Dani hugged Ruth good-bye again, she smiled through tears of her own. Ruth was amazing. In fact, she and her children made giving up Nana's home easy.

And so had the prospect of a future with Brighton, she had finally come to realize.

Over the past several months, he had become her anchor, securing her to the land of sanity. It had happened gradually, like the snowmelt before spring, so she hadn't recognized it until she'd been forced to reflect. The flood of realization had begun when she wrote the names "Garysville" and "Brighton" at the top of a sheet of paper, drawing a line down the middle.

Garysville had been first. She'd listed several items: wonderful people; simple, slow life; relaxing; peaceful; great job. After racking her brain for additional ideas, she had written "wonderful people" again and then moved her pen over to Brighton's column.

That was when the torrent had come. She couldn't move her pen fast enough to fill up the space: I love him; Good, kind, generous; close to the Lord; witty; charming; handsome; makes me happy . . .

The list went on until she had filled the column, plus an additional page. She had finally dropped the pen, knowing, like she'd never known before, that he was more than the champion of her little writing exercise. He was everything.

It really didn't matter where she lived, as long as she was with him. It was Brighton who was the essential ingredient in her recipe for happiness, and if he wanted to join a practice in New York City, well, she'd swallow her fears, take his hand, and follow him there—or at least to the nearest suburb. She did have future children to raise, after all.

But she also knew that Brighton would be conscientious of her desires. She knew he'd never ask her to live in a place where she wouldn't be comfortable. Just like she knew he'd make every effort to make her happy. He was considerate like that. And she loved him all the more for it.

Twenty-five

If Dani were to describe her relationship with her parents during the first seventeen years of her life, she would use the words neglected, ignored, shoved to the back burner, and uninterested. After she'd informed them of her college choice, it was more like volatile, argumentative, frustrating, and exasperating.

Now, at twenty-four and back home, it was the polar opposite. Her parents were attentive, understanding, interested, and almost smothering. Dani wasn't sure how to deal with their about-face, let alone understand it. Was it because they had gotten their way? Was it some new underhanded manipulation trick? Or could it actually be genuine?

It had been two weeks since she'd returned home, and Dani was becoming more and more perplexed with each new day. She'd played golf and racquetball with her dad. And her mother had taken her shopping, to the spa, or out to lunch nearly every day. Dani was determined to keep the peace, so she had accepted their invitations and tried not to speculate about the legitimacy of their intentions.

It would be another week before Brighton would finish up with his testing, and she couldn't wait to see him again. She ached to feel his arms around her, to watch his brilliant blue eyes when he spoke, and to spend as much time with him as his short break would allow. Her excitement at his imminent arrival was one of her few defenses against the mounting insanity brought on by her parents.

Another was the scholarship funds. Miles had finally gotten around to acquiring or creating all the necessary forms, and now it was her turn to deal with them. Who would have thought there would be so much paperwork? She rifled through the large stack of files on the desk in her room, hoping this wouldn't become an annual task.

"Danielle, dear." Paula poked her head through the opening in Dani's bedroom door. "I thought it might be fun to go get some pedicures this afternoon. What do you think?"

Dani studied the pile of forms in front of her. A pedicure was the last thing she desired at the moment. "Sorry, but I can't today. I promised Miles that I'd have these back to him as soon as possible." She wanted to have everything ready for Brighton to sign when he arrived, and she wanted Chad Rutling to find out he'd been selected for a full-ride as soon as possible.

"Oh." Paula sounded disappointed.

Dani sighed. As much as she would have loved a few hours of privacy, she felt compelled to say, "I could use some help, if you're willing."

"Really? Okay, sure. What do you need me to do?"

Dani handed her a file. "Here. You can sit in the armchair over there." Dani nodded toward the bay window. "Basically, each file contains information for an individual scholarship."

"The scholarships aren't all the same?"

Dani shook her head. "It would be a lot easier if they were, but after speaking with all the principals in the area, we realized there were more students who needed various kinds of help than we initially thought. So we adapted the scholarships to offer different levels of financial support. Chad Rutling, for example, will get something akin to a full ride with books and living expenses for four years, assuming he keeps his GPA above a 3.0. Another scholarship offers tuition only, and another, tuition plus books. And others, part tuition."

"I see," Paula said, taking the files. "What do you need me to do?"

"Proofread. Still want to help?"

"Of course. What am I looking for?"

"Everything, but mainly content. We need to make sure that the qualification requirements are specific, concise, and most important, make sense. Once we have the requirements and value all spelled out, we need to fill out this form." Dani held up several papers stapled together. "It will eventually become the application for the scholarship."

"Okay," Paula said, looking over the first page in her file. "I wonder if your father would like to help when he gets home."

Dani raised an eyebrow. "Not likely. In fact, I'm surprised that you want to help."

"Why do you say that?"

"Because when I was in high school, I once suggested that you and dad set up a scholarship fund of your own and your response was to practically ban me from visiting Nana again."

"Yes, I remember that conversation," Paula said, studying her daughter. "But there was actually more to it than you realized."

Dani waited.

"Do you want to know why your father and I wanted you out of Garysville so badly?"

"Besides the fact that it's a 'go nowhere' town, and I'd be wasting away my life living there?"

Paula ignored her daughter's sarcasm. "It's because that town took you away from us. My own mother took you away from us and brainwashed you into becoming just like her."

Dani was quiet, trying to digest the nonsensical words her mother said. How could someone take away an overlooked daughter? "Even if that were true, and you know it's not, what's so wrong with being Nana? She was an amazing person."

"I know," Paula said. "She was wonderful. But she was also so set in her ways. After Dad died, she wouldn't consider moving anywhere else, even though I desperately wanted to leave Garysville. I felt so trapped there. When your father offered me an escape, I took it and have never looked back.

"I achieved so much more than I ever could have if I had stayed. Look at my life. I now associate with people in the highest circles.

Your father and I are members of an exclusive club. We've travelled the world and seen places most people only dream about. We've sat on the front row for Broadway plays, dined at La Meurice in Paris, gone on an African safari, and sunbathed on a private beach in the Bahamas. Me—a small-town girl from Garysville, Texas." Paula leaned forward as if she were trying to make her daughter understand. "This world is a beautiful place, and when you have enough money, it's yours for the taking."

Dani was speechless. Yes, the world was an amazing place, and yes, she loved to travel and see new things, but could her mother really rate eating in the most expensive French restaurant or socializing with high-class people among the greatest achievements of her life? How was Dani supposed to respond to that? How could she possibly understand that way of thinking? She couldn't. So she bit her tongue and changed the subject. "What does any of that have to do with Nana or Garysville?"

"Don't you see? The more time you spent in that town and with your grandmother, the more content you became with that kind of life. You have no idea how difficult it has been for your father and me to watch you lower your standards. We want so much more for you." Paula set the scholarship file down and stood behind Dani, placing her hands on Dani's shoulders. "Your grandmother has given you a wonderful salary. Use it, Danielle! Go see the world and enjoy your life."

Dani sat there, mystified, as Paula left the room. Her mother was clueless—or crazy! Did she really place a higher value on vacations and luxury than she did on other people? In one afternoon of teaching a child to snowboard, fixing up a dilapidated farmhouse, or helping a high school student grasp a difficult concept, Dani had felt more fulfillment and joy than she had ever felt on a trip to the Bahamas. For the thousandth time, she closed her eyes and offered up a prayer of gratitude for Nana's influence in her life.

❋

Dani was on her hands and knees mopping the cold stone floor when the doorbell rang. Her head was covered with a bandana, pirate-style, and she was wearing some comfortable cut-off jean shorts and a faded black T-shirt. Standing to open the door, she winced when her foot throbbed back to life after falling asleep. She hobbled over, tugged the door open, and then gasped when she saw Brighton standing on her doorstep. Squealing in delight, she ran into his arms, her pained foot and unflattering attire forgotten.

"I thought you weren't coming home until tomorrow!"

"I'm sorry," he said, pulling back to study her. "Do I know you? I'm actually looking for Dani Carlson—not Jack Sparrow."

She grabbed his hand and pulled him inside. "How did you get here so soon? I thought you had a test this morning."

"I lied," he said. "I wanted to surprise you. I actually finished up last night and drove through most of the night. I caught a few hours of sleep but couldn't wait to see you again. Or do this." He pulled her to him and kissed her soundly.

"My, you're brave," she said when he drew back. "What would my parents say if they found me kissing a perfect stranger? I still haven't told them about you yet."

"You've had almost three weeks. Are you really that ashamed of me?"

"Quite the opposite, as a matter-of-fact. That's why I thought it would be better coming from you."

"Coward."

"Nobody's perfect," she said. "Have you had breakfast yet? Can I fix you something?"

"I'm starving, actually. I didn't eat anything before I left."

"You *were* eager to see me, weren't you?" She led him into the kitchen. "How about an omelet?"

Brighton hesitated. "Um, I'm not sure I'm that hungry. I've had your omelets before."

"Don't worry," she said. "I'm in a much better mood today, so it might be edible."

"Somehow that doesn't reassure me." He started pulling all the barstools down from the countertop where Dani had positioned them while she mopped the floor. Then he did the same to the chairs that were on top of the table.

Dani watched him as she whipped the eggs. "You're welcome

to finish mopping the floors while you're at it."

He shrugged. "Might as well." Kneeling down next to the bucket of soapy water, he picked up the rag. "Where do you still need to mop?"

"Where it's dirty."

Brighton looked up and down the floors before throwing the rag back in the water. "All finished."

"I don't think so."

"When you can't distinguish the dirty tiles from the clean ones, I call it clean." He picked up the bowl and carried it to the sink. "Anything else you'd like me to do that's already done?"

"Men," Dani muttered under her breath. "Has your mother never taught you to clean?"

He pointed his finger at her and accused, "You're a neat freak! How could I have not known this about you?"

"And how could I not have known you're a slob?"

"I'm not a slob," he said. "The floor is spotless!"

"How could it be? It hasn't been decently mopped for a week."

"Why are you mopping anyway?" He leaned against the counter beside her. "Don't your parents have a cleaning lady?"

"They do, and I gave her the day off."

"Why?"

"She'd been up all night with a sick baby and looked exhausted. I told her to go home, get some sleep, and accept the paycheck from my parents or else I'd have her fired."

Brighton shook his head. "Well, that was nice of you . . . I think."

When Dani's parents walked through the door three hours later, they found Brighton and Dani in the middle of a Monopoly game. The first thing Paula said was, "Where's Rosa? These floors aren't finished."

Dani gave Brighton a look that said, "I told you so," before responding to her mother. "It's Brighton's fault, not Rosa's. She did her job."

Unfortunately, her mother was not easily deterred. "I don't understand. How could it be Brighton's fault?"

"Aren't you going to ask who Brighton is?" asked Dani.

"I already know Brighton." She sounded exasperated. "What I want to know is why he is to blame for my dirty floors."

"Dani sent Rosa home before she could finish," said Brighton. "So technically, it's my fault for coming."

"Can we talk about the floors another time?" Dave asked. "They look fine to me."

"See?" Brighton turned to Dani. "They look fine."

Dani waved off his words and turned back to her mother. "How, exactly, do you already know Brighton?"

"They do not look fine," Paula said. "We have friends coming over for dinner tonight!"

"Oh, for crying out loud!" Dani practically shouted. "I'll mop the floors myself, just as soon as you tell me how you know Brighton. I've never even mentioned him!"

"That doesn't sound very flattering," Brighton whispered across the table. "Just for that, I'm putting a hotel on Boardwalk."

"He stopped by to introduce himself a few weeks ago," Dave said. "We got to know each other over dinner at the club."

"You what?" Dani turned accusing eyes on Brighton. "Why didn't I know about this?"

"I wanted it to be a surprise."

"You're just full of surprises today, aren't you?" Dani's head was beginning to spin. Why would Brighton meet her parents without telling her?

Paula picked up the phone on the kitchen counter. "I'm going to give Rosa a call and see if she can come back over and finish the job."

"Don't call Rosa!" Dani wanted the chaos to end. "It was not her fault."

Turning to Brighton, she pointed toward the front door. "As for you, I want you to go home and get some sleep. I have no idea why you felt the need to keep a secret from me, but you better have a good reason when you do come back. Meanwhile, I'm going to mop the floors, shower, and take a nap of my own."

❋

Dani fell back on her bed, wanting a few moments of peace to mull over Brighton's surprise visit to her parents. If they hadn't treated him with such cordiality, she would have thought he'd come to give her father a much-needed lecture. But her parents seemed to like him. Of course they did. He was Brighton.

So why had he come?

"You're getting married!" Paula said, walking into Dani's room without knocking. "I can't believe my only daughter is getting married. And to a future surgeon, no less!"

Dani's question was answered. "I take it that's why Brighton paid you a visit?"

"He didn't tell you?" Paula actually looked guilty, but only just.

"Nope."

"I'm sorry. I just assumed . . . Well, you'll just have to act surprised when he does tell you. In the meantime, we have a wedding to plan!" Apparently her mother refused to feel guilty for long.

"I'm not engaged," Dani said.

Paula waved away her daughter's argument. "I'm sure he'll clear that up soon enough. I just couldn't be more thrilled. You, a surgeon's wife! Who would have thought?"

Definitely not her mother. Dani moaned inwardly and stifled a yawn. So much for a nap.

"Your wedding reception will be the perfect place to introduce Brighton to all of the best doctors around. We will find a fabulous location, and it will be the event of the year. Think of it! You're on your way to achieving such honor and success. I couldn't be more proud of you. And once he's finished with school, Brighton can join a practice here in Colorado Springs, and we'll be able to do so much together! Parties, socials, luncheons, days at the spa, and travelling! Won't it be wonderful?" Paula's eyes glowed.

Dani stared at her mother in horror. "Stop! Please, please stop!" She took a couple of breaths to calm herself. "Mom, do you even know me? Do you know anything about me?"

Paula looked confused. "Of course I know you."

"No, you don't. If you really knew me, you would know that I want a small wedding at the temple with no reception afterward.

You would know that I don't care about parties, socials, or club memberships. You would know that I intend to live in a regular house, ideally in a smaller city. And you would know that I would rather Brighton become a farmer than a doctor.

"I don't think I'll ever understand you. You rate status and money above everything else—above character, even. It makes no sense. I want to raise my own children in an average home and in a nice, average neighborhood. I never want to give them a reason to think they are better than anyone else. I want them to learn to be frugal, to serve, and to treat others with love and respect, regardless of social standing."

Dani took a breath. She was a little worried that she had gone too far, but there was no stopping now. "You've chosen a life for yourself that makes you happy. And that's fine. All I'm asking is that you please let me do the same with my life. I love Brighton more than I thought I could ever love anyone. And together, we will decide our future—not you, not Dad, not anyone." Dani searched her mother's face. *Please, please understand.*

Paula raised her perfectly tweezed eyebrows, looking offended. "Are you done?"

"Yes."

"Good." She stood. "Like you said, you're not engaged yet, so we'll talk about this later."

"Mom, I meant what I said," Dani said.

Paula stared at her daughter. "If there's one thing I've learned over the years, it's that I can't keep you from doing whatever it is you please. And if Brighton is willing to sacrifice his success to make you happy, so be it. I just hope he doesn't live to regret it." She turned on her exquisite high-heels and left.

Dani groaned, turned over, and screamed into her pillow.

❇

An oversized Mayan hammock was nestled in a lush corner of the Carlsons' backyard. It was Dani's favorite summer reading and lounging spot, and she was there now, seeking refuge from her deranged parents.

Hearing footsteps, she opened her eyes to see Brighton approaching. He looked amazing, as usual, and she smiled up at him. "Hey there."

"Have you forgiven me yet?"

"I haven't decided," she said, scooting over to make room for him.

He slid in beside her and left one leg hanging over the side of the hammock. "I came to Colorado to ask your dad if I could marry you."

"I know."

"Who told?"

"My mother, of course," Dani said. "Future surgeon or not, I would have never thought they'd agree to anyone I picked out. Just how did you convince them you were such a good catch?"

"Easy. They heard the word 'surgeon' and practically called me son right then and there—even after I told your father where I'd be doing my rotations next year."

"Why would they care where you're doing your rotations?"

"Because I'm planning to do them in Dallas, a mere two hours from Garysville."

"You lied to my dad?" Dani asked. "Why?"

"I didn't lie. And he said that so long as we're married, you can live wherever you choose—even in Garysville. Though he and I both know there are no orthopedic practices there, so it was a safe concession for him to make," Brighton said.

Turning on her side, Dani propped up her head to get a better look at him. "What do you mean you didn't lie? Do you really have a rotation in Texas?"

"Four of my six rotations will be in the Dallas area. It was the closest location to Garysville that I could arrange. Of course it was all in the works before your father manhandled the situation and made a mess of things—but that's just the way my life's gone since I met you."

"Wait a minute. You arranged to be in Texas next year?" Dani asked, her heart warming. "For me?"

Reaching up, he tucked some loose hair behind her ear. "I love orthopedic surgery—it fascinates me to no end. But I also love you and would have happily completed my rotations in Garysville if it had been possible."

"You're amazing." She leaned over and kissed him before resting her head on his shoulder and nestling up against him. "I suppose I'll have to turn down my job offer then."

"What job offer?"

"A math teacher for a high school in Salt Lake. Thank goodness I haven't signed the contract."

Brighton looked momentarily surprised before he laughed. "We really need to work on our communication skills, don't we?"

"I blame it on the short battery life of cell phones."

Brighton stared into the tree above them. "If you can handle two years of rotations in Dallas and Salt Lake, as well as a brutal five-year residency, I think we should be able to settle into the kind of life you're hoping to have. Once I'm an attending physician, I can schedule my own hours, and since we won't need the money, I can take on as much or as little as I want—with the exception of the days I'll be on call.

"I've also been doing some research on an orthopedic practice in Denton. It sounds like a good one. I could try to do my residency there, and if I like them and they like me, it might just work out. That would put us as close to Garysville as I can get with my job, and Denton has some nice small suburbs."

Dani blinked at the tears in her eyes. "You would do that for me?"

"In a heartbeat," he said.

She swallowed the lump in her throat. Reaching her hand into her pocket, she pulled out the Brighton/Garysville list she had written all those weeks ago and had been carrying around almost ever since. She handed it to him and waited while he read through the pages. "I realized that even though I'll always love Garysville and the people there, I think I can be happy just about anywhere—as long as you're there with me. It's you I want the most," she said softly. "So how about we take it one day at a time and see where life takes us?"

Brighton refolded the papers and stuffed them into his pocket.

His jaw worked as though he was trying to control his emotions. Finally he cleared his throat and managed, "I like the sound of that."

Dani smiled as she snuggled into him, relishing a sensation of extraordinary joy. She felt so blessed, happy, and peaceful.

And then her stomach growled loudly, rudely interrupting the moment.

"How about we get some dinner?" Brighton released her and rolled from the hammock. Reaching for her hand, he pulled her up and wrapped an arm around her shoulders as he guided her around the side of the house. "I have another surprise I want to show you anyway."

"Please," Dani begged. "I can't handle any more surprises."

"I promise you'll like this one."

When they walked through the gate, the first thing she noticed was a prehistoric and battered pick-up truck. It was hideous, with splotchy dark brown paint and an orange stripe running down the side. Or maybe it was rust, she couldn't tell.

"Surprise." He gestured toward the truck. "Do you like it?"

"It's dreadful," she said. "Where's your truck?"

"This is my truck. I bought it this afternoon."

"You actually paid money for that thing?" Her eyes widened in disbelief.

"Well, not much. But she's got character, don't you think?"

"No." She shook her head. "I don't think. Why in the world would you buy another truck?"

"You were in a sour mood when I left you this morning. I figured I'd need an ace up my sleeve, should you refuse to marry me."

"Purchasing a piece of junk is your ace?" She peeked into the truck's passenger window. "Brighton, it's covered in rust, the upholstery is non-existent, and those tires are losing air as we speak. How in the world would that encourage me to marry you? If anything, I'm starting to think you're insane."

"You're such a hypocrite," he accused. "When we were back in college, you promised me that if I showed up in a beater truck, so long as I wasn't going bald, you would marry me."

She smiled at the memory and at how he had actually remembered their conversation from two years before. Or at least partially. "You need to get your facts straight. We agreed on ten years, not two, and I said I would date you—not marry you." She paused. "And I really think your hair might be thinning a bit."

"If it is, I'm holding you responsible," he muttered, wrapping his arms around her and pulling her to him. "I can't believe I'm going to ask you this after the way you've berated both my hair and my truck, but I'm going to anyway. Will you marry me?"

She pointed to the truck. "You better not have purchased that thing with my ring money."

"Dani," he warned.

Sliding her fingers up his arms, she laced them together behind his neck. "I don't know. I'm not sure I can handle being married to a gambler. Can you promise me that you'll never make another bet ever again?"

"Why should I? I won you, didn't I?"

"True," she said, pulling his head down toward hers. "You really must be lucky."

"You never answered my question." His mouth hesitated a whisper away from her own. "Will you please marry me?"

"You can bet on it."

Discussion Questions

1. Betting is a reoccurring theme throughout this book. How do you feel about that? Is it wrong to gamble when no money is involved—in the name of fun and adventure? Or do you feel that Brighton and his roommates should have found another source of entertainment?

2. Being raised by absentee parents, Dani formed strong negative opinions about having too much money. Do you feel she was justified in her feelings? Can too much money be a bad thing?

3. Dani developed a close relationship to the Rutling family and wanted to do everything in her power to help them. She came away from the experience with an almost addictive desire to continue giving. Considering the phrase "moderation in all things," do you feel that this sort of addiction could be wrong? Are there times when too much service or focus on others can be detrimental?

4. Nana felt she was right in keeping her illness a secret from Dani. Do you think her actions were right or wrong? Did she somehow deprive Dani or was her secrecy justified? What would you have done?

5. Dani thought her mother was crazy for placing more value on travel and prestige than people and service. What do you think? Is it wrong to enjoy some extravagances (assuming you can afford it) when others have very little?

6. If you were given a million dollars but you had to spend the money on someone other than yourself, how would you spend it? Would you donate it to one or more of your favorite charities or would you want to be more personally involved and choose the individual cases yourself?

Photo by Letha Grant

About the Author

❋ ˙●˙❋˙●❋●˙❋˙●˙❋˙

Rachael Renee Anderson graduated from Brigham Young University with a BS in business finance and a minor in psychology. She is currently employed as a wife and mother of four who enjoys writing in her spare time.

Rachael also loves reading and doing almost anything outdoors, with the exception of rock climbing, bungee jumping, or sky diving since her height phobias don't permit such activities. She does, however, enjoy running (okay, so it's more like jogging—maybe even a fast walk), hiking, biking, boating, skiing, tennis, and gardening—all with her family and friends.

If you'd like to learn more about Rachael and her books, please visit her online at www. rachaelreneeanderson.com or write to her at rachael@rachaelreneeanderson.com. She would love to hear from you!